ALL THAT MAKES
LIFE BRIGHT

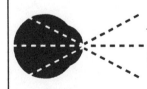

PROPER ROMANCE

All That Makes Life Bright

THE LIFE AND LOVE OF HARRIET BEECHER STOWE

Josi S. Kilpack

THORNDIKE PRESS
A part of Gale, a Cengage Company

Farmington Hills, Mich • San Francisco • New York • Waterville, Maine
Meriden, Conn • Mason, Ohio • Chicago

LIBRARY OF CONGRESS CIP DATA ON FILE.
CATALOGUING IN PUBLICATION FOR THIS BOOK
IS AVAILABLE FROM THE LIBRARY OF CONGRESS

ISBN-13: 978-1-4328-5428-7 (hardcover)

Published in 2018 by arrangement with Deseret Book Company/Shadow Mountain

Printed in Mexico
1 2 3 4 5 6 7 22 21 20 19 18

*To Lee, who has helped me
realize every dream.
How I adore you.*

INTRODUCTION

O, with what freshness, what solemnity
and beauty, is each new day born;
as if to say to insensate man, Behold!
thou hast one more chance! Strive for
immortal glory!
— Harriet Beecher Stowe,
Uncle Tom's Cabin

Before I undertook this project, Harriet
Beecher Stowe was a name I likely missed
on a high school multiple-choice test
twenty-five years ago. As I learned more
about her and her place in history, however,
I was struck by how relevant her story was
to my own. Almost two hundred years
before I was trying to balance family and
writing, Harriet faced the same challenge.

Like me, Harriet was often overwhelmed
by the demands of motherhood, and she
struggled to find a time and a place for her
writing, yet she fought passionately for both

7

of those things in her life. Like me, she married a man who could accept her creative side while also keeping her grounded. Like me, Harriet found success and contentment in her literary career, her family, and her marriage through trial and error, negotiation, and sacrifice.

Unlike me, Harriet accomplished all these things during a time when women could not vote, own land, speak in public, hold political office, or attend college. By the end of this project, I stood in absolute awe of Harriet's accomplishments and had no doubt that Calvin Stowe was her biggest fan as well as a primary reason she was able to have so much influence while still enjoying the blessing of raising her family.

The resources I used as my primary research gave varied accounts of the personalities of the people reflected in this book. Harriet was portrayed as awkward and shy in one account, but gregarious and outspoken in another. In one resource, Calvin Stowe was a pessimistic hypochondriac who was a thorn in Harriet's side, and in another he was a patient, long-suffering, forward-thinking cheerleader. I decided to base my version of their personalities on the results of their relationship, which was a supportive partnership that strengthened throughout their lives despite different temperaments that oftentimes exasperated them both.

Please remember that while I tried hard to capture these people, this is a novel, not a biography. I supplemented fact with fiction and changed some timetables for the sake of creating a good story. The "fullness" of Calvin and Harriet's marriage took longer to develop in real life than I felt I could show in novel form so I condensed the frustrations they both felt during the first decade of their marriage to fit within the eighteen-month period this story covers. I also showed a faster transition in Harriet's feelings of anti-slavery to abolition in order to include that detail of her character development which is so significant to the impact she made on the world. There are chapter notes at the end of the book that point out my specific changes as well as a bibliography that lists the sources I used should you want to explore Calvin and Harriet's remarkable lives in more detail.

I hope that by reading this story Harriet Beecher Stowe will become more than a name in history, that Calvin Stowe will be remembered as the remarkable man I believe him to be, and that you will feel the depth of their having been the perfect partners for one another.

CHAPTER ONE

January 6, 1836

Harriet Beecher looked around her bedchamber — which had been transformed into the bride's room for her wedding day — and found it ironic that all three of her bridal attendants had never been married.

Aunt Esther, her father's sister, and Aunt Harriet, her mother's sister and Hattie's namesake, had both mothered Hattie at various times in her life. Hattie had only been four years old when her mother died, and she was never quite sure if she remembered Roxanna Foote Beecher or had simply turned other peoples' memories into her own.

The third bridal attendant was Catharine, Hattie's older sister by eleven years. She was Hattie's mentor, teacher, mother in many ways, former business partner, and — sometimes — her dearest friend. Today, however, Catharine would not meet Hattie's eyes in the mirror as she did up the buttons on the back of Hattie's wedding dress she had borrowed from a member of their father's congregation. The tightness of Catharine's jaw reflected her disapproval that had begun when Hattie accepted Calvin's marriage proposal. Hattie had held out hope that Catharine's heart would soften in the months since — she had always wanted Catharine's approval — but her hope had been in vain.

"Well," Aunt Esther said, standing up straight and adding one more article of clothing to the armful of discarded linens she'd been picking up from around the room, "I shall check in on the kitchen and see what else needs to be done." She flipped open the pocket watch pinned to her apron. "You've almost twenty minutes until Henry will come for you, Hattie."

"Thank you, Aunt Esther."

Aunt Esther smiled and let herself out of the room.

"I'll see what I can do to help as well," Aunt Harriet said. "I do hope they have put the chairs where I told them to." She came to Hattie and pressed a kiss on her cheek. She smelled of the orange blossoms she'd used to make Hattie's bouquet. "You make a lovely bride, my dear." Aunt Harriet's smile rounded out her apple cheeks. She held Hattie's eyes a moment, and then turned toward the door.

Once Aunt Harriet left, Hattie took a breath and turned her attention to her sister. "Aunt Harriet is kind to extend the compliment, but I fear even a dress as fine as this one will never make up for what I lack."

Catharine concentrated on her task without responding. There were at least fifty tiny buttons.

How on earth will I get out of it later?

Hattie held back a laugh at the realization that it would be Calvin undoing those tiny buttons a few hours from now.

Goodness.

Is this truly happening?

Determined not to let her anxiety of *those* aspects of matrimony take over, Hattie attempted again to engage her sister. "I suppose it's a good thing Mr. Stowe has always been attracted to my intellect."

Catharine still did not respond, and Hattie's irritation rose. She had attempted to playfully engage her sister, and it had not worked. So be it. "If you are so angry, Caty, then go help Aunt Esther and send Aunt Harriet back. At least *she* is happy for me."

Catharine finally met Hattie's eyes in the

speckled mirror. "I am happy for you, Hattie."

If not for her dry tone, Hattie might have considered believing her. "Ah, I see. That explains why you are so morose and judgmental, then. My mistake."

Catharine pursed her lips and concentrated on the buttons again.

"Is this about the Institute?" If resurrecting that argument would fix things, Hattie would face the tired topic yet again. "I never wanted to be in the classroom, Caty. My being a teacher was your dream for me, not mine."

Before Calvin's proposal, Hattie had accepted that her future would likely be in teaching. She had invested time and money in Catharine's Western Female Institute when the Beecher family came to Ohio, and she had agreed to help it find its footing in this "London of the West." That the school had not grown as they had hoped, forcing Hattie to stay in the classroom instead of assuming a more flexible position of management, was not Catharine's fault. But the school had never been Hattie's dream, and marriage was a fair enough reason for her to resign her position.

"I have accepted your leaving the Institute, Hattie."

14

Oh, well, that is good. But if Catharine's sour disposition was not because of the school, there was but one reason left. During the previous three months they had rather expertly avoided it, like horse dung on the street or the smallest biscuit in the basket.

Hattie took a breath. "I am not going to lose myself in marriage, Caty, for all your worry that I will. I know I can make my own way but I am choosing not to."

Catharine finished the last button on the high neck of the gown and stepped to the side. She faced Hattie fully in the looking glass. "Yes, you are *choosing* not to. That is the hardest part."

Ah, they'd finally arrived at the heart of the matter. "I want to marry Calvin. I want to be his partner, and I want to be a mother."

"And waste your gifts — I know."

Hattie turned around to face her sister, struck by the caustic reply despite having braced herself for it. "Do you truly believe that becoming a wife and mother puts to waste what God has given me? Have we not taught any number of young women to embrace their God-given roles?"

"Because a husband and children are all they have to look toward for security," Catharine said.

"Are you certain that you are not simply envious that I am to have those roles after all?"

Catharine's neck turned red, and her jaw tightened. "I envy nothing you have, Hattie, except for the working of your mind. I am disappointed that you are giving up your writing, your potential, and your influence for what any other woman without such intellect and education could do in your place."

"I am not giving up any of those things! Mr. Stowe is proud of what I have accomplished already and promises to help me meet my potential, not hinder my progression."

Catharine was shaking her head before Hattie finished. "There is boundless irony in such a promise," she said, raising a hand to massage her temple. "The very things so attractive to him will be lost, mark my words."

"They will not."

"They will!" Catharine put her hands on her hips and looked at Hattie, her eyes tight and her jaw set. "Name me one married woman who has a voice left. Even in her own home she is drowned out by the cries of her children and the opinions of her husband. You will give yourself away piece by piece." She paused and blinked back tears. Catharine's emotions crashed against Hattie's growing anger, leaving her feeling unsettled.

When Catharine spoke next, her voice was soft and tired. "Mother gave up everything of herself for her family. The *second* Mrs. Beecher did the same, and, should Father marry a woman young enough to still bear him children, his third wife will become one more woman worn through. They were raised at a time when there was nowhere for women to go but from their father's hearth to their husband's bed, but *you* are different, Hattie. Times are changing. Women are being heard, and you have a gift that can make a difference. This isn't about the Institute or your being in the classroom; it's about who you have already become on your own and what you will now give up to become Mr. Stowe's wife instead."

Her voice was pleading, and Hattie wished she could concede to Catharine's argument in some measure.

Catharine's tone sharpened so that once again her words were a reprimand. "You are educated and capable, but you will throw away your potential for a girlish fantasy that will bury you."

A dozen arguments passed through Hattie's mind as she stared at her sister. She could hear the ticking of the old walnut clock counting down the minutes toward her marriage. Most of what Catharine had said was true — both their mother and the second Mrs. Beecher had worked themselves quite literally into the ground — but Hattie was not like them. She was herself, and until Hattie *proved* Catharine wrong there would be no convincing her. Hattie longed for the unity she once shared with her sister, and yet, it seemed obvious that her hopes to dispel the difficulties between them would not be realized. Not today.

The fight had left her, so Hattie looked away from Catharine's sharp gaze and fiddled with the folds of the cream-colored silk dress, trying to blink back the tears in her eyes. "Well, you've had your say then."

Catharine took a deep breath. "I'm sorry, Hattie. I had not intended to say such things on your wedding day. There is nothing to do but move forward. I will wait downstairs with everyone else." She let herself out of the room but did not take the heavy mood with her.

Hattie stared at the closed door and felt her solitude as sharply as the winter wind biting at the windows. The fire in the grate

18

burned off most of the chill, but winter was never completely forgotten in Ohio. Catharine's words were not easily ignored either. Hattie took a shivering breath and let it out slowly.

Am I doing the right thing?

When Calvin had first professed his feelings, Hattie had put him off for the very reasons Catharine had stated. She feared losing herself in the minutiae of daily family life. She had never been a domestic sort, and at twenty-four years of age, she had accepted a future that did not feature a family of her own. Her little geography textbook had done better than anyone expected, and she'd already written nearly a third of her next endeavor — a collection of short stories about New England life. Hattie felt called to write just as surely as Father felt called to preach and Catharine felt called to teach. And yet, even with that knowledge had come the whisper of another calling. God wanted her to marry. God wanted her to marry Calvin Stowe, the man she'd grown to love. And so she would. Doing so would not overtake the whole of her existence.

Hattie turned back toward the mirror and was startled by her reflection. It was strange to see herself as a bride, but she finally felt centered and calm. The angst of the preced-

19

ing weeks was gone, and her heart had shifted so there was room for Calvin where there had not been room before. *Calvin.* Dear Calvin who understood her desire to be a literary woman and who supported such a dream. Was there another man in all of the new America who would support her in such a way?

We will be happy.

A smile on her face did not improve her features any more than the dress did; the cleft of her chin remained, as did the squareness of her jaw and the roundness of her gray-blue eyes. Her plain brown hair was done up in curls on either side of her face for today's occasion. If she squinted her eyes and smiled just right, she almost looked pretty. Almost.

A knock at the door spared her a more critical assessment of her looks, and Hattie turned away from the mirror as her brother, Henry, peeked in. His best gray suit brought out the blue in his eyes, the same shade as Hattie's, and she thought him very handsome today. He looked around the room as though he did not see her, then startled when his eyes landed upon her. He put a hand to his chest with exaggerated drama.

"I'm very sorry, madam, I'm looking for my sister — Harriet Beecher? She's small

— only about this big." He put his hand at the level of his chin as he stepped into the room. "And easy to overlook until she opens her mouth. A rather large man with thinning hair waits to marry her in the parlor. Have you seen her, by chance?"

Hattie rolled her eyes but could not hide her smile. She crossed to the dresser and picked up her orange blossom bouquet. Thank heavens for Henry and his easy nature. "Am I to be escorted to my destiny by an idiot? Such an auspicious beginning."

Henry laughed and put out his arm with formal exactness while clicking his heels together like a soldier. "Ah, it *is* you. My mistake." He grinned, then leaned in and kissed her on the forehead. As he withdrew he whispered, "Calvin Stowe is the luckiest of men, Hattie. You make a beautiful bride."

Hattie could not speak around the instant lump in her throat. She squeezed his arm. He could not know how his compliment helped to heal the wound Catharine had left behind.

"Thank you, Henry." As they left her bedroom, Hattie realized that from this day forward she would be forever known as Harriet Elisabeth Beecher Stowe. She took a fortifying breath and lifted her chin. She would meet her future with confidence.

A new life.

A new future.

Calvin and I will flourish together, she thought as she and Henry reached the stairs that would take her to her destiny. They descended in silence and stopped in the doorway of the parlor. Hattie looked up to meet Calvin's eyes. He was dressed in a sharp black suit, waiting at the front of the room. He smiled at her, and the last of her anxiety softened into calm anticipation of this adventure they were about to embark upon. Together.

CHAPTER TWO

February 16, 1836

Calvin Stowe jotted down his final notes for tomorrow's lecture and placed the pages in their reserved space on the corner of his desk. He returned the pencil to the drawer, replaced the pen in the stock, and double-checked to see that the lid to the inkwell was good and tight. He stood to return *Tholuck's Commentary* to the expanse of shelving that filled one full wall of his office at Lane Seminary. Oh, how he loved German thought on religion.

As Calvin removed his coat and hat from the stand by the door, he made a final inspection of the office, verifying it was as tidy as it had been when he'd entered. The few papers in the bin would start tomorrow's fire in the stove. Assured all was in order, Calvin allowed his mind to move from his responsibilities as biblical professor to the evening ahead. Hattie would be waiting for him, and he was eager to see his new bride after such a long day. He was also famished, having only had tea and bread for lunch due to an afternoon class and faculty meeting. Hattie's father, Lyman Beecher, was not only the president of Lane Seminary but a minister besides, which made faculty meetings a combination of instruction, report, and pounding sermons.

He wondered how long he would stay at the Seminary.

The board and the trustees continued to argue over the results of the rebellions of former years, and the lingering difficulties were wearing on him. Lane Seminary had fulfilled very few of the promises they'd made when they'd recruited him from Dartmouth, and yet his roots were deeper than ever. The Beecher family was set upon the business of converting the West to evangelical Presbyterianism, and Hattie had no expectation of leaving the frontier. He would be well to do as Hattie often reminded him: "Count your blessings instead of your miseries."

Calvin buttoned his wool coat up to his chin and wrapped his favorite scarf — knitted for him by his mother years earlier — around his neck three times. He pulled his beaver hat low on his head to better protect

24

his ears from the February cold. The street-lights cast a heavy orange glow over the campus, and the metallic winter air smelled of wood smoke mingled with the aroma from various dinners cooking within the two dozen or so cottages that framed the campus. His mouth watered at the remembered promise of roast chicken for dinner. He and Hattie usually had remnants from her father's table or milk and bread for supper, so he was prepared to be effusive and gracious in order to encourage future dinners like this one. He craved normal routines and simplicity and hoped that Hattie — so carefree and flighty — was coming about to his way of thinking.

It was not a long walk across campus to Kemper Street, but even so Calvin's toes had begun to tingle with cold by the time he arrived at the door of the humble cottage. One of the promises Lane had yet to fulfill was for a larger house befitting his position. He stomped his feet on the doorstep to knock off as much of the mud-churned slush as possible, wiped his feet vigorously on the mat, then turned the knob and stepped inside. He stopped in the doorway as his breath caught.

The small parlor was usually furnished with a settee, a small table, and an upholstered chair near the fire — perfect for reading after dinner. However, the regular furnishings had been pushed aside to accommodate an easel, a folding table covered in paints, and a wooden chair from the bedroom. Sitting in that chair was his wife of six weeks, dressed in nothing but her shift — amply smeared with paint — and her head wrapped in a brown scarf. She held a paintbrush in one hand but paused to look at him, the brush a few inches away from the thick paper clamped to the easel.

He did not smell roasted chicken.

"Calvin, dear," she said, her face breaking into a smile. "Don't tell me the day has flown already."

Calvin stepped inside and closed the door before facing his wife. Thank goodness no one was on the street to see what he'd come home to. "Good grief, Hattie, what are you doing?"

She smiled indulgently and waved her brush toward the easel. "Painting, of course."

Hattie painted?

She returned to the unfinished painting before her, a summer landscape full of bright greens and yellows and reds that irritated Calvin. They were stuck in the churning gray of winter in Cincinnati, and no one had any business pretending otherwise! Fatigue and hunger and disappointment at not coming home to a hot meal knotted in his chest.

Hattie kept her eyes on her work while she spoke. "I awoke this morning fairly clutched by the needs of creation that had nothing to do with a pen. I went to Father's house and resurrected my mother's easel, which I have not touched since coming to Ohio, I'm horrified to admit."

Painting?

"The house is wrecked, Hattie," Calvin said, his irritation sharpening in his chest. The coal bin had been placed upon his chair, which currently sat in the corner like a scolded child.

"It is not wrecked." Hattie dabbed her brush upon the paper, widening the yellow patch already dashed upon the page and not looking up. "And I shall have it restored in a day or two, once this fit of artistry has passed me. It always passes, you know, but when it comes upon me, I've no choice but to surrender — like a story or an essay. You understand."

"A day or two!" Calvin exclaimed with more intensity than he meant to. Once it was out, however, he couldn't stop. "And where am I to sit until then? Where am I to read and recover from the trials of a long day?" His head began to throb.

Hattie finally seemed to realize his displeasure and looked at him first with surprise, then her eyes narrowed and her chin came up in defiance. "You may sit wherever you like. Simply move what might be in your way and *recover.* Really, Calvin. You are a grown man."

He took a breath that did little to invite calm. "A grown man who has spent the day by the sweat of his brow only to come home to this . . . chaos." He waved his hand around the room. "My wife sits in her underclothes, and . . . and . . . I do not smell any dinner." He had not come home to a home-cooked dinner in all the six weeks of marriage, in fact. Tonight was supposed to be a new beginning. He'd looked forward to it all day.

"I did not make dinner," Hattie said, sitting up straight and watching him with a challenge in her eyes. "I was not hungry, and I wanted to paint."

"Well, *I* am hungry! You said you would have dinner when I returned. You promised you would have it ready."

She shrugged and said coolly, "I changed my mind."

They stared at one another, Calvin's fists

clenched at his sides.

"*And,*" Hattie continued, "if you want dinner on a schedule then perhaps we need to hire that help I have asked for a hundred times."

Calvin unwound his scarf, refusing an argument about hiring help — Hattie knew they couldn't afford it — when he realized how warm the room was. His eyes went to the coal bin on the chair and then to the merry fire in the stove. He paused. "How much coal have you used today?"

"Enough to keep myself from catching my death, thank you very much." She put down her paintbrush and stood with her hands on her hips. There was a smudge of green paint on one side of her thin linen shift and a spattering of orange across her stomach that matched the swipe of color upon her cheek.

Calvin was acutely aware of the state of her undress, though it might have been more distracting had he not been so upset.

"And the paper and paints? Am I to believe you had them on hand for such an occasion as this?" The chance that such useful things would have survived at President Beecher's house was beyond consideration. The Beechers, for all their fervor and merit, were not as industrious or thrifty as Calvin had been raised to be, something he had not fully realized until after he and Hattie had set up a home together.

She lifted her chin in challenge. "I used my own income, Mr. Stowe. I've still some left of my final draw from the Institute."

That she would spend the last of her money on something as frivolous as paint was beyond Calvin's understanding. "And shall *my own income* pay for twice the day's usual ration of coal, then? And a new shift, household incidentals, and the like? Am I to have no say in what is considered necessary versus mere flippancy in my own home? And then I am to come home to no dinner despite your having *promised* me? How do you expect a man to conscience such things, Hattie?"

Her eyes flashed, more gray than blue. "I expect a man to abide a change of expectation from time to time."

"From time to time, not every night!"

She clenched her jaw. "You are capable of making use of the bread and jam in the cupboard. There are several jars of applesauce as well. Or heat the stove and make yourself some eggs." She sat before her easel again, dismissing him.

Calvin clenched his teeth and wound his scarf back around his neck as he glared at his wife, who looked as ridiculous as she sounded. He let himself out of the house, slamming the door as his way of getting the last word.

Hunching into his collar, he started across Kemper Street toward the college cafeteria meant for boarding students. If he was lucky, the doors would still be open and he could have himself a plate. If he was unlucky, Gilly's Pub served ham and potatoes most nights, but paying for it would further infuriate him. Calvin had become familiar with the meal options of Walnut Hills after the death of his first wife, Eliza. How he'd missed her; how he missed her still.

A wave of guilt attended the thought. He should *not* miss Eliza, not with Hattie sharing his name and his house and his bed. He loved Harriet. Of course he did. But some aspects of Hattie's character caused Calvin to remember Eliza's qualities from time to time. Eliza had been a fine cook, for one thing, and kept an efficient house. Duty came before frivolity for Eliza, whereas the opposite was true for Hattie far too often. Calvin shook his head to jar the thoughts out of his mind. He could not travel down the road of comparison. It was poison.

Calvin turned a corner and shuffled up the steps to the dining hall. The doors were still unlocked, and a smattering of students sat around the tables. He was embarrassed to be there. He was a married man, but instead of eating in his own home, he took a seat at an empty table on the far side of the room. Within minutes he had a plate of roast beef, squash, carrots, and a hearty slice of brown bread placed before him. His mouth watered as he unfolded the napkin and placed it perfectly square in his lap. With his fork in one hand and his knife in the other, he cut the meat into uniformly sized pieces and raised the first bite to his mouth. He would be better able to speak evenly with Hattie when his hunger pangs had abated.

Speak evenly, he repeated and felt the irony of those words.

When he and Hattie were aligned on a topic, there was no end to their invigorating discussions. The working of her mind was astounding, and, coupled with her wit, she was unparalleled in intellectual conversation. However, in a disagreement, she was a formidable opponent. A contentious household was nothing short of purgatory in his mind. The exact opposite of order and ease he thrived on. Hattie had to know he'd be vexed when he returned to the house after a long day and found no promised food upon his table. Or did she? Had she been so taken up with *painting* that she'd thought nothing of him? If that were the case, then the situation was more dire than he'd considered. If his comfort was of *no* consideration, what was he to do?

What if he had made a mistake in marrying Hattie? What if his loneliness after Eliza's death had pushed him to a hasty decision? And yet just considering not being Hattie's husband brought the sting of emotion to his throat. He loved Hattie. Even after only a month and a half of marriage he could not imagine life without her. She enlivened his mind and his senses; she brought color and laughter into his life. He longed for her company and opinions. But sometimes . . .

He turned his attention back to his plate and tried to push away the tense thoughts regarding his marriage.

After lingering as long as manners permitted, Calvin returned to his office at Lane. He needed to center himself in an environment of order rather than risk further agitation from the disarray of his home. To prove a point, he did not add more coal to the stove in the corner but instead kept his coat on. He pulled out an anthology of contemporary Christian thought and read about marriage, but he put it away when it placed too much attention on women remaining silent and subservient to their husbands. He and Hattie had agreed that they wanted a companionate marriage. Such a liberal ideal did not lend itself to submission on Hattie's part or dominance on his, but surely his expectation that she would fulfill the promise of dinner at the end of the day was within the realm of reason. He remembered something from a current periodical he'd kept for a future lecture and pulled it from his files.

"The companionate ideal, in short, raises the emotional stakes in marriage. The rewards can be great, but the potential for disappointment has never been greater."

Calvin groaned and threw the periodical on the desk, paused, and then picked it up and returned it to the file. *Every marriage has difficulties,* he told himself, and yet his marriage to Eliza had not. Their temperaments had been perfectly aligned, and, though he may have been overbearing at times and tended to "cultivate indigo," as Hattie had named his brooding moods, Eliza had been patient and accommodating, allowing him to feel all that he felt as deeply as he wanted to while still putting her effort toward his comfort.

He groaned again and pushed aside comparisons for the second time that evening. He attempted to distract himself with his notes for tomorrow's lecture and then, when he had run out of things to do, he bundled up and headed for home.

He wondered if Hattie's father might have some advice for him. Both of Lyman Beecher's late wives had cared for his children, managed boarders, and run household schools. Perhaps Lyman could help Calvin better understand how to inspire Hattie's compliance.

Braced as he was to face the madness, Calvin stopped just inside the front door and let his eyes travel slowly around the room, which had been somewhat restored to its usual condition. The settee was still against the wall and the easel was where it had been before, but both the fireplace chair and end table were in their usual places and the coal bin was beside the hearth. Light streamed from the kitchen, set to the left of the common room, and he smelled cooked butter in the air. Calvin warily removed his outer clothes before exploring further.

The kitchen was empty, but the lamp burning on the table illuminated a single plate filled with scrambled eggs and a slice of bread. A crock of butter sat beside a glass of water, and a jar of applesauce stood ready to be opened and poured into an empty bowl. The rest of the kitchen was a disaster, but she'd chosen him — chosen *them* — over her painting, and he could not ignore that olive branch.

With a softening heart, Calvin crossed to the bedroom and opened the door. The light from the kitchen illuminated a triangular portion of the bed enough for him to see Hattie's small form beneath the quilt. He entered the room and knelt beside the bed, reaching to brush a lock of her hair from her forehead.

Hattie blinked her eyes open, then smiled and reached a hand from beneath the quilt to lay against his cheek. Her touch felt like a kiss and made his skin tingle.

"I don't like it when we quarrel," she said in a voice husky with sleep.

"Neither do I." Calvin leaned in to kiss her full lips as the night's argument slipped away. When he lifted his head, Hattie put her hand behind his neck and pulled him back for an answering kiss of her own. Calvin was reminded from head to toe the ways in which he found marriage to Hattie extremely pleasing; her passions were not

36

limited to creative pursuit, and in matters of intimacy they were perfectly matched. Surely he ought to factor that compatibility higher than he had so far tonight. After some time, she put her hand against his shoulder and pushed him away.

"We shall be all right, I think," she whispered, grinning up at him wickedly. "Did you eat your eggs?"

The eggs were surely cold, and Calvin was full from his dinner at the cafeteria, yet she'd gone to all the trouble . . . "Not yet," he said, knowing he would eat every bite even if his stomach burst.

"Well then, Mr. Stowe, go on and eat." She pulled the blankets up to her chin once more. "When you're finished, come to bed so we might make up properly."

Calvin smiled with eager anticipation, leaned down for one more kiss, and then left the room so that he might eat his eggs.

CHAPTER THREE

February 29, 1836

The clock on the mantel of her father's home chimed four o'clock, pulling Hattie from the story she was trying to finish for that night's Semi-Colon Club meeting, the literary group she, Calvin, and several members of the Beecher family belonged to. The group was a little piece of New England intellectualism amid the Western Frontier — to socialize with like-minded and educated people was priceless. Hattie finished the sentence she was working on with a sigh. She still needed a summary paragraph, and she wasn't entirely pleased with the opening line, but in the fortnight since the "Painting Day" argument with Calvin, she'd been trying to do a better job managing the household and had promised herself she would leave her father's house at four o'clock.

She'd had dinner ready most evenings,

though she still borrowed from her father's table most of the time, and she tried to keep the house tidy even though it was tedious to pack away everything only to bring it out again the next day. She hoped that by applying herself as Calvin wanted her to — as Eliza had before her, though he hadn't said as much — she would find the same joy and satisfaction Eliza had. She had found some measure of satisfaction in having Calvin compliment her efforts, but she'd felt no real joy as of yet. Most of what she did day in and day out seemed like a waste of her time.

Hattie stood, and Catharine looked up from the book she was reading on the other side of the room. "Leaving already?" Catharine had written her piece for the club meeting weeks ago. Hattie had revised it and given some suggestions that her sister had promptly ignored.

"Calvin returns at five on Mondays." Did her tone sound bitter? She hoped not.

Catharine returned to her reading but her silence said enough.

Hattie bit back a defense and picked up the paper she'd been toiling over all afternoon. The meeting didn't start until seven thirty; perhaps she would find time after dinner was heated, served, and cleaned up to work on the final few lines. The hope was thin. She let out a sigh, then glanced at Catharine to make sure she hadn't heard. Catharine did not look up.

Hattie put her paper inside her leather writing folder while reminding herself that a delightful evening awaited her with Calvin and their friends at the meeting. She'd always enjoyed the Semi-Colon Club, but looked forward to tonight more than usual. Her days had become so tedious of late. Coming to the President's House — and enjoying the delicious luncheon the cook had prepared — had been a welcome reprieve from the work of the cottage. She fetched her coat from the rack in the hall and wound her scarf around her neck.

There had been some snow flurries that afternoon, not the heavy soggy kind, and a thin layer of snow preserved her footprints as she crossed Gilbert Street. The cold snapped at any exposed portion of her face, and she was grateful to see the doorway of her home. Calvin found the tiny cottage insulting — he'd been promised a full-sized home upon accepting his position nearly four years ago and was still waiting — but Hattie thought it perfect for just the two of them.

On the other hand, she wouldn't mind

better furniture whereas Calvin was quite satisfied with the heavy dark pieces that had been included with the house. She'd ordered new rugs against his wishes; they would come next week. She made a mental note to make dinner every night until then in order to earn some favor for when he learned what she'd done. New rugs were not extravagant, no matter what Calvin might think, and she was certain he'd like them once he forgave her the expense.

Hattie had left a pot of bean soup simmering that morning before she'd gone to her father's house. She would build up the fire when she got home to heat it through while she made some griddle cakes. She could be proud of her accomplishment in having made a full meal all by herself so long as she didn't think of all she'd have rather done with the time. She'd have likely finished her story if she hadn't had to attend to dinner. Keeping a house was an incredibly dull use of her time, but she was a wife now and had *responsibilities.*

Hattie stomped her feet on the mat and pushed through the front door, immediately realizing that the warmth which should have greeted her was not there. She took a hesitant step inside. She'd left enough coal in the stove, hadn't she?

She took another step inside and noted a hollowness about the house: an opening, a break. When she reached the kitchen, she saw snow, as fine as flour, covering much of the room. The back kitchen door gaped open, and, with a scowl, Hattie trudged forward and shut the door, listening for the click of the latch that she had apparently not listened for that morning when she'd gone out to use the privy. The wind must have pushed the door open as it had a dozen times in the last month. Without anyone to notice it today, however, it had *stayed* open. For hours.

Snow dusted the kitchen, thinner in the areas furthest from the door but still covering the table and chairs. The butter was frozen in its bowl on the counter. Hattie walked to the cold stove and took the lid off the soup. A layer of congealed fat covered the surface with bits of stray carrots and beans poking through the filmy crust. Hattie clenched her teeth and returned the lid with a snap. She looked around the kitchen with her hands on her hips. So much time sacrificed for the blasted soup only to have it come to this?

If Calvin would let her hire help, the room would be repaired in no time — many hands made light work. In fact, if Calvin would let her hire help, none of this would have happened because the servant would have closed the door straightaway and then made roasted potatoes for dinner and an apple pie for dessert. Her mouth watered just thinking about it. How much easier her life might be had she not married such a skinflint.

Be kind, she told herself, *be honorable.* She took a breath, elevated her thoughts, and then forced a smile. A little snow in the kitchen was a manageable tragedy if she approached it the right way.

"Emma, fetch me the broom," she called out to no one. She lifted her chin as a regal woman might. "Pearl, add some coal to the fire." Her words echoed back to herself, and she took a gliding step forward, her nose still in the air. "If we all pitch in, we can get this cleaned up in a thrice!" She pulled the broom from the closet and continued her imaginary counsels with her imaginary help. "And, truly, is it so very hard to make sure a door is latched? Is it so much to ask that you earn your pay by being attentive to such things? Indeed it isn't! I've half a mind to fire the lot of you, since it seems I have to do everything myself." The scenario made her smile, taking the edge off her emotions, and so she continued in her role of the grand lady she would never be.

"Ruth, are you finished with that chicken pie? You know Mr. Stowe likes his dinner hot, and you do make the most delicious chicken pie."

She swept the snow toward the door while instructing her fanciful servants, pretending she lived in a fine house and had no need to know how to run a broom herself. Once she had swept out as much snow as possible, she took a cloth and began wiping down the rest of the kitchen so the melting snow would not puddle and pool on the furniture. She threatened Emma when the insolent girl pouted about her duties, and reminded Ruth that she should be grateful for her position here — her references had not been without concern when she'd applied in the fall.

"I should like a cake to follow dinner too," she said as she bent down to rebuild the fire in the kitchen stove. "A cake would go a long way to earning my forgiveness of this horrible oversight, Ruth, and of course you have time to bake it. A cake only takes, what, two hours — three at most. Why, it will be done in time before we go to bed, and I shall give each of you a slice as thanks."

She lit the paper, closed the door of the

stove, and latched the handle before turning to see Calvin in the kitchen doorway. She jumped and put a hand to her chest. "Calvin," she said, smiling as her heart began to slow from the surprise and then warm at his being home. He had a way of making the house feel full, and she preferred it when he was with her. "I didn't hear you come in."

Calvin crossed to the table and put his leather bag on one of the still-damp chairs. "Who are you talking to?"

"Oh," Hattie said, laughing at herself and feeling the blush in her cheeks. "No one, or, well, I mean, myself, I suppose. I was —"

"You call yourself Ruth?"

Belatedly, Hattie realized that his expression was not jovial. Her own mood wilted, and her defenses rose quickly into place. "I was talking to pretend servants, if you must know."

"Pretend servants?"

Her irritation was fully locked into place. "Yes, pretend servants since we don't have any *actual* servants to help me when the wind blows doors open and fills my kitchen with snow. I've spent the last hour trying to repair the situation, so I made up a houseful of servants to admonish so that the task would not feel so much like the drudgery it is."

She put her hands on her hips, challenging him to say she was a grown woman who should not give into her flippant imaginations. Then she would respond that she was bored, with no outlet for her mind, and in need of some mental stimulation. With a little luck, they would have a row that would leave her feeling justified. Being irritated with her husband would save her from pining after the hours wasted cleaning the kitchen. She would of course eventually feel bad, ask his forgiveness, and perhaps see if she could tempt him to bed early to prove that all was right after all. But first, that argument.

Calvin stepped further into the kitchen, which showed no sign of either the snow she'd found or the effort she'd put into fixing it. He looked toward the back door and then raised a hand to his head and let out a groan. "You're making no sense, Hattie, but it's freezing in here."

Hattie still wore her coat, and between it and the warmth of her exertion, she hadn't noticed the lingering cold. She *should* have repaired the fire in the parlor and the fire in the stove first thing so the house would have warmed as she'd cleaned. She refused to apologize, however.

"It is cold because the wind blew the door open. By the time I returned, there was an inch of snow throughout the kitchen, Calvin." Not really an inch, but was it too much for him to commiserate the accident and praise her for having cleaned it up so well? She'd acted responsibly, which was something he always liked, so why not acknowledge it? Or laugh about it. Her desire for an argument dissipated, and she suddenly felt very tired.

Calvin let out a breath. "Why were you not here to shut the door?"

"I went to my father's house to work on my piece for the club meeting. I've found no time at all these last weeks and did not want to arrive unprepared as I did for the last two meetings." Since her marriage, she had not completed a single piece, which aggravated her to no end. She had worried out loud to Calvin that the responsibility of the household was affecting her ability to write, and he had replied that she should schedule time for her own pursuits in between her responsibilities and then stay to that routine. As though a schedule would solve the problem of having too much tedious work. As though creative writing could be done at a previously determined

47

time. Hattie needed to write, or read, or paint, or embroider when the mood gripped her. Talent could not be organized and catalogued like the books in Calvin's library.

Calvin left the kitchen without a word. Hattie followed a few steps behind as he entered the living room and fell into the chair by the cold fireplace. He raised both hands to his head. "I don't suppose you brought any supper home from your father's house, have you? I've a horrible headache tonight, Hattie. I can barely focus my eyes, but I am famished."

Hattie walked further into the room, her sympathies pricked by the miserable slump of his shoulders. "I left a pot of bean soup on the stove, but it went cold. I've lit the fire and hope to have it warmed through in time for us to eat before the meeting."

"I'm afraid I'm not fit to attend the meeting tonight, my dear."

Hattie's hands flopped to her sides, and her own shoulders slumped. "Not attend? After I worked so hard on this piece?" Which wasn't finished, she reminded herself, because domestic concerns had, yet again, trumped her individual pursuits. It was maddening!

"I am unfit for company," he said, mas-

48

saging his temples while keeping his eyes closed.

Hattie lifted her chin. "Well, I am not unfit."

Calvin opened his eyes, squinting at her a few moments, a look of disappointed acceptance in his eyes. "Then you should, of course, go without me, Hattie. I'll serve myself the soup when it is ready. Thank you for having it prepared." He reached out his hand.

The gesture seemed affectionate, but was he angry with her for leaving? Still unsure, she crossed the room to take his offering. When her small hand was in his larger one, he lifted it to his lips and kissed her palm. Then, with a sigh, he dropped her hand, closed his eyes, and grimaced as he seemed to collapse into the chair again.

Hattie watched him a few moments while debating what to do. Club members usually arrived in pairs, and Hattie had never attended a meeting alone. Catharine had been Hattie's partner in the beginning, and Calvin had been Eliza's; he did not attend in the months after Eliza's death until Catharine was unable to attend a meeting and Hattie had asked him to partner her. They were spending a great deal of time together by then, so it was a natural transition.

49

Calvin groaned again and raised a hand to his temple, his eyes clenched shut. Headaches beset him from time to time. There was nothing either of them could do but let them pass, right?

After watching Calvin for another moment, his eyebrows cinched in the middle of his forehead, Hattie decided that she *would* attend the meeting. Calvin had told her she should, and so he could not fault her for going. She fetched a blanket from her cedar chest and tucked it around Calvin's shoulders. He thanked her with his eyes still closed. She built up the fire in the parlor, stirred the barely warmed soup, and checked the damper on the stove. While Calvin huddled in the parlor, she went over her story in the kitchen and finished the final paragraph. Were her husband feeling better, she would read it to him for his opinion, but he was out of sorts, and she was trying not to feel guilty for leaving him.

At seven o'clock, Hattie set a bowl of just-warm soup on the table and kissed Calvin good-bye before running for her father's carriage that had pulled up in front of the house. Her own stomach rumbled with hunger, but Uncle Samuel's cook always made the most delicious finger foods for the guests. Far better than bean soup.

Hattie had not been at the club meeting more than twenty seconds before Aunt Elizabeth asked after Calvin.

"He is under the weather tonight," Hattie explained with appropriate wifely sympathy, just as she had when Father and Catharine had asked the same question in the carriage. "He encouraged me to come without him."

"Oh, dear," Aunt Elizabeth said. "I hope it is not serious." With regular breakouts of cholera in Cincinnati, illness was always of great concern.

"No, no," Hattie assured her, taking a sandwich from the tray set upon a small table. "Just a headache." She took a bite of the sandwich — ham and cranberry — delicious!

Mrs. Greene had joined them during their exchange, and her eyebrows lifted in response to Hattie's explanation. "Not one of those headaches that leave him low for days?"

"No, he did not have it this morning, only when he returned this evening."

Mrs. Greene shook her head, her round face pulled with sympathy. "I remember him explaining his terrible headaches to me once. He said it was as though a chisel were impaled into his skull and then hammered on for hours and days."

He'd never said as much to Hattie, but then he'd never had a headache in her presence before. Then she remembered a time when they were courting and he'd canceled plans three nights in a row because he said his head was hurting to the extreme. Hattie had sent him a note of condolence, and then accompanied her father on a trip to Hamilton where he proselytized to another minister's congregation. By the time she'd returned, Calvin was well.

"It is not so bad as that," Hattie assured Mrs. Greene, but she was uneasy about what she didn't truly know. Didn't many people get headaches?

More guests arrived, and Hattie found herself only thinking about Calvin when someone would ask after him. Mrs. Greene's sentiment and concern was repeated by most of the club members. "Remember that time he was down for a full week?" Mr. Allen, another teacher at Lane, said. "I don't think he ate a thing all that time. His belt could barely keep his trousers up when he came back to work."

The others in the circle nodded, though Hattie did not remember it.

"Thank goodness Eliza was there to tend to him," Father said with a nod. "She at least got him to take some tea and kept a cold cloth on his head."

Mrs. Bingham looked at Hattie. "Did you make sure he had some tea before you left, dear?" She caught herself, her cheeks turning pink with embarrassment as she leaned forward to pat Hattie's knee apologetically. "But of course you did."

Hattie nodded to save herself from any censure. She hadn't even thought to make him tea.

By the time everyone gathered for the readings, every member of the club had expressed deeper concern over Calvin's welfare than she had felt. Each of them seemed aware of his history with painful headaches, and several of them shared stories about their own headaches, or friends who had been laid low with similar complaints. Hattie hadn't hesitated deeming Calvin's complaint as one more shade of him "cultivating indigo," which he seemed to take a certain comfort from. She struggled to justify herself against the contrast of the unanimous concern surrounding her like a net.

"Well, then, who has something to read tonight?" Uncle Samuel asked as he stood at the head of the room.

Several hands went up, including Hattie's. Now maybe they could move past concern for Calvin and focus on the efforts put into tonight's meeting — parlor literature.

"Mrs. Stowe should go first," Mrs. Greene said. "So that she might return to Calvin as soon as possible." She patted Hattie's knee again. "I'll have my carriage take you home so that Mr. Beecher and Miss Beecher can stay a bit longer."

Heads bobbed in acknowledgment, and someone said, "Capital idea."

Hattie wished she could refuse. She disliked reading in front of everyone — Calvin often read her work in her place — and to be first made her stomach tighten.

With all eyes on her, Hattie walked to the front of the room and read her story with as much inflection as she could manage though her voice shook. Perhaps she should have stayed home and attended to her husband after all. The evening wasn't turning out anything like she'd expected.

When she finished reading, everyone applauded. A few members asked questions about the true story she'd based her work on, and Hattie felt they were well on their way to a debate about slavery when Aunt Elizabeth popped up from her chair and offered to make up a plate for Calvin. Mrs. Greene signaled for the footman standing at the rear of the room to order her carriage round.

As the next reader stood, Hattie followed her aunt into the kitchen.

"I do hope he'll eat something," Aunt Elizabeth said. "He needs to keep up his strength. You'll let me know what I can do, won't you, Hattie?" She took Hattie's hands and gave them a squeeze, her eyes bright with compassion. "I'm so glad he has you to care for him. We would all worry so if he were on his own. What a blessing you are, dear."

CHAPTER FOUR

Calvin had managed to make his way to bed and lay on the covers fully clothed, but he was still awake when Hattie came in. A rag covered his closed eyes while he repeated a silent prayer that the pounding in his head would end soon. Some headaches lasted only an evening, but sometimes it took days before he was restored. He had forced himself to finish his classes today; he didn't want to give the board of Lane Seminary any reason to deny his petition for the promised house again. Now, however, he regretted not coming home as soon as the edge of his vision had begun to crumple. That was always the first sign of an approaching menace, and lying down in a dark room sometimes meant he could avoid the worst.

Though aware of Hattie's return, Calvin's focus remained on his excruciating pain. The bed creaked when she sat upon the edge, and he reached his hand towards her, hungry for comfort of any kind. He found her hand and held it tightly, hoping she would stay. She did, and he swore the pain eased a fraction. A moment later, the rag was taken from his forehead and replaced with one so cold and brisk that his breath caught for a moment before his shoulders relaxed.

"Is it too cold?"

She spoke softly, for which he was grateful. Light was the enemy's cavalry in the battle taking place within his skull, but sound was a fearsome foot soldier. "No," he whispered back. "It is perfect."

"Aunt Elizabeth sent some ice. I did not know your headache was this bad, Calvin. I'd have never left if I'd realized."

Calvin squeezed her hand. He'd known as soon as he arrived home that she would go to the meeting without him. She'd had that determined look about her. Any resentment he'd felt toward her was forgiven now that she'd returned. And with ice for his head no less.

"Aunt Elizabeth also sent some brandy," Hattie said, her voice even softer. "She made sure that Father did not see."

"Bless her," Calvin whispered. Lane Seminary did not encourage indulgences, and though Lyman Beecher was known to open a bottle of wine on special occasions, he was not a supporter of keeping liquor in one's home. Calvin agreed with the sentiment — drunkenness was a cruel taskmaster — but a drink tonight would be purely medicinal, and he'd defend himself to the president if he had to.

It took a moment for Hattie to pour a glass, and then she helped him sit up enough to take a long swallow. He wasn't used to spirits, and so he coughed, which made his head feel as though it were exploding, but once he recovered, and managed a few more swallows, he felt his arms and legs softening into the mattress. His thoughts skittered away from the blaring thoughts of pain. Hurt. Agony.

Hattie replaced the cloth on his forehead. Calvin let out a long breath and believed for the first time that night that he might actually sleep.

"Thank you, dearest," he whispered.

"Of course," she whispered back, then laid down alongside him. He remained on his back and kept hold of her hand.

"What does it feel like?" she whispered. "Does it hurt to tell me?"

Calvin was touched that she wanted to understand. "It feels like my head is a nail beneath a hammer."

"How awful."

"As though my head were ice being chiseled to bits from the inside out."

"Terrible," Hattie commiserated.

"Like my brain is rising in my skull like bread dough without enough pan."

This time she said nothing, but her body shook slightly.

Calvin sighed dramatically and looped his free hand through the air. "She laughs at my pain." He cracked open one eye and looked at her, propped up on her elbow and staring down at him, trying to control her smile.

"I am sorry," she said, "but bread dough? That is not a very ominous analogy, Calvin. Once dough has risen, it simply falls."

"*Explodes,* you mean," he said, closing his eyes again. The pain was still intense, but between the brandy and Hattie's company he was not so focused on it. "Ruptures. Decimates."

She settled back beside him, snuggling closer. He took a deep breath, noting that she smelled of lavender. Had she put on the scent especially to help calm him? He was touched by the possibility. They laid in silence for a full minute before Hattie spoke again. "I'm sorry I went to the meeting. It was not very thoughtful of me to leave you unattended."

He gave her hand another squeeze, not wanting to dwell upon it. She was here now, and he was grateful. "Did you read tonight?"

"Yes."

"What was your piece?"

"Nothing notable." A sigh betrayed her disappointment. "I wrote a story about that slave woman Mr. Rankin told us about when we went to Ripley. Do you remember?"

"The one who crossed the breaking ice with her baby?"

"Yes, I tried to recreate the story, but I'm afraid it's lacking something. It felt more like a narrative than something . . . evocative."

"Why don't you read it to me? Perhaps between the two of us we can find the missing bits."

"You're not feeling well," Hattie said, but he heard the hope and hesitation in her voice. It surprised him how confident she could be one moment and how insecure the next. Especially when it came to her writing, and *especially* more when she had to read her work aloud. She'd explained once that as a teacher, no one had questioned her. As a writer, it seemed everyone did.

60

Calvin found the admission endearing. So often Hattie felt like a fortress to him, determined and resolute, without any weakness at all.

"Hearing your story will help take my mind off my poor head," Calvin said, squeezing her hand again. "Please."

The bed moved as she sat up. "Are you certain?"

He cracked his eye open again and saw her watching him with either concern or trepidation, he wasn't sure which. "I am sure."

Her expression relaxed and she nodded. "Let me fetch it."

She returned a minute later to sit cross-legged on the bed, skirts tucked around her knees. She read the story, barely two pages long and rather factual. "It lacks emotion," she said when she finished.

"I think it's compelling." Calvin could tell she'd been rushed in the writing; it did not reflect her usual voice. "I do not think it's far off from a very good piece."

"Only no one would believe the story is true, would they?"

Calvin opened his eyes again. Hattie was staring off into the darkened room, her forehead pinched. She must have felt his gaze because she turned back and met his eyes. "A slave woman jumping from ice block to ice block with a baby in her arms, risking the death of both of them?" She shook her head. "I don't know that *I* would have believed it if Rankin were not such a trustworthy source."

"There are fates worse than death that can compel someone to do unbelievable things," Calvin said. "And God's hand can reach for everyone in His time and in His way."

Hattie adjusted her position and looked at her paper as though it might fix itself if she stared hard enough. "After hearing so many stories of escaping slaves, I find it impossible not to believe such a miraculous thing. Edward heard about a mother jumping from a boat on the Ohio River with her baby after she was sold to a trader — drowning them both." She paused in appropriate solemnity, before continuing. "The man who told Edward the story had been on the boat. He'd seen the woman escorted onto the ship, and then he heard the splash in the night. It was only the next day when he realized what had happened. She hadn't been shackled on account of the baby." She paused. "Shackled," she breathed as though finding it hard to believe.

"Slavery is a cursed thing," Calvin said, nodding as best he could though it made the room spin. He closed his eyes again. "I am grateful we live in a free state so that we are not forced to endure the practice more pointedly."

He felt Hattie nod by the way the bed moved beneath him. The pain was sharpening. He may need more brandy. "Would you mind getting another cooled cloth for my head, Hattie? Then we can discuss the piece some more."

She fairly jumped off the bed and returned a minute later with a blessedly frigid cloth.

"Perhaps if you spoke more from the mother's voice than a narrator's, it would sound more like a story than an essay," Calvin suggested.

"I don't want to talk about it any longer," Hattie said, and her tone was resolute. "Not that I don't appreciate your thoughts, Calvin, I do, but I feel as though I am not ready to write such a thing. I'm not sure I understand it well enough."

"Understand slavery?"

Hattie paused. "Perhaps, but I meant . . . I don't think I can write about a mother when I am not one. I think it must be a thing that changes a person — makes her willing to jump on ice blocks across a river. I can't imagine taking that risk for anyone."

Calvin chose not to be offended that she

would not jump across the ice for him. He knew that wasn't what she meant. "Perhaps one day soon you will understand such a connection. Then you can return to the piece more aware of that kind of sacrifice and write it in a way that convinces your readers of its truth." Calvin was thirty-two years old and longed to be a father. He also felt a child would solidify this marriage, yoke him and Hattie together in such a powerful way that they would be united instead of too often wanting to move different directions. He longed for that solidarity with her, yet he knew he often went about it the wrong way. He didn't feel that distance now. In fact he felt closer to his wife than he had in some time. Because of her writing? Was that the common ground they held?

"Not too soon, I hope," Hattie said, laughing as though the idea of motherhood was impossible. They both knew better, but then Calvin and Eliza had been married three years and never been so blessed. Hattie lay back down on the bed and snuggled into his side again. She took a deep breath, then let it out slowly. "I prefer the meetings when you attend with me, Calvin. I think I shall not like to go without you ever again."

Calvin raised their joined hands and

kissed the back of hers. Her consideration was endearing and appreciated, but should another night like this one play out, he believed she would go to the meeting again. He settled their clasped hands onto his chest. "I'm glad to have you with me, Hattie. Thank you."

CHAPTER FIVE

March 24, 1836

On Thursdays, Calvin did not have a class until ten o'clock. He could stay in bed until eight if he chose. However, Calvin woke at six thirty every morning — even Sundays. Calvin ate two hard-cooked eggs for breakfast with a single cup of black coffee. Calvin felt Hattie's ambition of early to rise should match his own. It did not.

Sometimes Hattie was able to fall back asleep once the front door closed behind him, but more often than not she was too alert and would lay in bed for an hour before giving up and throwing back the covers with a grumble and a huff. One morning Calvin had come back for something just as she was making up the bed, and he'd given a triumphant smile that resulted in her making sure she was out with her friend Mary Dutton when he came home that night so he would have to forage for his own dinner.

Today, she rolled away from the unusually bright winter light streaming through the window of their bedroom, pulling the covers over her head and putting off rising as long as she could. If today was the same as the last eight days had been, she would be *certain* she was pregnant, and she did not feel prepared to face the reality. Her courses had not come. Her head spun when she stood suddenly. The smell of cooking meat made her ill. As an educated woman of twenty-four years, who had watched her stepmother navigate four pregnancies, she did not have the blessing of ignorance regarding what these symptoms meant.

Hattie clenched her eyes shut and tried to distract herself with thoughts about the essay she was writing about New England summer. She might submit it to the *Western Monthly,* which had published two of her prior pieces, and then use the money toward a new kitchen table that could also serve as her writing desk. She hated the table currently taking up space in the kitchen. A new table, smooth and varnished, would be a worthwhile addition to her household. Perhaps she would go to Findley's and see what they might suggest. If she ordered a table now, and sold another article in April, she could get matching chairs. Calvin had simple tastes and saw little value in things like varnished tables — or the new rugs she'd purchased last month. As predicted, he had not been pleased, which was why she would buy this table with her own income. Calvin worried too much about money.

Hattie drifted in and out of sleep for another hour, until the need to visit the privy made it impossible for her to doze any longer. The late Mrs. Beecher — not her mother, who had died when Hattie was four, but Lyman Beecher's second wife who'd been dead these last nine months — had sometimes gone to the privy twice an hour when she was pregnant. But that had come later, when the babe took up every bit of space, she'd said.

Though Hattie had never been particularly close to her stepmother, she missed her right now. She was the only woman Hattie felt she could have talked to about this. But Hattie's stepmother was gone. Hattie's mother was gone. Hattie's sister Mary was a mother herself, but she lived in Connecticut. The idea of telling anyone else made Hattie's face catch fire. She'd been married just over two months — *two months* — and already she was expecting.

Catharine would be upset, but only show it with a tight look and an even tighter smile. Father would be ecstatic; he thought she needed a child to take her focus off herself. And Calvin? What would he think? Certainly he would be happy — but why? For the same reason as Father? Because he hoped a child would settle Hattie's racing thoughts and unfocused ambition? Or would he see a child as a gift from heaven — a part of her and a part of him bound together in legacy? The warmth of that thought calmed her, and she pushed herself into a sitting position amid the tangled bedclothes. A baby. A child. Her own.

The room spun, and she took a few breaths to settle her balance before swinging her legs over the side of the bed. Her feet did not touch the floor, making her feel too young and childish for this phase of life. But she was twenty-four years old. Some women her age had two or three children already. She'd wished to have at least a year to find her way as a wife before she had to find her way as a mother. Catharine's words from her wedding day about being drowned out by her husband's opinions and the cries of her children pricked at her like pins. Hattie was determined to prove Catharine wrong, but she was already struggling.

A mother.

Hattie put a hand on her still-flat stomach. At what point did a soul attach itself to the child growing within her? Was she already more than just Harriet Beecher Stowe? She stepped off the bed, let her balance return, and then found her dressing gown in a heap near the chair where she'd thrown it the night before. Her habits of housekeeping, which she'd been so attentive to following the "Painting Day" incident, had suffered these last few weeks as the newness of the intention wore off and hints of spring pulled at her interests. It simply wasn't in her temperament to need things so tidy and exact. She'd told Mary Dutton, "Every woman has different gifts and housekeeping does not happen to be mine." She liked walks through the woods of Walnut Hills, however, and was contemplating starting a flower garden in the sorry patch of dirt behind the cottage. She'd ordered four different magazines to help with her preparations, and kept them hidden so Calvin would not ask how much they cost.

Hattie tied the robe around her still-slim waist — that would not change for some weeks, she knew — and slid her feet into her slippers. The chamber pot was always an option, but without hired help, she would have to take responsibility to clean it. She preferred the biting cold of the outside privy to that. She wished again that Calvin would let them hire a girl of all work. It continued as a source of contention between them, but maybe an upcoming third member of their household would convince him of the necessity. She'd tried everything else to sway him — poor meals, cluttered rooms, undone wash — maybe this child would finally bring him to her side of the argument.

It was noon before Hattie was dressed for the day with her hair pinned up respectably. She'd managed some toast for breakfast and then spent some time working on the New England article while sipping her morning tea.

She struggled to focus on the writing, but eventually finished the draft and then entertained herself by writing a satirical version of the same piece with lobsters chasing tourists on the beach in July and heat capable of boiling water without a fire. She would take this second one to the next Semi-Colon Club meeting. Thinking of the next meeting, however, made her think about the last one, when she'd left Calvin home with a headache that had kept him prostrate for two days. She felt guilty every time she thought of how dismissive she'd been at first, and how hard it had been to be by his side as nursemaid in the days that followed. Both at the club meeting and at church the next Sunday, people had brought up how wonderfully attentive Eliza had been to Calvin when he'd been similarly ill during their marriage.

Eliza. Thoughts of her dear friend and Calvin's first wife brought an array of emotions. What would Eliza think of Hattie carrying Calvin's child? A child Eliza had wanted so much and never had. Hattie usually told herself Eliza would be happy that she and Calvin found comfort together, but there were days when Hattie's awareness that Calvin still held affection for Eliza rose like a specter. Prayer, studying the Bible, and remembering the assurance she'd felt of God's approval would usually silence her guilt, but today the fears roiled inside her like the churning wheels of an undertaker's carriage.

Had Eliza lived, Hattie would be teaching, writing — unmarried and unpregnant. Had Eliza lived, Calvin would only be the husband of Hattie's friend, and he would enjoy dinner on the table every night, and pressed pants and clean shirts in the closet every morning. Perhaps Eliza *would* have given him a child by now. When headaches laid him low, Eliza would tend to him without a thought for herself.

Would Calvin be happier if Eliza had been the only Mrs. Calvin Stowe? Would Hattie? Was Catharine right? Had Hattie entered a phase that would lead to the demise of being her own person? Anxiety wrapped around her until she found herself sobbing at the splintery kitchen table.

Eliza. Eliza. Eliza.
Calvin. Calvin. Calvin.

Was she living the wrong woman's life?

"Hattie?"

Her head popped up, and for an ethereal moment, she didn't know where she was or who had said her name. The room spun for an instant before the front door closed, and Hattie realized that Calvin had come home early. As his footsteps came toward her through the parlor, she sat up straighter and wiped frantically at her eyes.

Too soon, however, Calvin stood in the kitchen doorway — filling it as though it were built to his measurements exactly — and grinned at her. *Grinned?* In the same moment Hattie realized he'd come to tell her something exciting, he seemed to realize he'd interrupted something quite different than what he expected. It wasn't like Hattie to turn into puddles. In fact, she couldn't remember the last time she'd indulged herself in so much emotion. Another change this pregnancy had brought into her life. Another *something* to come to terms with.

"What's wrong?" Calvin asked, hurrying to slide next to her on the bench. He put an arm around her shoulders, and she melted into him, led away from her embarrassment by his kindness.

For a few seconds she tried to control the emotion that had overtaken her, but the pull was too great and soon she was sobbing into his shoulder. Maybe if she fully expelled this burden she would be able to think clearly again. Calvin held her against him, rubbing her back, and whispering that whatever it was would be all right. And she believed him. The words burrowed into her, casting out the shadows, freeing the dark places in her mind, and replacing her equilibrium. Perhaps this *was* exactly what she and Calvin needed to smooth things between them. Maybe a child *would* calm her sometimes-frantic nature and free his sometimes-unbending one. It was some time before Hattie dared lift her head, her insides soft and her heart open in the light of his compassion. He did not even know why she was crying, yet he'd held her and comforted her wholly.

"I'm so sorry, Calvin," she said, wiping at her wet cheeks. His coat had taken the worst of it. She shook her head in self-recrimination. "I don't know what's come over me." Except that she *did* know, and the reminder nearly unhinged her all over again. How would she tell him? What would he say? Surely he would be happy, wouldn't he? And his happiness would balance her own wobbling thoughts, wouldn't it?

Calvin took her chin in his hand and used his handkerchief to wipe away the last of her tears. His eyebrows were furrowed, his blue eyes heavy with concern. He really was so kind. Her chin began to quiver again.

"What's the matter, Hattie? What's happened?"

What's happened? A newly married couple filling long, cold, Ohio nights *happened.* Two people who struggled to find common ground together during the day but had no such difficulties once the bedroom door closed behind them *happened.* "I'm pregnant, Calvin. We're going to have a child."

Calvin went so still she feared he'd stopped breathing. His expression, so concerned a moment earlier, went slack, and his eyes widened as he stared at her. She took two shuddering breaths. He said nothing, and she felt tears well up in her eyes again. What if he *wasn't* happy? What if all he saw was the difficulty and embarrassment and responsibility that loomed ahead of them? What if he did not want a child that was part her and part him?

And then tears came to his own eyes and he smiled as she had never seen him before — she did not know he could smile so big. He put his hands tenderly on her shoulders. "Are you certain?" he asked in a whisper, in a breath.

Hattie nodded, and he let out a shivering exhale as he pulled her to him and held her tight. She felt his tears against her neck, and her fear receded again. The crying turned to laughing and then he began asking questions: How was she feeling? What could he do to help? How long had she suspected? Was she certainly, entirely, unquestionably sure?

"When will the child come?" he finally asked.

"October, I think," Hattie said, smiling too as she caught hold of his excitement and clung tightly.

Calvin's expression went slack and his shoulders fell. "October?"

"I know," she said, shaking her head. "Everyone will know that we wasted no time at all. It's humiliating."

He shook his head and pushed a hand through his thinning hair as he turned and stared at the table, his expression troubled. "It's not that."

"Then what?" Hattie said, her fears returning. It made her feel vulnerable and weak to see him wavering.

Calvin pulled a letter from the inside of his coat pocket. He handed it to her but explained the contents before she could read for herself. "The plans for my trip to Europe have come through," he said.

More than a year ago, Calvin had been asked by the Ohio state legislature to travel to Europe to research their schools. Lane Seminary had agreed to continue his salary if he would also gather books to make their library the finest one west of Harvard College. At one point she and Calvin had decided to wait to marry until after the trip was finished — he would be gone eight months, at least — but then when delay after delay made the trip feel more like fantasy than reality, they had finally chosen not to wait. Weeks had passed since they had talked about the trip at all, and now it had come at the worst time.

While these thoughts stomped through Hattie's thoughts, she could see in Calvin's face that he was considering rejecting the offer — was all but asking her to give him reason to do so. It was tempting. She needed him here; they were only just married and would soon have a baby. But she knew the importance of this trip. Calvin was hesitant to put himself forward for such opportunities. He tended to hang about in the corners while other men were promoted around him. This trip of a lifetime had come to him, and if he did not go, he may never get another chance.

Hattie took a deep breath and insisted that the emotions she'd already entertained too much of today did not take over. She pushed a smile to her lips. "Oh, Calvin, that is wonderful."

His expression showed the slightest bit of confusion, and perhaps disappointment. She looked away so he would not read too much in her eyes. She opened the letter, scanning quickly so that she might say something more before the lump in her throat prevented her. "June?" she said, hating that her voice shook. He would set sail a week before her twenty-fifth birthday. She couldn't fall to pieces again. He needed her for strength in this moment just as she'd needed him a few moments before. When she had contained her objections, she looked up at him and spoke the details he already knew. "You sail from New York in June."

"Perhaps you can come with me as we once considered," he said. "I can talk to —"

Hattie put a finger to his lips. "I will be four months pregnant in June. I cannot cross the Atlantic." Oh, but if she were *not* four months pregnant . . . what an adventure it would be! To tour Europe? To see the world?

Oh, God in Heaven, help me not to hold this against my child.

"Perhaps the trip can be postponed," Calvin said. "They have already waited this long."

If only. Hattie straightened her spine. "And then you'll leave me all on my own with a baby? I don't think so, Mr. Stowe. If I am to be left to my own care, I should rather have less responsibility at my feet than more during your absence."

Calvin let out a breath, deflated. "If I go I shall miss the birth of my child."

"But you will return soon after, and he will not know the difference."

"He?" Calvin said, looking shocked again. "You can tell already?"

Hattie laughed, bringing some ease to her heart. "Or she." She took Calvin's hand, so

79

much bigger than her own, and held it between both of hers. "I shall move in with Father and Aunt Esther when you go. Then I'll have all the help I could want when the baby comes. By the time you return, I shall be recovered and our baby will be eager to meet its father. What a reunion we will have."

He let out another breath and his shoulders fell another half an inch.

"This trip is the opportunity of a lifetime, Calvin, and you cannot reject it. When you return, we'll be a family — all three of us."

He looked up, and she could see that he was accepting what the decision must be. Good. *She* had little choice but to do so, and if they could move forward together, they would be stronger for it. Was there, also, perhaps a bit of relief that she would have some time to herself while he was gone? She could gather strength for being a wife *and* mother. Time apart would be a chance for her to get her feet beneath her once again. Such thoughts were for no one but herself, of course, and she was glad for keeping quiet when a smile spread across Calvin's face once more. He leaned in, took her face in both of his hands, and kissed her soundly.

"I love you, Hattie Stowe, and you have

made me the happiest of men."

She kissed him back, and then they turned their attention to the details of the letter. He would leave for New York in May, barely six weeks from now. Lane would pay for his sea travel and book purchases, in addition to a portion of his current salary, and the state of Ohio would pay for lodging, land travel, and meals. Calvin would be responsible for incidental expenses, clothing, and any personal luxuries. But Calvin did not indulge in anything, and he assured Hattie he would spend very little of their personal funds. She believed him and decided to leave their discussion about how much money Hattie would have available in his absence for another day.

When the clock in the parlor chimed one o'clock, Calvin startled. "Gracious, I've a class waiting for me." He jumped from the bench and picked up his hat. "I had meant to come over for just five minutes. How could I have known how much news was waiting for me?"

Hattie smiled and rose to her feet. She walked him to the door and held it open as he stepped onto the street. He took two steps, then turned back to her, still beaming. "If it's a girl, I would like very much to name her Eliza Tyler, do you mind?"

Hattie froze for the space of a heartbeat. He wanted to name their child after the wife he'd buried?

"Eliza had wanted a child so dearly." The sentimental tone in his voice reminded Hattie why she'd been in tears when he'd arrived, and yet she knew he would not understand the offense of this request. He would also not feel it if their roles were reversed because there was no room in his heart for petty jealousy. For all her complaints, he was a good-hearted man.

Calvin lifted his eyebrows, waiting for her response. Hattie forced her smile bigger and nodded. What else could she do? Calvin nodded in relief, then turned and took long strides toward the Seminary. Hattie closed the door behind him, leaned her back against it, and cried all over again.

CHAPTER SIX

April 19, 1836
Calvin was teaching when the classroom door burst open.

"A fight in the square!" a young man shouted before disappearing as quickly as he'd arrived.

"A fight?" one student repeated. He was halfway from his chair when Calvin told him to sit.

"We've ten minutes left of class," Calvin said, standing from his desk and giving his students a hard look. Once the students stilled, he returned to his instruction regarding the death of Joseph and the enslavement of the Israelites by the Egyptians. The restless air continued to fill the classroom, however, and when Calvin looked up from his notes, the young man he'd ordered to sit was slipping through the open door and two others were en route.

Calvin glared at the young men and took

off his spectacles. "Whatever squabbles are taking place outside of these four walls are not our concern," he said, even though he couldn't help but think of the racially motivated scuffle in town last week or the campus riots of a few years earlier. His heart began to race despite his determination not to think the worst.

"But, sir," the student closest to the door said, "what if it is more than a fight?" The faint sounds of distant yelling could be heard beyond the classroom.

Calvin did not have time to formulate a response before the second young man already on his feet bolted for the door. The other student followed, and simultaneously another half a dozen men began shutting the covers of their books.

"Conduct yourself as Lane students, all of you," Calvin said before waving the rest of them to the door. He would not keep their attention now — assuming he *had* before the announcement. Even though the Lane students came for theological training, it was a challenge to keep their attention on events that had happened thousands of years ago on days even without such juicy distractions.

The room cleared quickly, and Calvin gathered his materials, hoping that the fight was nothing serious. The Lane Rebellion, as the anti-slavery events of 1834 had come to be known, were not so long ago as to be easily forgotten. The student debates that had grown into rioting on campus had resulted in a loss of both enrollment and sponsors. For every person who felt Lane had been too conservative in their final judgment to refrain from officially supporting abolition there was another person who felt Lane had been too liberal for allowing the debates to go on as long as they had. Calvin had agreed it a wiser course to keep Lane focused on a theological education and to not fully side with the abolitionists, but he was not always comfortable with the fact that their decision showed up as support of slavery itself. If slavery was evil, which he believed it was, shouldn't any Christian institution take some official stance against it?

Calvin left the building, considering whether he should follow the shouting — louder now that he was outside — or report it to administration. Someone called his name, distracting him from the decision for a moment.

Lyman Beecher was coming toward him at a brisk pace. Calvin's misgivings rose. "I pray you are not bringing me bad news," he said when Lyman was near enough to hear.

Lyman smiled, putting Calvin's mind at rest. "Nothing of the sort. Did your class desert you?"

"Entirely. Do you know anything about the tussle?" He nodded toward the sound of yelling emanating from the western side of the campus. It seemed to be fading.

"Already breaking up," Lyman said, waving a dismissive hand. "Thankfully."

Calvin nodded in relief. "Racial?" he asked, almost not wanting to hear the answer.

Anti-slavery groups were getting bold in Ohio again, which only caused the merchants dependent on Southern trade to bellow. A new abolitionist newspaper — the *Philanthropist* — was the most recent bone over which the two sides were fighting. Lane was still attempting to maintain neutrality.

"Not this time," Lyman said, the grateful tone still in his voice. "Young men fighting over the affection of a woman. Ordinary things that burn themselves out rather quickly."

"Thank heavens for that," Calvin said. "I'm still hoping that what we saw in Cincinnati last week will be the worst of this latest round." The men began walking toward Calvin's office.

Lyman was silent a moment, his great steely eyebrows pulled together. He shook his head. "I think we both know that wishing last week's breakout to be the worst we'll see is a hope beyond even our level of faith." He caught Calvin's eyes. "I fear the discord will get worse before it gets better — especially in Ohio, poised as it is between slave states and Canada. Did you hear about George?"

Calvin shook his head, surprised by the turn of topic to Hattie's brother. George currently lived at the President's House and attended Lane, though he'd received prior education at Yale. "I can't say that I have. One never hears much about George."

Lyman huffed a laugh at the joke, but the smile did not last for a second breath. "He's gone and joined the abolitionists."

Calvin stopped walking. "You don't say. I am rather impressed."

"Well, I am not." Lyman bristled and faced Calvin. "He's made himself a target, that's what he's done, and you know as well as I that my household needs no more scandal." He looked at the ground and toed a sprig of grass flourishing in the mild weather of spring.

In that moment he looked quite contrite — an emotion Calvin rarely saw displayed by his sixtyish father-in-law who was larger than life and louder than most voices in whatever argument he found himself debating. And Lyman was often in the center of a great many debates due to his progressive Protestantism and unfailing opinions. Twice he had been called to defend his teachings to a Church heresy court. Then the Lane Rebellion had ended with more than half the theology students deferring their placements, and a similar number of potentials refusing scholarship, and it was Lyman who had been blamed for not putting a stop to the debates before they got out of hand.

Yet this was the first Calvin had ever seen of something close to remorse from Lyman. That he was speaking of it at all revealed how vulnerable George's new affiliation must have him feeling.

Calvin began walking again in hopes of reclaiming the more casual tone of the earlier conversation. "I think George will handle himself with calm and decorum, as he always does. Besides, the abolitionists are gaining converts every day, which strengthens the whole of them. More and more people feel the need to make their position clear."

"Openly proclaiming oneself only heats the pot," Lyman said, shaking his head. "I'm as certain of the evil of slavery as the next man, but making blacks equal citizens will never work, and it only sets back the necessary changes that *could* undo this great wrong. If George is so determined to join a cause, why not side with colonization? Everyone knows that's the most reasonable option with the highest chance of governmental support."

Actually, everyone did *not* know that colonization — sending the blacks to some new colony in Haiti or Libya or some other distant place — was the answer to slavery. Calvin himself did not favor that option. It seemed costly and devoid of the order the blacks would need to establish a society of their own. He knew a number of free blacks who proved the race as capable and moral as any white man — better than many hotheaded frontiersmen he'd met in Ohio, in fact. They deserved citizenship and equal rights, which is exactly what the abolitionists were fighting for. But he was not one to argue with the formidable Lyman Beecher. A great measure of wisdom was in knowing when *not* to speak.

"I'm worried about Henry joining up too, now that George has opened the gate," Lyman said, shaking his head again. "For George to cross over is one thing. As you said, he is calm and levelheaded. But Henry is outspoken, and as serving-editor of the *Journal,* he has a built-in platform from which to proclaim his position. It could be very dangerous for him."

Truly, Henry did not seem overly caught up in any social issues. He was not quiet and thoughtful like George, but he also was not pressing an agenda. Lyman, on the other hand, had made good use of Henry's position as editor by often bullying his son into printing his opinion regarding a variety of issues on the pages of the *Journal.* Lyman was entitled to be loud, but no one else was.

"When I last spoke with Henry on this topic, he was moderate," Calvin said. "Henry seems determined to keep his place as editor and knows that he cannot do that if he begins taking too firm a stance on either side. I don't think he would risk his position, and, as I said, I don't think George's affiliation will be of the demonstrative type."

"And Hattie?"

Calvin turned quickly to look at Lyman. "Hattie?"

"George seems to think she's all but put in with the abolitionists, too."

"Well, certainly not," Calvin said, his neck

getting hot. "I would know if her sentiments were that extreme, Lyman."

"And if they were?"

"I would rein them in." Even as he said it, he could imagine the fury on Hattie's face if she heard his declaration that he would control her feelings.

"So you favor colonization, too."

How had Calvin become trapped so quickly? He took a breath and gathered his thoughts. "You know I am antislavery, Lyman, but I have not put in with any campaign. Neither has Hattie."

Lyman's eyes narrowed, proving that he had been attempting to force conviction from Calvin for his views of colonization. Those Beechers! If there was not one entanglement, there was another. Hattie was all the Beecher he could manage, and even then he did a faulty job of it much of the time.

Calvin strove for calm. "Hattie and I are very focused on our own household at present, and while I am well aware of the strength of her opinions, I can assure you that she is not throwing in with the abolitionists any more than I am — and I am not. I understand your fears for George's involvement, especially regarding the current temperaments hereabouts, but I believe he will act as his nature dictates, with ease and thoughtful intention. The *Journal* is a grounding force for Henry, and Hattie and myself are no reason for your concern, I assure you."

Lyman seemed to consider Calvin's words with deep thought. Finally he nodded, though he looked only slightly appeased. "I am glad to hear it. You'll tell me if you sense any changes in opinion, though, won't you?"

Calvin hesitated — he was neither a nursemaid nor a spy — but he nodded because he did not foresee that he would have any changes to report. There was little room for anything but Calvin's impending trip to Europe and Hattie's pregnancy for the little Stowe family at present.

Lyman placed a hand on his shoulder and squeezed. "Thank you, Calvin."

Despite himself, Calvin wanted to please this man. Without a father of his own, Calvin often looked for placeholders in his life. He'd been privileged to know many men who set an admirable standard. Soon to be a father himself, Calvin was more determined than ever to draw from those men whom he admired so he might be the kind of father his child deserved.

With a final nod, Lyman turned and cut

across the grass, already intent on some new task.

Calvin continued to his office and spent the remainder of the afternoon preparing for the next day's lecture about the Egyptian order of government, which would now need to include the last quarter of today's lecture.

Calvin returned home in the evening, and his shoulders fell when he smelled no dinner even though he wasn't surprised. He'd come to expect that he would fend for himself most nights. Hattie's pregnancy was the newest reason why she was unable to make dinner, or keep up with the wash, or pick up after herself. Calvin spent many evenings trying to set the house to rights himself. There was little point in complaining with the time so short between them, however, and Calvin had become quite adept at making himself bread and milk for supper. Sometimes Hattie would apologize for not having a meal for him, twice she'd broken into tears over her self-recriminations, but usually she did not seem to notice. Surely this child would help her fully accept her responsibilities. Surely he would return from Europe to find things better than this.

The scratching of a pen from the kitchen

confirmed that Hattie was home, so Calvin set his case beside his chair, currently draped with a tablecloth for who knew what purpose, and found his wife at the table bent over a large paper filled with fold marks — likely one of the Beecher family letters which they would all add to as it traveled from one family home to the other. He admired the way the Beechers stayed in contact, even if sometimes he felt burdened by the way they were always looking over one another's shoulders.

Calvin came up behind her and kissed her neck, eliciting a mewing sound that never ceased to invigorate his senses. Before he allowed himself to become distracted, he set about making bowls of bread and milk for both of them. Hattie had likely only nibbled on tinned biscuits today. She was not nearly so driven by hunger as he was, probably because she'd been raised with plenty to go around while he had often feared there would not be enough food for his brother, his mother, and himself. He remembered well one winter when he and his brother had traded off the days they would eat. It had left a lasting impression on his mind and his stomach.

"How is the Beecher clan?" he asked as he broke the remaining loaf of bread into

94

two bowls. "Hearty and hale, I hope."

"For the most part, yes," Hattie said, straightening. "Would you like to hear?"

"Certainly."

She tucked her feet underneath her and read the letter, stopping to explain some detail and then laughing at a passage about how William had prayed for a horse to be healed for the sake of their child's faith. "And it was," she read. "Within two days that horse was springing from its pen, and my son looked at me as though I was Christ himself, though I did not let the impression last for long."

She accepted the bowl Calvin set before her and continued reading between bites. When she finished the letter, she set the paper aside with a satisfied grin. "I do love to know the goings-on in peoples' lives. I shall add my part tomorrow and give it on to Catharine."

"Will George add his news?" Calvin asked.

Hattie looked at him with a guilty expression. He wished it didn't hurt him to know she'd kept something from him. Was he so untrustworthy?

Calvin set down his spoon. "Why did you not tell me?" He hadn't wanted the hurt to color his tone, but it did.

"It wasn't that I didn't tell you, I just

hadn't yet. I didn't want to upset you or give us cause to argue."

"You think we would argue about George joining up with the abolitionists?" Granted, they argued about a great many things.

"I knew you would not agree with his making such a formal commitment."

"Which means you *do* agree and therefore believed we would be on different sides." He'd been so sure he knew Hattie's mind on this topic. Now he wondered where his confidence came from. Was she closer to the abolitionist camp than he'd believed? Had she hidden more than just George's level of determination?

Hattie stirred her soggy bread in the bowl before she answered. "I admire George for owning his convictions, that is all."

"Your father is concerned."

Hattie looked up sharply. "*Father* told you about George?"

Calvin hesitated, surprised by the snap of her response and worried that he should have kept the conversation with Lyman to himself.

"It *was* him, wasn't it?" Hattie set down her spoon, bristling like a cat. "What did he say? Is he very upset? Henry was certain he'd be furious when he learned of it."

Which meant Hattie had discussed George

with Henry. Calvin swallowed his jealousy of her turning in every direction but his and relayed the gist of the conversation he'd had with Lyman, working up to the end. "He's also worried about you and me — afraid we'll throw in with the abolitionists too."

Calvin had hoped Hattie would be shocked at the idea, but she simply went back to her lackluster meal. Calvin waited her out and finally, she looked at him and spoke. "I do not feel ready to throw in with the abolitionists. They are too rowdy and aggressive for my tastes. But I do feel the hatred of slavery rising up in me more and more, Calvin. I read the articles and hear the stories, and my heart is nearly fit to burst from my very chest at the atrocities that take place every day under the banner of this allowance. Sometimes I fear that my not standing up and speaking my mind makes me as bad as any slave owner taking a whip to his human possession."

Calvin reached across the table and took Hattie's hand, all the while trying to keep his surprise from showing too strongly. Hattie could be volatile when her emotions were engaged, and these days, between the pregnancy and her passionate feelings, she was emotionally engaged much of the time. He needed to speak carefully so as not to get her ire up even more. "Hatred is a very strong word, Hattie, and it will eat you up long before it will influence a change the magnitude of this one."

To his relief, she nodded, and then used her free hand to wipe her eyes. Calvin prayed for help in knowing what to say that would keep her calm but help her feel supported. Some days the eggshells he tread upon were more fragile than others, but the longing to be united with his wife was ever-present. "Your feelings are commendable and good. I admire you for feeling as you do."

She smiled gratefully at him, which strengthened his own confidence.

"I told your father that he has no need to fear, that you and I are focused on our family so much that there is little room for politics."

She didn't seem to like that as well, and he hurried to continue. "We both must think of more than just ourselves right now. You are growing our child, a great miracle from heaven, and I am preparing for a journey to distant shores and new cultures. We will be apart for so long." He paused, a lump in his throat and fear in his chest at what this separation could mean for them. How much harder would it be to build their marriage when they were on opposite sides of the world? He took a breath, remembered his faith, and continued. "I feel we need to make the most of our time together, and not let the ugly portions of the world outside our cottage touch us. Do you agree?"

Hattie half shrugged and half nodded. "Change will never happen if everyone only focuses on their own lot and never looks to the lot of their neighbor, Calvin."

"But one must have their own house in order before they can expect to make any changes elsewhere."

She considered that, but the nod she gave him was not convincing. He sensed, however, that, like him, she was increasingly aware of the limited time left for them to be together. Two weeks from now he would be traveling to New York. He could pretend contentment with bread and milk for dinner, and Hattie could agree with him on this so that these last days together stayed easy between them.

Calvin patted her hand, hoping it would put an end to the discussion. "So, then, tell me what you did today. Did you read anything interesting? Did anyone come by for a visit?"

Hattie was hesitant, clearly aware of his

concerted effort to change the topic, but after a few short answers, they were discussing a neighbor whom they suspected to be operating his own still outside of town. Calvin had never been so grateful for gossip to detract from the potential pricks of marital discord. He would repent of it at a later date, but for now he reached his hand across the table. Hattie took it, softened, and his mind eased. So much was happening so quickly, more than they had expected, and he was glad they were both trying to keep things positive.

He needed to believe their impending separation would allow them both to find their feet and would prove them more united when Calvin returned. He liked that she was proud of him for having been chosen for this trip, and he looked forward to making her even prouder by how he would take advantage of this opportunity. He would miss her so very much, and yet he believed they would both grow into themselves and their marriage while he was gone. They needed that growing. Much like the child Hattie carried, they needed some time to become who they were meant to be.

All is well, he said in his mind as Hattie's conversation moved on to Mary Dutton's visit that afternoon. *All is well.*

CHAPTER SEVEN

June 8, 1836

With a great blast from the foghorn, the steamship *Montreal* pushed away from the New York pier. Calvin held on to the railing while the people around him waved and called out good-byes to the loved ones who had accompanied them to the docks. Calvin had no one to say good-bye to; his Ohio farewells had taken place almost a month ago, and he'd stopped to see his mother in Massachusetts for a few days before traveling to New York alone.

As the ship began its journey, he took one of the peppermint candies from his pocket and popped it in his mouth. Hattie swore the treat would help combat seasickness. He'd been on boats before and suffered no ill effects, so he had reason to feel confident in his health, but he'd always liked peppermint. Calvin sucked on the candy and remembered Hattie tucking the small sack into the pocket of his coat.

The ocean settled into a pattern of color and rhythm, always moving with a lulling smoothness. Many of his fellow passengers lost interest with the disappearing shoreline and moved on to explore other parts of the ship.

Calvin keenly felt the separation of home and country the further out to sea the ship went. He'd left his home. Left his work. And he missed Hattie; his throat tightened each time he thought of her. The last weeks before he'd left had been the happiest of their short marriage. She had been eager to spend time with him as every day brought them closer to separation, and he was better able to ignore her clutter and idleness for the same reason. A very small rounding of her belly was the only solid evidence of their child, but he had kissed Hattie's tender skin the morning of his departure and left his blessing that all would go well in his absence. The longer he was gone, however, the harder it was to keep such optimistic thoughts. What if all did *not* go well?

His solitude since leaving Ohio felt similar to the weeks following Eliza's death, when he would think a hundred times a day of what she would be doing if she were there. Now it was Hattie he thought of. If Hattie had been with him when he'd walked Central Park, she would have wanted to buy a flower from that vendor. Or if Hattie had come with him to the pier, she would beg him to buy some stale bread to feed the seabirds. Would she have cried as the ship moved out to sea? Would she have waved a handkerchief while tears rolled down her cheeks?

It was a blessing to miss her, but the vulnerability of their connection made him aware of the potential dangers ahead of them. Though Calvin had not lost Eliza in childbirth, a great many men *had* lost their wives through that travail. Hattie was hearty, and her family had a history of healthy births, but she was small and too often inattentive to details she deemed unimportant, such as eating regularly. What if she did not care for herself the way she should? Calvin had been a large baby. What if she did not survive the birth? What if she lived but the baby died? Could she carry on with such heartbreak alone?

At such a distance, should the worst happen, Calvin might not know until weeks or months after the fact. Watching Eliza fade through the last few days of her life had been excruciating, and Calvin had been steeped in guilt for bringing her from the comfort and climate she knew in New Hampshire to the harsh conditions of Ohio. So many times he felt Eliza would have been better off had she never met Calvin Stowe. Would Hattie, too? Already their marriage had been peppered with numerous arguments and quarrels. She did not bow to his authority as patriarch in their home, and he was irritated with her determination to pursue hobbies rather than responsibilities. What if marrying her had prevented them both from happiness they could have found elsewhere? The thought stilled him, ached deep within his gut, and he shook his head, refusing to accept such a possibility.

A lump rose in his throat, making it difficult to breathe. He could arrive back in America eight months from now as a father or a widower for the second time.

The sea air whipped at his coat. He put his hand on his hat to hold it in place and began making his way through the remaining crowds still gathered on the deck. Many of the passengers were becoming acquainted with one another. Calvin had little interest in striking up friendships.

Dinner would be served in one hour's time, but he needed distraction from his morbid thoughts and, ironically, Hattie had already provided it. He wound through the narrow hallways and stairwells until he reached his cabin, let himself in, and then rifled through the pocket of his bag until he found the letter she'd given him at their parting. It was crumpled and crushed from having accompanied him thus far, but he smiled at her familiar script across the front: *My Darling Calvin.*

"Promise me you won't open this until you are on the sea. Promise me, Calvin!" She'd stared at him — there would be no negotiation.

He had promised her, and although he'd received a packet of letters and journal entries at his hotel in New York just three days ago, he had not yet opened *this* letter. He sat on his firm bunk — glad that the man sharing the tiny room was still on the deck above — and broke the seal, which had already begun to crack.

He unfolded the paper.

Dear Calvin,

I hope you have waited, per your promise to me, to open this letter upon your departure from our American shores. I imagine you are feeling the separation between us already and questioning your choice in taking this adventure. That is why I wrote this letter to assure you that you are precisely where you need to be. The Good Lord has brought this opportunity to you, and I am as pleased as I can be to boast of my world-traveling husband in whom so many have placed their wise trust.

Now, my dear, you are gone where you are out of the reach of my care, advice, and good management so I will caution you on some considerations. You are of a disposition to persistently think of the worst of a situation. (Do not argue this point for you know it to be true!) Should you do as much on this journey, I've no doubt you will find a great deal to complain about as the people and places will be so different from what you are used to. Don't you do it! There is no space in this adventure for you to culti-vate that indigo or fall into a fit of hypo — no space at all. Instead, you must keep your spirits up by seeing all that you can, and writing about all the won-derful things you experience so that your poor wife might live vicariously through your travels. For I will be here, waiting for your return with our little one. I feel the Lord's hand in all of this, and I will play my part to perfection. Only think of all you expect to see: the great libraries and beautiful paintings, fine churches, and, above all, think of seeing Tholuck, your great Apollo!

My dear, I wish I were a man in your place; if I wouldn't have such a grand time! Have a grand time yourself, won't you, and return with a lifetime of stories and experiences with which to fill our home and fill my heart all the days of our life together.

With loving affection,

Hattie

Calvin read the letter a second time, smiling to himself, then folded it and placed it in the inside pocket of his coat. He would keep it there throughout the duration of his trip. How could she know exactly what he needed to hear? He would do as she said and not play into the blue spaces his mind could so easily wander into. He would look for the good, the lovely, and the beautiful so that he might tell Hattie all about it. Her thirst for knowledge and experience would make her a perfect audience, and he took pride in being counted on to bring her such news as she would never know otherwise. In that way, they would be together here.

CHAPTER EIGHT

Dearest Calvin,

We had a lovely Independence Day celebration here in Cincinnati, though it was scorching and humid and what have you. None of that will surprise you, I'm sure. There was the parade and the footraces, too many sweets for children and too many colorful things for ladies. I admit I bought a new shawl, but I spent almost nothing for it, and it is as fine a thing as any other I own. I daresay you will like it, when you return.

Today I will go to town with Henry and see the colored folks have their celebration. The passions have not dimmed since April's protests, and I will not put myself in harm's way, but I do like their singing and should like them to know that not every white man (or woman) is set against them. I wonder if one day they might celebrate on the same day and in the same places as the rest of us. Does it not seem possible? And yet, sometimes it feels like nothing but fantasy to imagine such a thing.

I shall report in tomorrow's letter. I know that you have likely just arrived in England as I write this and that the travel would delay any letters you have sent, but I have not heard from you since the last letter you sent from New York. That seems a very long time ago. I do hope you are writing back to me. I should like to know you have not forgotten me completely!

Yours truly,
Hattie

"Ah, here they come," Henry said, leaning to the left so he could look down First Street though Hattie could tell he still did not have a clear view. The singing was barely audible, but already rich as the parade marched in their direction. It would not be a parade as the white citizens had enjoyed yesterday with bright banners and flags, fiddles, dancers, and decorated wagons. Just black folks marching and singing, mostly.

Hattie smiled from the other side of the

blanket she and Henry had put down in Lincoln Park and stuffed the oil cloth back into the lunch basket. Chicken sandwiches, cherries, and Aunt Esther's corn salad. "I wish there was a vendor selling ices or lemonade," Hattie said, looking from under her parasol in every direction in case one had suddenly appeared. "Every vendor in the city was here yesterday."

"Every *white* vendor, you mean. White vendors for white celebrations. Black vendors for black."

Hattie frowned and turned the handle of her parasol. "There are no black vendors in Cincinnati."

Henry nodded with a grin still on his face. "Precisely my point."

Hattie looked toward the sound of the robust hymns once again. "What is the point of being a free state if blacks and whites are still set apart from one another? What kind of freedom still dictates your class based on the color of your skin rather than the state of your soul?"

Henry sighed, showing his fatigue of this discussion. "I wish your husband would return so he could occupy your mind and divert you from your obsession for social injustice."

Mention of Calvin caused a twinge in

Hattie's heart, and one hand went to her rounded belly, impossible to hide even though she was only just half way through her pregnancy. More than one woman had said she was too big. What was Hattie supposed to say in response?

Inside her belly was the child she and Calvin had made before he had boarded a ship and sailed for distant shores. She wondered for perhaps the hundredth time if she shouldn't have encouraged him to go. In the two months he'd been gone, he'd sent only one letter, asking Hattie to edit the enclosed article he'd written for the *Cincinnati Journal* about his travels thus far. Other than closing his letter with "Your loving husband" there had been little sentiment, and she'd suspected he'd written it in a rush.

Hattie wrote him multiple times each week and had already sent three different packets with letters and copies of her journal pages. It was a strange thing to be married and pregnant, but without a husband. Sometimes it was easier not to think about Calvin so that she did not miss him so much. Other times she did *not* miss him. Like today, when she knew they'd have bickered about her wanting to watch the colored celebration.

"Calvin would agree with me on having mixed-race celebrations," Hattie said as she picked at a loose seam on the homemade quilt. She wasn't entirely sure that was true. A few weeks before his departure, Calvin had all but told her not to make abolition an issue between them. He felt they should focus on their family and not get pulled into the political turmoil. Hattie had conceded, but since his departure, tensions had increased in the city. Hattie could not go a day without encountering some opinion or another on the issue of slavery. To ignore the topic, as Calvin seemed to want her to do, was impossible, and in the process of discussion, her own views were becoming crisper and easier to articulate. Her brother Edward had officially joined the cause in Illinois, and William and his wife, Katherine, had all but thrown their hats into the ring in Putnam as well.

"I've read Mr. Birney's paper, Henry," Hattie admitted, though she did not look at him during her confession. "And I object to very little of what he's said. I'm glad he's moved his press to Cincinnati, and I hope he makes more converts to his cause by doing so." James Birney was a slave owner-turned-abolitionist on a quest to convert the country to his belief that slavery should be abolished, no matter the difficulty it might create. Proclaiming his stance had created a great deal of difficulty for Mr. Birney already, and yet he was not backing down. His determination impressed Hattie. What's more, she knew Henry's heart was with hers on this issue, and she wanted him to trust her with his own thoughts.

Henry held her eyes a few moments, then plucked at a blade of grass. "Birney is too divisive," he said. "Besides, I am a newspaper editor now, and he is my competition." His grin was back — the grin that hid his seriousness of mind and discomfort with injustice.

The singing voices were louder now, and although Hattie had been anticipating the group rounding the corner for some time, she wished they were just a few minutes slower now so she might extend her discussion with her brother.

Henry rose up slightly. "Ah, there they are."

Hattie saw the first line of brown faces with bright white smiles breaking through as the parade turned the corner. She could not help but smile back. The rhythm of their singing distracted her from her unpleasant thoughts. One impossibly large black man had a child of five or six on his shoulders, and the two of them seemed nearly to pierce a hole in the sky as the child waved a handmade Ohio flag. The singers were clapping as they sang toward heaven, and Hattie put down her parasol so that she might clap along. Henry did not join her, and she knew that her clapping made him nervous. But what would anyone do to the pregnant wife of a Lane professor and the daughter of the seminary's president?

She did not know the song — some slave song, no doubt — but that didn't bother her. Such songs belonged to the black men and women who had created them as a relief from the bondage some of them had experienced before coming to Ohio. Most of these people had once been owned by other men and now were not. Hearing them celebrate Independence Day, even without ices and lemonade and equal rights, burrowed deep in Hattie's soul with rightness. Hattie was so caught up in the singing that she startled when Henry's hand gripped her shoulder. She looked up to his face. When had he stood?

"We need to go," he said, then picked her up by her elbows, hoisting her to her feet.

"What are you doing?" she said once she had her balance.

Henry let her go and gathered the quilt

and food into a sloppy bundle before smashing everything into the basket. His movements sent her parasol tumbling, and she moved as quick as she could to pick it up. When she turned back to face her brother, he'd already picked up the basket. He reached his free arm around Hattie's shoulder and steered her toward the newspaper office a few blocks west. "Henry," she said as she struggled to keep up with his steps while keeping hold of the parasol. She put one hand under her belly as though that would be any protection if she stumbled. "What are you about?"

Then she heard shouting where the singing had been. She tried to look back toward the parade, but Henry pushed her forward and her five-foot frame was no match for him. "We'll be safe at the office," he said, looking over his shoulder.

Hattie tried again to glimpse what was happening, and this time she saw a blur of movement — white faces among the black, people falling out of formation in the middle of the street. She heard a woman scream, and her heart suddenly matched the rhythm of her hurried steps.

"What's happened?" she asked, no longer objecting to the escape. She dropped her parasol. It bounced on the street once, and then she was too far ahead to consider where it might end up. She put both hands over her belly. She'd had no sense of danger when she'd asked Henry to take her to the parade and felt foolish for not anticipating this. Had her determination to show her position put her in danger? Put her child in danger?

"I saw a few men calling out to the crowd," Henry said breathlessly. Hattie could relate to the condition. They were all but running, and yet the angry voices behind them were getting louder.

"White men?" Hattie asked, though she didn't need the clarification. Of course it was white men heckling from the sidelines. It was a common occurrence when any one black was on the street, to say nothing for when there were hundreds of them.

"A black man came after them," Henry said.

If Hattie could have afforded the breath, she'd have caught it in surprise. They turned a corner, muting the sounds of fighting behind them and bringing the newspaper office in view. Relief drowned out the chaos for a moment.

"We'll be safe in the office," Henry said again, and Hattie nodded, wishing they were there already. She thought of the child she'd seen on the big man's shoulders. The white men wouldn't hurt a child, would they? She thought of her own child and imagined what Calvin would do if someone threatened it. She knew Calvin would go to blows, even as mild and self-possessed as he was, but *he* would have the law on his side. A black man — even a black father — had no such consolation. He could not accuse a white man for any reason, and even if some man were brought up before the law, a black man could not testify against him in court.

Within seconds, Hattie and Henry crossed the office threshold. Henry slammed and bolted the door behind them. They tried to recover their breath amid the smells of machinery, ink, and paper. A worker setting type for the next edition hurried upstairs to watch the events from the window. "We'll stay here," Henry said, pulling shut the blinds but then peeking through. "I should never have allowed you to talk me into this."

Hattie nearly argued with him. It was only supposed to be a parade, but she cut off the protest as the child within her shifted, objecting to her hurrying, no doubt. She spied a chair and crossed the room before collapsing upon it. Her hips hurt from the frantic pace Henry had set.

"Birney's there!" the worker called from

upstairs. "No wonder everyone's in such a lather."

"Oh, Birney," Henry said, peering through a crack in the blinds. "When will you learn to keep away from the hornets' nest?"

CHAPTER NINE

July 17, 1836

Dearest Calvin,

The mob madness is certainly upon this city! There have been meetings and more meetings. More homes have been destroyed on the west end of town, and I would be scared and anxious if I weren't so angry about it all. A mob broke into Mr. Birney's office last week and pulled apart his press in an attempt to put an end to his paper, *The Philan-thropist.* (I have sent you earlier editions and have enclosed the very paper he printed not two days after the attack on his property!) He promptly patched up his equipment and went on with the next edition. What a smile that brought to my face, and yet it is hard to smile too much as things are not at an end. I hope the man stands his ground and asserts his

119

rights that are most assuredly being violated.

What possesses any man to count their neighbor below them in such a way as to justify breaking through the front door of his home and ransacking his belongings? And I am not talking about black men's homes being raided, though that has happened far more than it should. You will remember Mr. Chase, of course, from our beloved Semi-Colon Club. He himself blocked the entrance into Birney's boardinghouse the night they looted his office, telling the mob to get on home. The mayor and Mr. Chase and a handful of other men with some power have attempted protest, but do you think any of the wrongdoers have been brought to justice? Certainly not. If you ask me, the mayor is turning a blind eye to the whole of it. I can truly say that, for the first time since coming to Ohio, I feel as though I am on the frontier. This primitive justice and spirit of lawlessness turns my stomach. All this mob justice will result in converts to abolitionism since the opponents act against our very constitution, mark my word.

Today, however, is bright and calm,

and I am meeting Mary Dutton to walk our city and show the citizens that we are not all quaking. Of course Father is out of town and you are not here either to counsel me otherwise, but I have thought much about it and must break free of these four walls — though I love them. This will be the last letter I include with this packet, as I will stop at the post on my way to see Mary. I hope it reaches you in good health and joyful spirits.

Do write to me, dear husband. I long to hear of more civilized things and distant places. What visits have you made already? What books have you acquired? When it is late and the city's lights go down, do you miss me the way I miss you?

Your loving wife,
Hattie

"Thank you for the ride, Henry," Hattie said as he helped her from the carriage in front of the post office in Cincinnati. There was a post office in Walnut Hills, but as she wanted to come to the city today anyway, this errand gave her one more reason to do so.

"Father would hang me for it after what

happened the last time I brought you to town."

Hattie rolled her eyes. "There is no potential for protest today." She looked around the street, noting how quiet it was compared to their last visit when the parade had turned into a riot. All the more reason to help set precedence by living life again. "And we will seek refuge if there should be the slightest change in temperament."

Henry shook his head. "Come back to the newspaper office when you finish so that I can drive you home."

"And spare me the first exercise I've had in weeks?" Hattie lifted her eyebrows. "I would not hear of it. It is only two miles back to Walnut Hills, and I shall rejoice with every step."

He shook his head again before jumping from the seat and helping her from the wagon. Once she was safely on Market Street, he continued to his office. Hattie smiled to herself all the way into the post office, then shared the smile with Mary Dutton, who stood from the wooden bench out front where she'd been sitting. Mary held the letter she'd been reading at her side.

"I hope I did not keep you waiting," Hattie said as she embraced her friend.

"Not at all. I arrived only a few minutes ago." Mary lifted the letter and continued reading, her eyebrows furrowed behind her spectacles.

"Is everything all right?"

Mary did not look up from her letter as she sat back down on the bench. "Yes, I've just received this letter from Catharine."

From her expression, it was clear that the letter was not a friendly note centered on Catharine's summer travels to New England. "Let me post my things, then you can tell me all about it."

Mary nodded absently. Hattie went to the counter and posted the packet of letters and journal entries to Calvin. It was the third she'd sent in as many months. She'd received a short letter a few days ago, sent his first night in England to assure her he'd been a good little sailor throughout the crossing — not a moment of seasickness if she could believe it. In fact, she wasn't sure she did. Calvin seemed to coax illness so often, worrying that he was getting sick or another headache was coming on, that she felt sure he'd be green in his berth for the whole trip. She was glad he felt well, but disappointed that it seemed his time away from her was so much more invigorating than when they were together.

Once she'd finished the arrangements, she thanked the clerk and returned to Mary, squinting slightly after the dim interior of the post office. Mary stood, folding the letter. They easily fell in step together toward Shillito's Dry Goods on Main Street to choose a gift for Mary's sister in New York. What they could find at a dry goods store in Cincinnati that was better than what her sister could find in New York, Hattie did not know.

"Catharine's letter does not seem to have brightened your day," Hattie noted.

Mary huffed slightly. "Not in the least. I have always admired Catharine's shrewd mind, but I never expected to bear her teeth marks myself." She handed the letter to Hattie.

Hattie read through the letter, eventually stopping along the boardwalk to better focus on the words. Catharine was worried about the school: enrollment was down, prospects were low, and investors were hesitant to financially support the endeavor. Catharine expected Mary to make up for the shortfall by teaching an additional class in the fall as well as taking responsibility for the first week of Catharine's classes since Catharine was extending her trip to meet with a potential investor in Philadelphia.

When Hattie saw her own name, she slowed her reading to make sure she didn't miss a single word.

I regret that so much of the responsibility falls to you, Mary, but with Hattie abandoning us I have only you to rely on. When there were three of us, there was not so much division of labor that any one of us felt so burdened, but Hattie has gone her way and left us holding the basket. We shall do the best that we can.

Hattie wasn't necessarily surprised by the words, but she was still hurt by them. She folded the letter and handed it back to Mary, who watched her as she tucked the letter into her handbag.

"I'm sorry the burden falls to you," Hattie said as they began walking again.

Mary looped her arm through Hattie's. "I don't blame *you.*"

"But if I were still teaching, you would not have to shoulder so much of the load."

"Catharine is divisive," Mary said, surprising Hattie with her candor. "She has offended too many investors who want more accounting of her curriculum. She wants everyone to trust her and that is simply not how it works." She shrugged as if letting the difficulty slide off her shoulders. "The Institute is in early years yet. I suppose I don't mind picking up an additional course."

"Then why did the letter upset you?"

"Because Catharine doesn't ask, she orders. We're supposed to be partners, but she makes all the decisions as though I am some first-year teacher." She looked at Hattie. "Has she returned your investment yet?"

"She says she cannot until enrollment improves." Hattie shrugged as though it was not important, but in truth it bothered her a great deal.

The majority of Calvin's salary had been forwarded to him upon his departure so he would have funds on the other side of the Atlantic. Ten dollars a month was made available to Hattie for spending, seeing as how she was back living at the President's House and her day-to-day needs were therefore met.

Her allowance was not nearly enough, in Hattie's opinion. The first month Calvin was gone, she'd spent the remainder of her own funds on dresses and shoes that would see her through her pregnancy. Calvin would see such necessities as frivolous; he didn't understand a woman's need for pretty things. Not when he wore a black suit every day and made do with a single pair of shoes. She couldn't ask him for more money — not with finances being such an issue between them since day one of their marriage — so she had hoped Catharine would return some portion of Hattie's two hundred dollar investment in the Institute.

When they reached the end of the boardwalk, Mary took Hattie's hand. "I'm sorry for all of this," she said, softer than she usually spoke. The lines around her eyes and the graying curls that peeked out from around her bonnet reminded Hattie that Mary was thirty years old and unmarried; she had nothing but her career as a teacher. If the school failed, it could affect Mary's future teaching prospects. That was why Mary would run the school in Catharine's absence and teach an extra course without complaint. She'd left everything she'd ever known in Connecticut in order to come to Ohio. Yet here was Mary looking at Hattie sympathetically and apologizing on Catharine's behalf.

Hattie gave Mary's hand a squeeze. "It will all turn out, somehow," she said, realizing it sounded like a platitude even though she did not mean it as such. "Trust in the Lord and do good."

"Yes," Mary said, her expression softening, which made Hattie glad she'd spoken her thoughts. "He is mindful of all things."

The women turned to lighter topics: Mr. Maple had purchased a new carriage from New York — had Hattie seen it? The Carringtons' pigs had been running amuck at the wharf on Thursday. Cincinnati would never live down its nickname of "Porkopolis" if there was not better control of the little beasts.

They reached the dry goods store and, after some searching, found some nice tallow candles scented with vanilla that Mary was certain her sister would love. Hattie didn't have the heart to point out how rustic they looked, but maybe her sister would like that: *"Oh, look at these lovely handmade candles my sister Mary sent from the frontier. Aren't they quaint?"*

The women parted ways at Sycamore Street and Third, Mary heading toward her boardinghouse and Hattie continuing back toward her father's home in Walnut Hills. Aunt Esther had warned her against excessive exertion, but the heat was not yet unbearable and time alone with her thoughts was hard to come by in the bustling Beecher household. It always had been. Her half-siblings were all home from their respective schools for the summer, and with Henry and George residing at the President's House, too, she was eager for some solitude.

Hattie continued toward the east end of town, glancing in shop windows and stopping to talk when she passed an acquaintance from church. She was just stepping off the boardwalk to cross the street when a young man came running around the corner, narrowly avoiding a collision with her. Hattie squeaked as she jumped to the side, her hands protectively on her pregnant belly.

"Sorry, ma'am," the youth said, then shoved a printed flyer in her hand before continuing past. She turned to watch him, wishing she'd reacted with the dressing-down he most certainly deserved, only to see him push papers into the hands of every person he passed. She turned her attention to the tract.

FUGITIVE FROM JUSTICE, $100 REWARD.
 The above sum will be paid for the delivery of one James G. Birney, a fugitive from justice, now abiding in the city of Cincinnati.
 Said Birney in all his associations and

feelings is black; although his external appearance is white.

The above reward will be paid and no questions asked by OLD KENTUCKY.

Hattie caught her breath and looked around to see if anyone else appeared as incensed as she felt. Some tracts had been dropped by other recipients, the summer breeze already tumbling them to the south side of the street. A few people were reading the flyer, two women nodding to each other as they did so.

Hattie folded the paper and tucked it into her reticule. Henry would want to see this latest addition to the fires of temper burning in their city. She turned toward Henry's office near the city center, deeply troubled by the increasing vigilante justice. Hattie tried to increase her pace, but the child within her made it impossible. She had planned for a leisurely walk today, and her body would allow little else. The awkwardness of her body reminded her of other limitations. As a woman, her opinion meant little, and her voicelessness was aggravating. Not for the first time, she wondered why God had given her such a passionate heart if she were meant to be silent. And now she was a wife. And soon she would be a mother. Those familiar pangs of one calling pulling down the other gripped her tightly before an oddly satisfying thought took center stage.

Are you a wife now — where is your husband?

Are you a mother yet — where is this child?

Though she admitted it to no one, Hattie had enjoyed much of her independence in Calvin's absence. With no one to answer to, she lived without responsibility to anyone but herself. Her child was warm and fed and growing. In a few months' time, that independence would be gone forever. She no longer resented that potential, and she missed Calvin enough to feel excited about his return and accepting that she would once again be responsible to care for him. But he was not here right now, and she did not have a child to swaddle and coddle and care for. What she *did* have was time, and words, and a passionate heart she believed God had given to her for a reason.

By the time Hattie reached *The Journal,* her intent was twofold. First, she would show Henry the tract and hear his thoughts, but then she would present him an idea. Henry had to maintain public neutrality, yet he published any number of letters to the

131

editor each week and had even allowed their father to print his explanations when he'd come under censure last spring. Henry was careful to print opinions from multiple sides of any issue when possible, but often lamented the poor quality of the editorials received. Just the other night over dinner he had proclaimed, "It is not just what is said, but how it is said that makes an impact. How I wish I could print something well presented — on any side — so that the opinions were not so easily dismissed as fragmented thoughts of frenzied minds."

Hattie's written opinions — printed under a man's name — might be the very thing Henry was looking for without even knowing it. The style could be casual, domestic even, but it could say more than any other article had thus far in the debate. Hattie might not be able to sign it with her name, but her voice would shine through all the same. She was sure of it.

CHAPTER TEN

July 21, 1836

"Now, my friend, do you think the liberty of the press is a good thing?"

"Certainly — to be sure."

"And you think it a good article in our constitution that allows every man to speak, write, and publish his own opinions, without any other responsibility than that of the laws of this country?"

"Certainly, I do."

"Well, then, as Mr. Birney is a man, I suppose you think it's right to allow him to do it in particular?"

Hattie read over "Franklin's" editorial in the day's *Journal* twice, smiling to herself and feeling invigorated at seeing her words in print. Until now her printed work had been specific to a few magazines, Christian mostly, and distributed from New England.

She had never been prouder, however, than she was of *this* work written for the citizens of her own city in hopes they would see reason within the fictional conversation between Franklin and his friend, Mr. L.

Hattie touched the name "Franklin" printed at the bottom of the piece and felt no regret. Men would not hear the sentiments increasingly dear to her heart if the work bore a woman's name, and she felt safe in her anonymity, something Calvin would appreciate if he were here. She read the editorial once more, then carefully cut it from the paper and folded it for the next packet she would send to Calvin.

Calvin. Her heart ached to think of him. He'd been gone nearly three months, and the distance between them felt like more than miles and time. If Calvin were here, however, would she have had her thoughts published in the paper? Sometimes she would tell herself that he would support her; he'd said more than once that she should be a literary woman. This was simply her pursuit of that goal, and in such, they were united.

This was the first printed work she'd done that was political, however, and Calvin was not one to put his own political thoughts on the line. He would not favor her doing so.

134

Were he here, there would have been arguments, and one of them would win and one of them would lose. It had been seven months since she'd joined her life to his, and yet she had lived without him almost as long as she'd lived with him. What would it be like when he returned? Would all the arguments avoided during his absence rise up between them, or would a new fondness have grown that put those arguments firmly into the past? The longer he was gone, the more insecure she felt about his return. She couldn't picture it and did not know what to expect.

Hattie had written to him about the ongoing protests and riots, yet explained her editorial as a light sketch. When he read the actual work, he would see right away that, though the style was light, as was her trademark, the content was meant to inflame the reader; it was meant to make people think.

The folded article lay innocently on the table, and she bit her lip, wondering if perhaps she should not include it in the next packet of correspondence she sent across the sea. She would not be there to explain — assuming she *could* — why she'd given a diluted impression of the truth when she'd first mentioned the work. The thought of

Calvin being angry with her while so far away was uncomfortable. Were all marriages as difficult as this one? Surely most grooms did not sail across the world so soon after matrimony, but it wasn't the distance that worried her. He expected her to be sitting still and idle in his absence, not charged as she was by the disputes filling the air in every room in the city.

The child moved within her, and she leaned back in her chair and rested her hands on her belly. Her heart softened, and she felt her shoulders relax. She must not lose faith or forget that both she and Calvin had covenanted not only to each other but also to God. He had a hand in all of this, and she felt sure He knew her heart, even if Calvin may not. He would help mend things, and she must not lose hope in that promise.

The front door of her father's house suddenly flew open, startling her. Hattie craned her neck to see who had come home.

Henry hurried past the doorway of the parlor, and Hattie called out hello. She heard him stop just past the doorway and then come back her direction. "Hattie, there you are," he said as he came into the room and sat on the footstool in front of her.

"Here I am," she said, smiling. "Why are

you in such a rush?"

"There's been a good deal of response to a certain editorial in today's paper." The triumph in his voice caused the same shiver of self-satisfaction she'd felt upon reading her article to roll through her a second time. Henry continued. "It was a wise decision on the part of the editor to publish the article on the very same day a certain meeting is to be held concerning recent unsavory action on the part of several Cincinnati citizen groups."

"Oh?" she said, playing coy.

"Mr. Peterson has already come in asking after the man who wrote it. He would like to talk with this man, *Franklin,* about this conversation he overheard and see if he might make the evening's meeting. I told him I was quite certain Mr. Franklin was indisposed."

"A pity," Hattie said, and meant it. How she would love to walk into that meeting, take the podium, and share her thoughts on the constitutional rights being violated left and right in this city.

Henry continued. "Salmon Chase also dropped by to ask me to pass on this note to the writer should I have a chance."

He held out a note. The heavy paper was folded in half but not sealed, which meant

Henry had already read it. Hattie took the card and opened it.

Mr. Franklin,

Thank you for sharing what you "overheard" in today's article. I wish more of our citizens could see the further-reaching difficulties of our present circumstance and relay their thoughts in such an easy-to-understand manner as you have. I hope that you might have more to say on this subject as I find your voice a very necessary one within our present society.

Sincerely,
Mr. S P Chase

"He suspects me as the author," Hattie said when she finished. "I'd known he might." As a member of the Semi-Colon Club, Salmon P. Chase had been in the audience to a similar essay she'd brought for their group a few years earlier — a pretend letter from the imaginary Mr. Howard that used a similar tone. Other members might recognize her written voice as well, and she wondered if that was something she should be concerned about. Not every member felt as she did about slavery. Would a contradicting member

138

expose her?

"I want you to write another piece," Henry said, eagerly shifting forward on the stool, his eyes glittering. "As Franklin of course, but expand on these ideas. You've done exactly what you hoped to do, and *The Journal* supports you fully."

"I imagine you've received some criticism too." She was nearly as eager to hear complaints as she was to hear compliments since her words had not been meant to activate only those who agreed with her position.

"Oh, yes," Henry said, smiling widely. "Three letters to the editor already, and one subscriber came in to demand a refund."

Hattie watched him carefully. "But you are not dissuaded?"

Henry shook his head. "The newspaper must hold as neutral a position as possible — never mind the criticism I receive daily for not siding in one direction or another. Only through editorials are we able to share a specific viewpoint, and your style has captured more attention than any article I have printed for months. You'll do it, won't you?"

"I hadn't considered writing more," Hattie said, though her mind was already racing with thoughts that expanded on her views.

Henry held her eyes a moment and then

looked around the room. When his gaze lit upon the writing desk, he jumped to his feet, talking as he crossed the room. "Now, where are your paper and pens, Mr. Franklin? And what can I do to help you get started on a follow-up to this first proclamation? I am at your service."

CHAPTER ELEVEN

August 25, 1836

Dear Hattie,

I am concerned regarding this last round of letters I have received. It seems you have involved yourself in sentiments which are not our affair. While I understand your passionate heart, you are not Catharine Beecher. You are a wife and soon to be a mother, and I would caution you — with all the affection and concern of a loving husband — to remember the most important use of your feminine qualities. I am quite distressed and wish that your father and your brothers would be more careful with my greatest possession.

Please, if you have not already, put away your pen for the present and take no risk of public opinion against you. No one likes falseness and, while I understand your reasons for posing as a man for this endeavor, I find your having to lie about your identity as one more indication of why you should have avoided this venture in the first place. Should you be found out, I fear greatly for your safety as well as for our child. Now is not the time for this. I beg you to stop.

Do take care of yourself, my dear, and be wise with your ambitions, especially at this delicate time. My heart and prayers are with you while my arms and bosom ache to hold you close. Know that my counsel comes from a place of love and protection. Be wise and be well.

Your loving husband,
Calvin

"She is here," Isabella shouted from the window before hurrying to the front door and throwing it open. "Catharine is back!"

Hattie did not share her fifteen-year-old half-sister's exuberance. Things had been strained between Catharine and herself since her marriage, and they had not improved when Hattie requested a return of her investment in the school.

The letter Catharine had sent Hattie in reply included a complicated explanation of why Hattie in fact *owed* money to the school. Hattie had been too furious to respond, knowing Catharine would be home in a few weeks and hoping for a sufficient argument by then. She hadn't managed to prepare that argument, which cast further trepidation over the upcoming reunion.

Hattie pushed herself to her feet — a bigger trial every day — and lumbered to the doorway of the parlor.

Not only did Hattie not feel the excitement of Catharine's return, she did not particularly understand where Isabella's came from. Catharine was not particularly playful or affectionate, but perhaps the child's enthusiasm said more about how sedentary Hattie had become these last weeks. According to the midwife, Hattie had several weeks left of this suffering called pregnancy. Hattie was good for little more than playing cat's cradle with her younger siblings these days. Her huge belly prevented her from even sitting at the table and being able to reach a hand of cards.

Hattie wished Catharine's homecoming had not coincided with Calvin's letter of reprimand she'd received that morning. His words had left her feeling small and burdened. She hated to be curtailed in her actions, but she also hated disappointing her husband. She imagined him in Europe, meeting with important people and doing important work while worried that she was putting herself and their child in harm's way. She didn't want him to worry about her or distrust her ability to use sound judgment for her own behalf. But there would be time to ponder on the letter later, and she needed to welcome Catharine.

Hattie had not even reached the hall before Catharine stood framed within it, holding Isabella's hand while the girl looked up at her older sister with the same adoration Hattie had once felt for her sister. Not that she did not adore Catharine still, but she was tempered in light of their recent difficulties.

"Goodness," Catharine said, her eyebrows lifting in raw surprise as she looked Hattie over. "It really is as bad as Aunt Esther said."

Bad? Hattie planted a less-than-polite smile on her face. "Lovely to see you as well, dear sister. I shall return to the parlor now that this affectionate greeting is concluded." She turned, but within two steps, Catharine had put a hand on her arm, prompting Hattie to pause and look back at her.

"I am sorry," she said in a tone that begged to be believed. "I did not mean it to sound that way. It is lovely to see you, Hattie. I've missed you." She put both of her arms around Hattie's shoulders, though she had to bend forward to embrace Hattie over the belly between them.

Hattie could not resist softening. Her sister's arms had given her comfort and encouragement so many times in her life. She returned the embrace, and for a moment she pretended there was no trouble between them.

Catharine pulled back. "I do think you should return to the parlor though. It must be uncomfortable to stand for very long in your condition."

Hattie let Catharine lead her to the parlor where she helped her into the leather chair by the window and brought a footstool for Hattie's feet.

"Thank you, Catharine." Hattie lifted first one swollen ankle onto the footstool and then the other.

"Of course," Catharine said, waving off the thanks. "Bella, fetch Hattie a glass of lemonade from the kitchen, and ask cook about having tea early today." Isabella left, and Catharine announced that she would be back after seeing to her trunks. For nearly an hour Hattie sat alone, useless and silent, while Catharine dashed this way and that, directing her trunks and tea. She had the entry table moved to a different position since its current place was "ridiculously inconvenient, don't you think?"

Henry came home to welcome Catharine, and Aunt Esther returned from visiting a neighbor. Everything was merry and light, making it almost possible to believe that the hardships between the sisters did not exist. The afternoon was a whirlwind — they had tea, Catharine recounted her travels, Henry returned to the office, Bella scampered off to a neighbor's house with a gift of New England maple sugars, and Aunt Esther went to lie down for a short nap — until finally it was Hattie and Catharine alone in the parlor with no one but each other.

"So," Catharine said, sitting on the settee and putting her hands in her lap. "I suppose it's time to clear the air between us, then."

Hattie recognized the authority in her sister's posture and wished that she could adopt the same. Feeling very much like a squash, however, made it a vain hope.

"I don't owe you or the Institute any money," Hattie said. Much as she was tempted to put off the ugliness of this subject, she'd been preparing for it for days. "I never drew a regular salary and —"

"You never *earned* a regular salary," Catharine interjected. "We all agreed to donate fifteen hours a week, and you barely did that yet you *did* take payments now and again."

"I worked far more than fifteen hours a week," Hattie said, bristling but unable to sit up straight in the chair. Her belly seemed to have settled into her hips, turning her into a giant sandbag. "I was there every day through December."

Catharine gave an indulgent smile. "But the school term continued until May, which means by averaging out the hours you put in over the course of the whole of your contract, you did not quite meet the minimum."

Hattie let out a breath. "You are exasperating, Catharine! I gave you notice of my leaving a full three months in advance."

"But your contract was through May of this year."

"Yet you are just now bringing this to my attention? Why not make mention of it in the letters we've been exchanging all summer?"

"It's very simple." Catharine was a master at staying calm in order to keep the upper hand in an argument, and Hattie detested her for it at that moment. "Your letters made reasonable arguments that sent me back to the agreements. I saw your point in regard to the initial investment and remembered that you had agreed to teach courses that first year only, so I concede that point. However, in my research, I discovered the clause regarding donated time and also found that you had agreed to help find a replacement if you opted out of teaching. You did opt out, but you did not find a replacement."

"Because you said you did not need one, that you and Mary would continue the teaching portion since enrollment was lower than originally expected."

"I said that I could not *afford* a replacement, not that I didn't need one. And you did not seek to find one."

Perhaps it was a good thing that Hattie could not move or else she might have wrapped her fingers around her sister's throat. "So your position is that I should have hired a teacher you didn't need and pay her salary myself?"

Catharine avoided a direct answer. "What I've done is factor in your investment against you not facilitating a replacement, and in averaging out your donated hours against the length of your contract, I have realized that you don't owe any additional money toward the venture. You are free and clear of it, and I shall attend to the additional particulars on my own. There is a small portion of your investment that you may be entitled to; however, you agreed not to withdraw it until the doors were closed or there were sufficient funds that would allow a repayment without a negative impact on the school. Since we need every bit of capital to keep the school going, we are unable to reimburse you at this time." She smiled. Sweetly. Confidently.

Hattie was struggling to sort through not only what Catharine had said now, but what she'd said in the letters. Her mind settled on one aspect. "You agree I don't owe you anything?"

Catharine nodded. "Yes, that is what I said."

"And I will still receive a portion of my initial investment. How much?"

"That cannot be determined until the school either closes or we reach five years of practice. Then we may evaluate the assets and longevity of your investment."

Hattie rolled that around in her mind. If she didn't owe Catharine any money, she would not have to explain it to Calvin. She would not feel responsible for additional discord between her husband and her sister, to say nothing of additional discord between her husband and herself. To be sure, Hattie wanted her investment back, but she'd become used to her allowance of ten dollars a month. Besides, she could not go anywhere to spend money right now anyway.

Calvin's concerns regarding her behavior in his absence were a heavy enough burden, and she wanted nothing else to incur his disappointment in her or her family. She could see that Catharine was setting up the inevitable announcement that Hattie would get none of her investment returned — that was why she would not give a dollar amount despite all her "factoring." But was Hattie willing to give up this fight in exchange for not having to start a new one with Calvin?

"I would like to put this agreement in writing," Hattie said as evenly as she could manage. "With a copy for each of us."

"You don't trust my word?" Catharine raised her eyebrows.

"I would like to put the agreement in writing," Hattie repeated in order to avoid saying she did *not* trust Catharine's word.

Catharine considered for a moment and then nodded. "Very well. I shall write something up. And then we shall never speak of it again, agreed?"

"Agreed."

Catharine relaxed her shoulders. Hattie

relaxed, too, though surely no one could tell as she felt as though she'd grown into part of the chair.

"Good," Catharine said, and her voice was soft again. "I would like very much to return to simply being sisters, Hattie. I feel that is the best connection we have ever had. Business and family creates far too much of a risk, I have decided."

"I agree."

When Catharine had convinced Hattie to first begin teaching at her Litchfield Female Academy in Connecticut, Hattie had been reluctant. Though she was a good teacher, she did not enjoy giving instruction and had continued in the profession far too long in order to please Catharine. It seemed now, finally, that Catharine could accept that Hattie had a different future. Never mind that Hattie felt less ready to face that future with each passing day.

"Very good." Catharine stood and began gathering up the tea tray. "I shall have an agreement ready tomorrow, but for now I shall see to the kitchen. I'm afraid things have become terribly inefficient in my absence."

Hattie didn't even bristle. She'd known this dominating side of her sister was coming. She even found it endearing in its own

151

way now that she was not the center of Catharine's storm.

"Be mindful of Aunt Esther's feelings," Hattie warned. "She has had a great deal to do this summer seeing after all of us."

"Oh, I've no doubt of that." Hattie felt the accusation but did not rise to it. "And I am always mindful of other people's feelings. I'll lobby no complaint at Aunt Esther, to be sure, only institute a more sensible system than the one operating now."

Meaning, of course, that she would lobby complaint toward Hattie instead, who was supposed to have helped with the household management but had not. Hattie didn't care that Catharine was making a backhanded accusation — so be it.

Catharine put the last of the cups back on the tray and then lifted it. "Oh, and I should have said this when everyone was gathered, but I guess I'll tell you first instead and announce it to the others at dinner. Father has found a widow to marry. The deed shall be done next week and then they will return to us the week after that. Her name is Lydia Jackson, and though I have not met her, I hear she's a fine woman and will be a good companion for Father. Some men simply need a woman to take care of them."

She left Hattie with this news hanging like

a wet rug about her shoulders. Father would be married? There would be *another* Mrs. Beecher?

Only when the shock had passed did Hattie pick up the additional implication of Catharine's words. This new stepmother would take care of the minutiae of their father's life as his other wives had done, and as Hattie had chosen to do when she married Calvin. In Catharine's opinion that was what wives did — they took care of their husbands in place of their own pursuits.

Hattie looked out the window, but the street was quiet and there was nothing to detract from her rising self-pity. She had no husband to care for right now, and Calvin was unhappy with how she'd spent her time during his absence. She had not made Calvin's life easier, as this new Mrs. Beecher most certainly would for Father, and in that moment, Hattie felt like a burden to everyone.

The face of Hattie's first stepmother came to mind. Harriet Porter Beecher had been dead little more than a year and already she'd been replaced, just as she had replaced Hattie's mother so many years before. It seemed wives were easily exchanged by the men in Hattie's life. She had stepped into Eliza's shoes just as Lydia Jackson would step into Harriet Porter's and Harriet Porter had stepped into Roxanna Foote's.

And yet Hattie was well aware of the many ways in which she did not fill those shoes the way Calvin wished she would. Eliza would never have written inflammatory editorials under a man's name, let alone felt so strongly on an issue to want to write about it in the first place. She'd been mild where Hattie was extreme, patient where Hattie was excitable, and easy where Hattie continued to be complex.

A tear on her cheek surprised her, and Hattie hurried to wipe it way, accounting her emotion to her pregnancy, the stress of Catharine's return, and her own uselessness.

"He loves her," she said to the panes of glass, but even as she said it, she wasn't sure if she were assuring herself of her father's love for this third Mrs. Beecher or trying to convince herself that Calvin loved her still, even after all they were going through — or *not* going through. At least not together.

She could not sort her thoughts or situations, but neither could she push away the sorrow. Better that she let it wash over her, perhaps then it would find another place to rest. A second tear followed the first and then a third while her heart ached to please her sister and her husband and to know there was a place in their lives that was all her own, that she would not be so easily replaced should she somehow disappear.

CHAPTER TWELVE

September 12, 1836

Dear Calvin,

Things are calming here in Cincinnati. Whether that is because the protesters have made little progress or because the Anti-Slavery Society here in Ohio is better organized, I cannot tell. I do think a great deal of the lawlessness has converted some to the anti-slavery camps as the tactics of the protesters are so abhorrent — as I predicted it would. Our friend Salmon Chase is a full supporter, as I am myself, though silently. I have not written a "Franklin" letter for some weeks; truth be told, I have not done much of anything. I do not think you would recognize me were you to see me face to face. I have swelled into a pumpkin and spend most of every day as a piece of furniture.

True to her word, Catharine has brought order to the household, and Aunt Esther — bless her soul — has stepped aside. In truth, she seems relieved of the burden, reminding me that Aunt Esther is not a young woman. She needed the help, and since I am completely worthless in my present state, I am glad Catharine is here for her sake.

It is strange to think that you will return to an entire family, not just me. How I hope you will be pleased with both of us. The midwife says I am still at least a month from welcoming our child, but I wonder how I am to survive even one more day in this state. I marvel that our species has managed to propagate at all given the circumstance of my body and mind. How on earth does any woman go through this more than once? Perhaps it is easier to say with your being gone so long, but I sometimes fear I shall never enjoy those nights we spend together now that I know what might come of it!

Be well, dear husband, and work hard. God willing, you will have two sets of arms ready to embrace you upon your return.

Affectionately yours,
Your Hattie

Hattie dusted the letter with sand, then tipped the fine grains back into the tin box before blowing the paper clean and folding the letter. One would think that with so much time on her hands, she would be writing Calvin every day as she had in the beginning of their separation, but since she heard from him so rarely, she wrote him once a week now, when she felt as though she had something to say.

It was the receipt of his letter on August 28 that had given her reason to write this one. He said he'd written it the day after sending the reprimanding one that had broken her heart, worried he had been too terse. Though he restated his concerns regarding her affiliation with the anti-slavery movement in Cincinnati, he apologized for his harshness and ended the letter with several lines about how lonely he was without her and how eager he was to return home. The ocean between them made communication so difficult, and more than ever she longed for her own house with her husband at her side.

Thinking back on shared evenings by the fire, when she would do handwork and he would read his German out loud made her heart hurt with longing. Such a simple thing felt like heaven now, and as time marched steadily forward, she realized more and more that those days would never come again. Would that she'd made better use of them when she'd had them so easily at her fingertips. But she could not very well reprimand Calvin for cultivating indigo if she allowed herself the same.

Hattie was closing the drawer of the parlor's writing desk where she was collecting her correspondence for Calvin until she had a packet ready — next week probably — when she heard the crunch of carriage wheels in front of the house.

Hattie took a deep breath as she tugged at the skirt of her dress. Only one dress fit her now, but she did not want to alter another one when she would only need it a few more weeks. This one was faded and unattractive, but then again nothing could present her much better in her current state. Still, she smoothed her hair and pushed herself up from the desk. Today was the day she would meet her new stepmother. She wished she could make a better impression than this. She felt bloated and clumsy and big as a house.

From the other side of the front window her father laughed as he came up the walk — laughed! — and it did an odd thing to the undeserved prejudice Hattie had been feeling toward the newest Mrs. Beecher.

Catharine's voice from the hall did not allow Hattie's thoughts to linger long, however.

"Yes, yes, you here, and you . . . Yes, you stand here. No, Aunt Esther, you go into the parlor with Hattie. Only the staff need greet the new mistress of the house. Honestly."

A moment later, Aunt Esther came into the parlor, shrugging good-naturedly as she crossed to Hattie. "Why are you standing, dear? You should rest your feet."

"I've only just come to my feet, and trust me when I say it wasn't easy. Let me take some steps before I get sewn into a lumpy cushion again, please."

Aunt Esther laughed and took Hattie's arm as they took a turn around the room. Hattie hadn't left the house in two full weeks, not even for church. While she didn't need Aunt Esther to support her walking, she didn't mind the companionship. Catharine could organize the troops and Aunt Esther could keep her company every hour of the day and she'd be content with the arrangement.

The two women looked at one another nervously when they heard the front door open and listened to what unfolded in the entryway. Catharine introduced herself, let their father introduce Mrs. Beecher, and then the four servants each greeted their new mistress. It was a rather formal practice for the staff to turn out in welcome, especially here in Ohio, but it made Hattie feel as though they were a family of consequence. She hoped it made a good impression on the new Mrs. Beecher.

After the introductions in the hall were finished, Catharine led the way into the parlor, where Aunt Esther and Hattie waited with polite smiles on their faces. Hattie looked past Catharine and felt her heart leap in her chest. She had not seen her father for months. Her increasing state of pregnancy had softened her heart in many ways, making her feel toward her father the way she had when she was a child, dependent and eager for his approval.

"Papa." She moved forward spontaneously as though she could skip across the room as she'd done when she was young. Her feet felt stuck in mud, however, and Aunt Esther interpreted the resulting lunge as Hattie losing her balance. She pulled back on Hattie's arm, gasped slightly, and asked if Hattie was all right.

"I am fine," Hattie said, but she felt her cheeks flush with embarrassment. Only then did she look at the woman holding her father's arm. Her first thought was how grateful she was that Lydia Jackson was not young enough to add more Beecher children to the family. Though she would share the thought with no one, she had not forgotten Catharine's words on her wedding day about their father having worn out two wives already. The new Mrs. Beecher was nearly fifty, pleasantly stout with somewhat sharp facial features. She looked around the room with a rather critical eye before stopping on Aunt Esther and Hattie. Catharine managed the introductions.

"A pleasure to meet you," Mrs. Beecher said.

"The pleasure is all mine, I'm sure." If Hattie were honest, she did not feel much pleasure. There was a tightness about this woman that was off-putting. Perhaps her prejudice was not so undeserved after all.

Father came to Hattie and kissed her on the forehead before they embraced. Hattie rested her head on his shoulder, wanting to soak up the affection she felt particularly in need of right now. As soon as he released her, however, Mrs. Beecher stepped right up beside him and put her arm through his. The woman was making a point, and Hattie wished she dared say, "Yes, I know he belongs to you now."

"We shall have tea in a thrice," Catharine said, waving toward the sofa and adjacent chairs. Everyone followed her direction, and Hattie tried to settle into her chair with as little awkwardness as possible. Even so, once she was seated and caught her breath, she noticed everyone watching her, except Catharine, who had fetched her footstool and was even now ordering Hattie to lift her legs.

"When Catharine said you were as big and round as though the baby would be here tomorrow, I thought she was exaggerating," Father said.

Hattie shifted so the baby didn't sit squarely on her bladder, but realized she should have used the privy while she'd been standing. She shifted some more and the pressure eased. Still, she would not be drinking tea.

"I'm sure it only looks that way because my frame is usually so small," Hattie said, echoing what other women had said to comfort her after exclaiming over her size.

"Or you've more than one on the way."

Hattie shifted her gaze to Mrs. Beecher, who had her eyebrows pulled together as though Hattie had done something wrong. "I feel sure that's not the case," Hattie said as politely as she could. Other people had made similar comments, but she never considered the idea for long. Childbirth was fierce business and adding another child into that equation often meant death to one or all. "My mother-in-law says that my husband was a large baby, and so I believe his son is likely taking up more room than is his due."

"For your sake, I hope you're right."

The room went silent at this woman's talk of such dark things when they had only just met. Hattie, however, knew how to level the playing field. "Besides, my mother birthed nine children and was hale as a horse for each one. I'm sure I am just like her."

The women held one another's eyes. Father cleared his throat and asked after Isabella and the boys. Mrs. Beecher looked away a few moments later when the tea tray arrived, and Hattie was content to let the conversation move on without her. Hattie had never been close with her first step-mother, but they'd shared a mutual regard. This woman, however, was cut from different cloth, and Hattie felt her hackles rising more and more with every minute in her company. Why did her father have to marry again? Did his children not take good enough care of him to have him feel he could give up matrimony after having put two wives in the ground already?

Hattie came back to the conversation in time to hear Aunt Esther address Father's new wife. "Everyone calls me Aunt Esther," she said sweetly, choosing a shortbread from the tray. She looked up. "May we call you Lydia?"

"Certainly not. You shall call me Mrs. Beecher." She met Hattie's eye, and Hattie thought again of those nights in her small brick cottage with Calvin and his German readings. She missed them more than ever.

CHAPTER THIRTEEN

September 29, 1836

"I need to get another dish of cool water," Hattie said softly, as though speaking loudly would break the reverence of the sickroom. She dabbed the coolest of the cloths against Aunt Esther's fevered brow. Cholera had come to Cincinnati again, and the least deserving of the affliction had fallen prey.

Aunt Esther, pale and gaunt and more skeletal than usual, had been sick for three days now. She nodded without opening her eyes. Though it was morning, the blinds were shut tight, leaving the room in shadows that were at odds with the autumn sunshine outside the window. Hattie put the dish of water, warmed by the heat coming from Aunt Esther's body, on the side table, took a breath and then pushed herself upright, using all her strength to do it. She tottered a moment on her feet, gained her balance, and went to take a step. She must have knocked the bowl of water because liquid drenched her skirt and pooled on the floor at her feet.

"Gracious," she muttered. "As though what we need right now is my clumsiness." She attempted to step away from the water all over the floor, noting that it seemed a good deal more than what had been in the dish, when she knocked the *actual* dish, still on the side table, and watched the patch of water widen. She looked with confusion from the bowl to the water to the side table to her skirts, trying to make sense of what had happened. And then she felt something deep and twisting in her hips and back.

She cried out and leaned forward to grab the bedpost as she felt sure her hips were about to crack. The room spun. Somehow she made it back to the chair. She heard feet on the stairs and a shout from the doorway.

"Hattie," Catharine called out again as she ran across the room. "What's wrong?"

"I . . . I . . ." Hattie groaned. She wanted to pull her knees to her chest though she hadn't been able to do that in months. Catharine took her hand, and several seconds later, the twisting in Hattie's back eased enough that she could blink open her eyes and try to orient herself to the room.

She saw the dish she thought she'd spilled twice and the water on the floor and her delirious thoughts jumped to the reason she'd stood in the first place. "Aunt Esther is still burning up." She attempted to stand again, and this time Catharine helped her, with one arm around Hattie's back and the other at her elbow. Aunt Esther lacked the strength to even open her eyes to see what was happening.

"I will fetch the water," Catharine said as they exited the sickroom.

Hattie wondered at the tone of panic in her voice — Catharine never panicked.

"Henry!" Catharine yelled toward the first floor once they were in the hallway. "Mrs. Beecher!"

"Why are you calling *her*?" Hattie said, shaking her head. The two weeks they had lived as one family in this house had not gone well. Not that Hattie, Catharine, and Mrs. Beecher openly objected to one another, rather Hattie stewed and judged while Mrs. Beecher glared and dictated and Catharine scowled and rolled her eyes.

Catharine led Hattie past the stairs.

"Where are we going?"

"My room," Catharine said. "I don't dare take you down to yours."

"Your room? I don't want to go to your

room," Hattie said, reviving from the onslaught of such odd sensations and occurrences. "Aunt Esther needs more cool water."

Heavy footfalls on the stairs preceded Henry's sudden arrival on the second level. Catharine continued guiding Hattie toward her room while she spoke over her shoulder, her voice decidedly calm. "Someone needs to be bathing Aunt Esther with cool rags, and we need to call for the doctor."

"Has she taken a turn?" Henry asked. "What's wrong with Hattie?"

They had reached the doorway, and Catharine turned to meet Henry's eyes. "Hattie is going to have a baby, and Aunt Esther is not improved. We need that doctor, and I need some help."

Hattie is going to have a baby? "Oh my goodness," Hattie said, thinking of the water that hadn't come from the dish and the pain and . . .

She clenched Catharine's hand. "I can't have a baby! Not like this."

"It will be fine," Catharine said in that mothering tone Hattie knew from her childhood. "Your body says you are ready and so you are." She walked Hattie into the room but still spoke to Henry over her shoulder.

"Get Father from school, set Mrs. Beecher

in with Aunt Esther. Keep Bella downstairs and get that doctor."

Henry didn't say another word, but his feet pounded down the stairs as he raced off for his errands.

Catharine ordered Hattie to stand while she stripped the fine quilt that had been made by their mother from her bed and laid it over the steamer trunk set against the wall. She began helping Hattie out of her wet dress.

Hattie's mind became more frantic. "I can't have a baby today, Catharine. I'm not ready, and the midwife said she is not available until next week."

"You are ready. Stay calm. Everything is fine."

"It's too soon. It won't live."

"Don't think such things," Catharine reprimanded, lifting the skirt over Hattie's head. She made short work of Hattie's wet petticoats and drawers.

Hattie began to shiver though the day was not cold. "My waters broke?" she asked as she hugged her naked self. "I thought I'd knocked over the dish."

"You did that too." Catharine pulled one of her own nightgowns from a drawer and put it over Hattie's head as though she were five years old again and their mother had just died, leaving sixteen-year-old Catharine to manage the seven children left behind. But Hattie was *twenty*-five years old now, her mother had been dead for decades, and her own child was coming. A surge of emotion rose up, and she began to cry. Catharine took her in her arms and held her. "It's all right, Hattie. Everything is all right, don't cry."

"I don't know how it's done."

"Of course you don't," she said, almost laughing, which only made Hattie cry harder. "You've never done this before."

"I want Calvin." She wanted his strong arm around her back, his voice of encouragement in her ear. She'd been missing him so strongly these last weeks. She could not have his child without him.

Catharine pulled back and held Hattie's face between her own. "Calvin is not here, but if he were, he would tell you the same things I am telling you. God made you for this, Hattie — do you believe that?"

Hattie blinked, and her chin continued to tremble. Calvin would tell her to be strong if he were here. But Calvin was not here, he couldn't be. Yet she wasn't alone and that was a blessing. Even in her distress, she knew she was lucky to have her family around her. "Do *you* believe it, Catharine?"

Catharine's smile was soft, and her eyes were wet. "I do believe it, Hattie. You are to be a creator as Eve was, as our mother was, and you can do this as they did it — with grace, and faith, and strength. You *can* do this, Hattie, but you've got to set your mind to it."

Hattie nodded. *Grace. Faith. Strength.* She was nearly convinced of her capability when her hips seemed to pull together again, drawing her spine to the very center of her body. She cried out and bent forward. Catharine caught her and adjusted Hattie's arms around her shoulders.

"Relax, Hattie," she said softly and soothingly. "Take a breath. . . . Hold it. . . . Let it out. Relax. . . . Take a breath. . . . Hold it. . . . Let it out. Relax . . ."

Hattie felt as though she had no choice but to obey even though the instructions seemed the opposite of what her body wanted her to do. It wanted to clench and tighten, but she did as Catharine said because she could not think her own thoughts.

When the tightness receded, Catharine led Hattie to the bed and helped her lay down.

"I'm going to fetch some towels and sheets and things," she said gently.

"Don't go!"

"I'll be right back, I promise, but I need some things if we're do to this properly."

Hattie nodded, suddenly exhausted. Her whole body relaxed, and she felt as though she were sinking into the pillow and the tick.

Catharine left the room, closing the door behind her, but betraying her fear as she broke into a run down the hall. Hattie couldn't hear the words but an anxious conversation was taking place on Aunt Esther's side of the wall, then she heard footsteps going down the stairs, heavier ones coming up, shouting from downstairs, and all Hattie wanted to do was sleep. She began to drift off while repeating Catharine's affirmations.

Grace.

Faith.

Strength.

Your body was made to do this.

And then she was screaming again.

CHAPTER FOURTEEN

Hattie lost track of time, but it felt like days instead of hours before the doctor — going between Aunt Esther and Hattie — delivered Calvin Stowe's baby. Hattie fell back against the sweat-soaked pillows and felt strangely disconnected as excited voices swirled around the room.

"It's a girl, Hattie," Catharine said, then under her breath added to the doctor, "She is so small."

Small? Hattie reflected on the months she'd felt three times her usual size. The baby was *small?* Pondering was cut off by a shrill scream, and Hattie opened her eyes to see the squalling pink thing at the end of the bed being rather roughly wiped down by Catharine. Thin arms and legs protested in time with the hearty cries.

"A girl?" Hattie asked, looking at the baby with a sense of wonder. This morning they had been one person, and now they were two. Pride swelled through her, and she wished more than she had ever wished all these past months that Calvin was there. Wouldn't he be astounded! Catharine exchanged the towel for a blanket and quickly swaddled the baby like a package ready to take to the post. Only a tiny pink face peeked out at the world.

"A girl." Catharine handed over the tiny bundle that was now merely whimpering.

"Eliza Tyler Stowe," Hattie pronounced. She'd been practicing this moment for months, determined to support Calvin's name for the child. If Hattie were a tiny bit disappointed that the baby wasn't a son she did not have to name after Calvin's first wife, she would bury it deep beneath the love blooming within her. Hattie gathered the child in her arms, awed at how familiar it felt to hold her though she'd never done it before. The name settled about her, leaving no room for regret. This baby reminded her of Eliza in fact, small and delicate with a calm disposition. Little Eliza blinked her eyes to look around her, but did not cry.

"Are you certain you want that name, Hattie?" Catharine asked in a quiet voice. "You can make your own choice. You've done all the work."

"Her name is Eliza Tyler Stowe," Hattie

said as she touched the finely shaped nose and ear. She had a daughter. She was a mother! "It feels right."

A moment later, however, that tightness in her hips returned, and Hattie hunched forward, clasping the tiny bundle to her chest.

"There's another," the doctor said. Hattie had nearly forgotten about him.

Eliza was taken from Hattie's arms, and she went back in time to the hellish minutes that preceded Eliza's welcome. Hattie collapsed when the tightness passed. The doctor told her another baby would come with the next contraction and she should gather her strength. "Second one's bigger than the first — happens sometimes. Be ready to give it all you have, Mrs. Stowe."

All I have? I have nothing. And another baby? Two!

It seemed impossible. How could there have been two all this time and Hattie not known it? There was no time to think of how many people had mentioned the possibility before the next contraction hit. Hattie gave this one moment in her life all the effort she possessed. The deep growling sounds accompanying the doctor's coaching were her own, but they felt as though they belonged to someone else. She'd never made such unfeminine noises in her life.

"A bit more," the doctor said.

"You're doing fine," Catharine said, gripping Hattie's hand while still holding Eliza tucked against her side.

The doctor continued his coaching. "Keep pushing . . . keep on. . . . Almost there . . . and . . . we've got it!"

The release and relief and pure exhaustion caused Hattie to cry out with a scream, part victory and part surrender. Then she collapsed, feeling as though her bones had crumbled. Her body throbbed. Her head ached. She felt like she was dying, and the room began to turn. She closed her eyes and tried to catch a full breath as a second infant's cry filled the room — heartier than the first. *A-wah, a-wah, a-wah.*

"Another girl," Catharine said, her voice high with shock and surprise. "Fairly twice the size of the first."

"Eliza." Wait, had she said that already? Hattie struggled through disconnected feelings, afraid she would fall asleep and never wake up. "The first is Eliza. Tell Calvin I did as he asked."

"Of course," Catharine said.

Hattie opened her eyes and watched a repeat of what she'd already seen: Catharine rubbing down plumper legs, a head the size of a small melon instead of a large apple as the first had been. This baby was nearly red, rather than pink like Eliza. Catharine wrapped the baby in another blanket that seemed to come from nowhere and, like Eliza, this second creature's cries turned to whimpers and then to merely a sniffle. Catharine put the child in Hattie's arms that had regained enough strength, it seemed, to hold this child as she had the first.

Hattie wondered briefly where Eliza was, but she stared into the dark eyes of her second baby and felt that same blossoming feeling of love all over again. There was room for both of them — room for many.

The bed jostled, and Hattie looked up at Catharine holding Eliza but looking down at the baby in Hattie's arms. "Twins, Hattie. Can you believe it?" Tears ran down Catharine's face, and Hattie felt the emotion welling up in her own eyes while letting go of any lingering resentment she'd felt toward her sister. When Hattie had needed her most, Catharine was there, holding her hand, encouraging her forward, and showing none of the envy Hattie sometimes suspected.

"We've work to do yet," the doctor said. Hattie had managed to forget him again.

"Not another one!" Catharine said.

"No, afterbirth and such, but two babies presents the need for meticulous attention. You may take the babies elsewhere, and I'll finish the work in here."

"Yes, of course," Catharine said. She looked between the babies as though considering holding them both, and then shook her head. "I'll return with another set of arms."

She took Eliza with her, leaving Hattie with the unnamed one still held tight to her chest. She touched the child's perfect lips and nose just as she'd inspected Eliza. She had only allowed herself to think of one girl's name and therefore had nothing to name this one.

"Isabella," she said, thinking of her sister who was as excited as anyone to be an aunt. Hattie had always liked the regal name. She leaned forward and christened the name upon her infant with a kiss to the baby's forehead, soft as silk. The infant mewed like a kitten, and Hattie laughed as she pulled back to look at her again. Two babies. Two daughters. The miracle of it all filled her with a connecting light to Heaven she'd never felt before. Would Calvin feel it, too, if he were here? Her heart ached with wishing. She'd been so certain that his going to

Europe and her having her family around her would be enough, but it wasn't. She needed him to cry with her and be astounded with her. Why had she thought his missing this was of no matter?

The bedroom door opened. Hattie looked up to see her stepmother's severe face and felt some of that light leave her. Mrs. Beecher came to the bed and took the child from Hattie's arms without a word. She bounced on her feet and smiled softly into the infant's face, but then turned sharp eyes back to Hattie. "Didn't I say it was twins?" With that, she turned on her heel and left the room, pulling the door shut behind her and leaving Hattie and the doctor to do the rest of the work.

CHAPTER FIFTEEN

January 20, 1837

Calvin stepped off *The Gladiator* at the New York pier only to spend an hour arranging the transportation of the crates that had accompanied him across the Atlantic Ocean. He had four to add to the three he had shipped from Europe earlier in his tour. The last of the books he'd collected for the library would arrive at Lane nearly a week before he did.

Standing on American soil again increased his eagerness to make his way to Cincinnati immediately, but there were investors in Boston he needed to meet with first, as well as a council he'd been asked to attend on behalf of the church and Lane Seminary. Agreeing to these meetings while still in Europe had seemed ordinary. He'd no accounting at the time how weary he would be by the end. Nine months away, and a wife and, God willing, a child were waiting for him. Yet he would be two more weeks in the East and then endure two more weeks' travel to reach them. The waiting was agonizing. Between a last-minute change of his itinerary and the extended ocean travel, which had been tumultuous, he had not received a letter from Hattie since September — four months ago — just after the new Mrs. Beecher had set the household on its ear.

Surely Hattie had had their child by now. Was it a boy as he sensed she wished it to be, or did he have a daughter? Would Hattie remember to name her after Eliza?

A crisp wind came off the ocean, and Calvin caught his breath. He turned up the collar of his coat, tucking the scarf from his mother tighter against his neck. The temperate winter he'd experienced in Europe might be the only thing he'd miss.

"Need you some help with that trunk, sir?"

Calvin looked around and caught the eye of a dark-skinned porter standing near the dock. Calvin smiled gratefully and gave the young man the name of his hotel. "Do you deliver there?" His breath came out in puffs of frost.

"Ye'sir," the porter said with a crisp nod. "I's have it there in an hour." He waved toward a cart nearly full with other trunks.

"It be the third stop on my loop if that set well with ya."

"Well enough, yes," Calvin said and pulled out the proper coin to pay the man. Half now, and the second half of payment would be left at the front desk of the hotel to be paid when the trunk arrived.

Once the transaction was finished, Calvin took out his pocket-sized notebook, removed his leather glove from his hand with his teeth, and entered what he'd paid the porter into the pages set aside for "Lane Expenses." Porter services were considered a necessary travel expense. He'd filled pages and pages with the details of his expenses. He would need to get them totaled and submitted for reimbursement as soon as possible.

It had been a far more expensive trip than he'd expected, and he'd spent more of his forwarded salary than he'd have liked to. Receiving, and therefore having to pay for, Hattie's packets of letters and journal entries were a good example of expenses he had not expected to incur. Thank goodness he'd put Hattie on a budget before he left. It was the only reason he was not out of his head with worry over their finances. At the thought of Hattie, his heart melted in his chest with longing. When would he see her?

Would he see her at all?

The darker thoughts about what might greet him in Ohio settled about him during his walk to the hotel even though he told himself that if something tragic had occurred he would have been informed. Only how? He'd been at sea for nearly three months thanks to rough seas and an inexperienced crew. The nightmare of returning to Cincinnati to find Hattie buried beside Eliza had woken him on more than one night. Prayer and work and acquiring more literature than he could read were all that kept him from falling into complete panic over the possibility. At his core, he felt Hattie was well, but when he reached the hotel he would know for sure. He'd left his forwarding address with his last hotel in Europe and told Hattie to send any correspondence to this hotel after October 15 so that he might meet up with it as easily as possible.

It was a cold, fifteen-minute walk through the snow, but Calvin was reluctant to spend any money on a hired carriage. Lane would pay for the hotel, of course, and his meals, porter, and necessary travel, but additional expenses, especially those of convenience, came out of his pocket. At the hotel, Calvin shook the snow from his hat and stamped his feet on the mat before letting himself inside.

"Professor Calvin Stowe," he said to the lanky man behind the counter who was dressed in a white shirt and black vest. Calvin hoped the room Lane had arranged included a fireplace.

"Aye, Professor. We've set you in room sixteen, just down the hall." He pointed to his right. "And we've got a fire ready for you at no extra charge."

Praise the Heavens! Calvin thanked him and left payment for the porter along with instructions to deliver the trunk to his room when it arrived. The clerk slid the guest book across the counter, and Calvin signed his name and date on the page covered with two dozen other signatures. "Have you received any correspondence for me? I've had some things forwarded."

"Let me check in the office, but I think we do have some post for you."

The clerk disappeared through a narrow door behind the desk, and Calvin tapped his fingers impatiently. When the clerk returned with a thick stack of letters tied together in a bundle, Calvin snatched the bundle and then apologized for startling the man. "I've been three months without news from home, you understand."

"Of course," the clerk said, but he seemed to harbor some offense.

Calvin paid the amount owing with barely a wince before hurrying to his room. He checked the letters as soon as he'd closed the door behind him. Six of the letters were from Hattie, one was from Lane, and two were from his mother. Arranging them in order of date allowed him to breathe more freely as his eyes were drawn to Hattie's fine script across the front of her letters. She'd last written him just two weeks ago, which meant she had come through childbirth. A great weight slid off his shoulders, and he felt he could draw a full breath for the first time in months.

The other letters were dated back to the middle of October, and though he was tempted to read what she'd most recently sent, it didn't seem right to read the letters out of order. He settled himself in the straight-back chair, then stood and removed his coat when he realized the room was quite warm from the crackling fire. Once settled again, he extracted his penknife and opened the first letter, expecting the usual news of family, her continued discomfort with pregnancy, and likely a great deal more about Hattie's new stepmother. Instead, the opening line took his breath away, and he

186

shot to his feet.

"I am a father!" he said, only just resisting cheering out loud. His eyes jumped and skipped through the next several lines, pulling a word here and a phrase there.

"Twins?" he breathed to himself, then laughed out loud. Of course Hattie would have twins! It was exactly her nature to do what no one would expect. He sat on the edge of the chair and read more slowly, every muscle in his body was taut as a wire. Emotion rose in his chest as he realized the enormity of this blessing. Twin daughters — Eliza and Isabella.

He read the names again, touched that Hattie had remembered his request to use Eliza's name, but stopped on the name Isabella. It was a lovely name, of course, and likely in tribute to Hattie's sister, whom she adored. But it didn't set right with him.

"Harriet," he said, letting the name fill the room. "Their names should be Eliza and Harriet." He smiled to himself — twin wives and twin daughters. He would send a letter first thing tomorrow. Oh, how he wished he could jump in a coach right that instant and make his way to them. *Them.*

Calvin continued reading Hattie's account of the girls' birth but found the words blurred until he had to stop reading, cover his face with his hands, and cry as he had not cried since Eliza's death. So many times he'd been afraid to dream of the future, fearful of looking ahead too far in case he would light his mind on an expectation that could not be realized. But the grandest dream of his life had been granted him. He was a *father.* He had a family to raise and care for as his own father had been denied. Hattie, dear Hattie, had given him what he so often had feared would never be his. How could a man absorb so much all at once, especially at such a distance from those he loved above all else in the world?

"Dear God in Heaven, help me be worthy of this blessing," he prayed out loud when he found himself on his knees before the fire. *I thank Thee with all my heart for the chance.*

CHAPTER SIXTEEN

January 30, 1837

Dearest Hattie,
  Eliza and Harriet! Our girls must be named Eliza and Harriet!

Hattie read through Calvin's letter post-marked from New York on January 21, but despite having been so happy when she'd received it, by the end she wasn't sure what she thought. She was glad Calvin knew he was a father, and glad he was happy about the girls, but could he not have included some praise for Hattie?

She had brought these daughters into the world, after all. She had toiled — and was toiling still — to care for them day in and day out, night after night after night. It had been three months, and yet she could not account for any single particular day since their birth. All the days ran together as she struggled to regain her physical strength and manage two infants who seemed to always demand something. She'd waited more than three months for a letter from her husband acknowledging that he knew all that had happened. Was it too much for him to ask how she was faring? Was it selfish for her to want him to tell her what a remarkable thing she'd done?

"It *is* selfish," she told herself and folded the letter. "Just as it is selfish to want to sleep for four hours in a stretch, selfish to ask others to lend a hand when possible, and, most selfish of all, to want for anything in life but your two precious angels." Mrs. Beecher had been quick to offer such reminders whenever the chance arose. Yet, Hattie *was* surrounded by helping hands at her father's house. What would she do when all the work was upon her shoulders? Well, her and Calvin's. It was hard to imagine how he would fit into the pattern of their family after having been apart from it for so very long.

Hattie looked at the cradles, side by side on the other side of the room, and felt her heart melt as it did a hundred times a day. Despite her fatigue and frustration, her daughters *were* precious angels, and she felt guilty for thinking anything contrary. She had never known how much love a person could feel until she'd become a mother. She had also never known how tired a person could be, how absolutely drained and cavernous. Sometimes it felt like loving her daughters was the only feeling she had left. Except, it seemed, irritation with her husband for not asking after her welfare.

Eliza stirred, reminding Hattie how priceless the moments were when both girls slept. She hadn't thought she was squandering the time by reading the first letter she'd had from their father in months, but now she was cross, which made her feel ungrateful. Fatigue pulled at her like an anchor. Did she have the energy to be cross?

Hattie looked from Eliza's cradle to Isabella's — who Calvin wanted to name Harriet. She should feel complimented that he wanted a namesake for her as well as for Eliza. At that moment, however, it felt like one more reminder that she shared his heart with another. Would his two daughters feel the same?

Hattie moved across the room to stand at the foot of Little Isabella's cradle. "Shall you like to be a Harriet?" Hattie whispered to her second born. Isabella was still bigger than Eliza, but both girls were healthy and growing at a steady rate, thanks in part to the wet nurse Hattie had hired to help keep the girls fed. Father had agreed to pay for it from Calvin's wages not already forwarded, and Calvin had better not lodge a complaint. "I can't say the name has ever been *my* favorite. Isabella was a queen, you know." She let out a breath. "But never mind that. It seems you shall become as I am — common and ordinary. It is what your father wishes."

Her words brought back Catharine's words, voiced on her wedding day: *You will give up your gifts to do what any other woman could do in your place. . . . Name me one woman whose voice is not drowned out by the cries of her children and the opinions of her husband.*

Had Catharine been more prophetic than Hattie wanted to believe? Was she being swallowed up in the people she loved? Did they love her back half as much as she loved them?

Such thoughts threatened tears, and Hattie shook her head to clear it. "No more!" She was determined to rise above the constant emotions that had come with motherhood. She would not become maudlin and melancholy. "Calvin will come home, and we shall build a life for ourselves that fits us just as it ought."

Her words echoed through the room, and she moved to the writing desk Father had purchased for her as a gift upon the girls' birth — a thoughtful, if not ironic, gift. Hattie had not picked up a pen for months aside from her letters to Calvin and her contributions to the family letters that passed from one Beecher household to another. The desire to pen a new article or essay had been growing within her for weeks. Usually it was exhausting to even entertain the thought of writing, and she would push the desire away, but if she were to be a literary woman, she would need to find a way to make the time for it. And both girls were sleeping right now.

She settled herself in the chair that felt unfamiliar and pushed down the anxiety that demanded she fill whatever time she had with something brilliant and perfect. There was no time to write a rough draft or explore a topic before finding the right approach. She uncapped the inkwell and dipped her pen. She let it hover over the paper as she tried to think of what to write. Perhaps something for her New England collection she had all but abandoned. Nothing came to mind. New England was a lifetime ago. The only things she could think of writing about were diaper balms and burping techniques. No magazine would include such vulgar topics. Surely she could think of something else.

Her mind moved to the continued conflict between the anti-slavery campaigns that she followed through Henry's reports at the dinner table. Maybe that was what she should write about. Her brothers were all beginning to support different anti-slavery groups and preach with more fervor from their pulpits. Catharine's article *An Essay on Slavery and Abolitionism with Reference to the Duty of American Females* had been accepted for publication amid great praise for its ideas. Could Hattie add to what had already been said? She wanted to, but did she have fresh thoughts after months of doing nothing but attending her babies? And would Calvin approve? She frowned. She'd wasted nearly a quarter of an hour already.

Anything, she told herself desperately. *Choose a topic and write!*

Isabella-Harriet began to whimper. Hattie tried to ignore her. Perhaps she would fall back asleep; she was the better sleeper of the two. But then the whimpers turned to cries, which awoke Eliza, whose cries were always quicker in volume and higher in pitch. Their crying competed with one another while Hattie let out a breath, recapped the ink, and returned the pen to the stock.

She pushed herself out of the chair and turned toward the fists swinging in the air above the cradles.

Maybe tomorrow.

CHAPTER SEVENTEEN

February 6, 1837

"They've just arrived, Hattie!" Catharine called up the stairs.

Hattie inspected her hair from one side to the other. *Why must I have this sudden influx of vanity now?* It was surreal to think she'd readied herself as a bride in this very room just over a year ago, and here she was, preparing to see Calvin all over again.

She moved a final curl in place, secured it with a pin, and then stood from the dressing table and shook out her skirts. All the missing him and irritation toward him and loneliness for him and eager anticipation of his return had become mixed and stretched and rolled and sorted a hundred different times over the last few weeks. The list of grievances she'd been collecting during his absence had become misplaced, and all she felt now was the spirit of rebirth and reunion. How she longed to lie in his arms and know she belonged there.

A soft cooing distracted Hattie from any further adjustments to the dress or her hair, and she turned in the direction of the cradles — one empty, one rocking gently in response to Little Harriet's movements. Eliza was already downstairs, having been taken by Catharine when Hattie proclaimed herself in desperate need of repairing her presentation one more time.

With gentle hands, Hattie scooped her daughter into her arms, settled her in the crook of her elbow and adjusted the lace bonnet she'd chosen for the day that her four-month-old daughters would meet their father. Calvin had been picked up from the dock some thirty minutes ago, and the household had held dinner so that they might give him a proper welcome. All these months without a home-cooked meal or family at the table would surely make tonight a perfect homecoming.

Will he find me too much changed?

She thought of her new figure, still small but now filled out and womanly. She thought of the changes to her attitudes regarding civil rights and equal treatment; she was growing increasingly uncomfortable standing on the sidelines. The role of "wife" had been packed in a closet with dishes and rugs, ready to be brought out with the other items of domesticity. Would she be better in that role than she had been before he left? There were parts of her domestic life she was eager to return to: having her own space, setting furniture as she liked it, keeping the drapes open in the evening if she chose to. But she continued to cast a wary eye toward other parts, such as having no help, which meant all the household chores — and two babies — would be up to her. She had grown these last months, and Calvin had likely experienced new things that had honed him as well. Only time would tell if that growth would bring them together or create a distance they could never close. The thought was terrifying.

Hattie forced herself to walk slow and careful as she descended the stairs and followed the sound of voices into the parlor. In the doorway, she was caught short at the vision before her. Calvin, dressed in his simple black suit and unpolished shoes, sat on the settee, holding Eliza as though she were made of glass. He stared into Eliza's face as though he'd never seen a baby in his life. She had hold of his finger, and he smiled with such raw joy that Hattie's throat tightened. He loved that baby in an instant, just as Hattie had when she'd first held their child in her arms. She'd been so afraid he would not feel the same thing she had, but she could see in his face that her fear had been misplaced.

After a moment of silent observation, Calvin looked up and saw Hattie standing in the doorway. The air froze between them, a moment that spanned the months and distance they'd been apart. He smiled, crinkling the skin around his eyes and causing Hattie's heart to nearly burst in her chest. She swallowed the growing emotion. Calvin — her sweetheart, her partner, her love — was a few steps away and she could hardly believe it. Calvin wrapped both arms around Eliza as though she might leap from his grasp like a frog and stood.

Hattie swallowed as she crossed the floor toward him, then she lifted Little Harriet in her arms and let Calvin get a look at his other daughter. He stared at Little Harriet just as he had Eliza, his expression reverent, then reached a hand out to touch her cheek. Little Harriet wrinkled her nose. Hattie choked on a laugh, completely overwhelmed.

"I am astounded," he said under his breath, but not soft enough to hide the crack in his voice.

Hattie felt the tears rising and wished she

had time to warn him that she'd become a virtual watering pot since last he'd seen her. When she met his eye and saw tears there too, the shame drained away. He leaned into her, and she read the cue as though they'd seen each other just that morning. Uncaring that they had an audience, though she noted that her family was in the process of leaving the room, Hattie leaned across their daughters and met Calvin's lips in a tender kiss that seemed to heal every wound she'd ever harbored. The edges of past offenses became as smooth as a river stone and as light as a snowflake. All she wanted was to be with him and their daughters.

"Welcome home, Mr. Stowe," she whispered against his lips.

They were a family. Hattie wished she could gather up the spirit of this moment and put it in a jar to keep.

CHAPTER EIGHTEEN

February 24, 1837

Hattie bounced from one foot to the other in the parlor, shushing and soothing Eliza, who was determined to be heard for the injustice being inflicted upon her. "It is nearly your turn, darling," Hattie said as she added a few dance steps to her bouncing, turning a quick circle in the process. The unexpected motion seemed to leave Eliza in question of what she'd been crying about, but only for a moment before her wails started up again. Hattie began to sing softly until she smelled the stew burning.

"Gracious," she said and hurried into the kitchen of the new house Lane Seminary had given them now that Calvin was returned.

It was bigger than the first cottage and had two bedrooms, both on the second floor, but the rooms were smaller, the stove older, and the furnishings less impressive than the last. Lane promised they would have a suitable house ready by summer, but Calvin was irate that they hadn't fixed the housing issue while he was away. He'd been home more than two weeks and still had battles with Lane almost every day regarding his expenses of the trip, the house, and the fact that they'd let a student leadership group use his office while he'd been away. His orderly space had been left in disarray. Plus two volumes of *The History of the Church* were missing.

The bliss Hattie felt at Calvin's return still survived in moments between them, but reality could be sharp at times as they tried to build what felt like an entirely new relationship.

Hattie moved the wailing Eliza to one hip, still bouncing her, and picked up the spoon she'd left across the top of the pot. She could feel a burnt layer on the bottom of the pan so she was careful not to scrape. Putting down the spoon, she picked up a kitchen towel and pulled the pot off the stove only to realize that if the stew were burning, the corn bread likely was too.

"I'm sorry, Lizzy," she said to the still-screaming infant as she moved to the opposite end of the narrow room and used one hand to grab the blanket she'd tossed over the chair earlier and spread it on the wooden floor as best she could. She laid Eliza down and returned to the stove while the baby redoubled her efforts of protest.

The corn bread was brown but not burned, and Hattie placed it on the counter to cool. Next she sampled the stew and made a face at the acidic tinge it had acquired. She must have run the stove too hot. It was so hard to keep the right temperature for the right duration. What she would not give for a cook!

"Miss Harriet is finished."

Hattie turned to the doorway where Mina, her wet nurse these last five months, held a very contented baby in her arms. Hattie looked around for where to put the spoon before putting it across the top of the pot again.

Mina was five years older than Hattie and likely capable of nursing half a dozen children if she had the time. Hattie nursed the girls during the night and at their midday, but Mina came every morning and evening. Hattie had told Calvin that she was unable to make enough milk for the girls, and he hadn't argued such a womanly point, but the truth was that she *might* be able to maintain both girls if she were willing to tether herself to the task. But she wasn't.

"Thank you, Mina. What would I do without you?"

"I wonder," Mina said, then laughed heartily at her joke. She looked at the corn bread and took a deep sniff of the air.

Hattie chose sheepishness over offense. "How does any woman manage a home and family?"

"Practice and necessity." Mina shrugged her heavy shoulders, looking around the room until her gaze settled on Eliza on the floor. That the women could have any bit of conversation over the child's wailing was evidence that they had both had a great deal of practice already. "I'm a commin', Miss Lizzy," Mina said, shaking her head as she headed for the baby. "Hold your pretty little hosses." She picked up the child and left Hattie to her semblance of cooking.

Usually Mina was gone before Calvin returned from the University, but the snowy weather made her late for this evening's feeding. Hattie adjusted the blanket closer to the stove now that the stew was lost and settled Little Harriet in the very center. She fetched a rag from the sideboard and soaked it in the water she'd pumped that afternoon. The water was still cool, and she handed the rag to Little Harriet, who took it eagerly and began sucking and chewing on the article.

"Be ye therefore easily en-treated," Hattie said, smiling at her revision of scripture and addition of a pun. She turned back to the stove and put her hands on her hips. How might dinner be salvaged? To keep the corn bread from drying out any more than it already had, she spread butter over the top and added a sprinkle of sugar. She also tried adding a little sugar to the stew. It helped some, but not as much as she'd like. She searched her packets of spices spread throughout her kitchen — the cinnamon had spilled all over the shelf above the stove — and added a bit of dried thyme and some more pepper. The seasonings covered the burnt taste but brought in a new, stranger flavor that might be worse.

She was adding a bit of powdered onion when she heard the front door open and sighed in surrender. She'd been trying so hard to have dinner ready when Calvin returned home each night, and in two weeks of their living as husband and wife again, she had succeeded exactly once. That day, Catharine and Aunt Esther had come and helped with the babies and housework so that there was nothing for Hattie to do but cook with a singleness of focus. She knew it had pleased Calvin to have the house in order, the babies calm, and a well-prepared dinner waiting for him, but she had not been able to recreate that evening since.

Hattie stayed at the stove, hoping the appearance that she was hard at work would earn his favor. He came into the room and paused in the doorway. Little Harriet threw aside the rag, put her hands up, and began babbling a greeting. Both girls had taken to Calvin quickly once he was a constant presence in their life.

"Ah, here are my angels!"

Hattie looked over her shoulder in time to see him reach down and scoop up Little Harriet. Two babies had helped him to quickly overcome his lack of experience. He planted a noisy kiss on her cheek and smiled at Hattie. "Smells like dinner got a bit overcooked."

Hattie's hand tightened on the wooden spoon as she turned back to the spoiled stew. She clenched her teeth to keep from saying something cantankerous.

Her silence apparently said plenty since a moment later she felt a warm kiss on the back of her neck. "Forgive me," he whispered, sending shivers down her spine. "How is my sweetheart?"

Her eyes seemed to close of their own power, and the forgiveness he asked for overrode her complaints.

Hattie tapped off the spoon and laid it across the pan so she could turn and face him. He was holding Little Harriet on one hip, but Hattie snuggled into his other side, and he put his arm around her shoulders. "I'm better now that you're here."

He smiled and kissed her temple just as Mina came in with a now-content Eliza in her arms. Calvin quickly stepped away from Hattie, directing all his attention to Little Harriet.

Hattie wiped her hands on her apron and hurried to take Eliza. "Thank you, Mina."

"Certainly," Mina said, but she stayed standing in the doorway.

Hattie pulled her eyebrows together while settling Eliza on her hip. "I'll see you in the morning?" she said.

Mina blinked, but still did not move. "I beg yer pardon, Mrs. Stowe, but it's Friday."

Friday? Hattie felt her cheeks heat up. Friday was the day she paid Mina for the previous week. "Oh, I'm sorry! I completely forgot. Give me just one minute."

Hattie looked around for somewhere to set Eliza, but Calvin was bouncing with Little Harriet on the far side of the room and the blanket on the floor had become wadded against a chair leg. There was nowhere to put the baby. Mina stepped out of the way, and Hattie took Eliza upstairs to her and Calvin's room. She put Eliza on the bed — where she instantly began screaming again — and pulled her money jar from the second drawer of the bureau.

Calvin had increased her monthly budget to twenty dollars, though he did the grocery shopping himself and managed the household finances. From Hattie's portion, she paid Mina and was responsible for household goods, including clothing for her and the girls. She ended up with less spending money than she'd had when Calvin was in Europe. She counted out Mina's wages of three dollars for the week, picked Eliza back up, and returned to the main level where Mina waited in the hallway.

She handed over the coins. "There you are. I'm so sorry I forgot."

"No trouble, thank you, ma'am."

Hattie returned to the kitchen. "I need to serve dinner before it gets cold," she said to Calvin as she laid Eliza on the blanket. Eliza was not pleased and balled her tiny fists like a pugilist. Hattie barely gave the crying child a second look as she pulled bowls and plates from the cupboard and arranged them on the table. Calvin said something but she couldn't hear him over the wailing.

"What?" she shouted, looking at him in hopes she could read his lips if he repeated himself.

Calvin shook his head and bent down to pick up Eliza in his other arm. With a baby on each hip, he danced and bounced around the table while Hattie finished setting out the dishes. In the back of her mind, Hattie knew this was a pleasing scene, the type of moment she would look back on with fondness, much like she looked back on the first moment she saw Calvin holding Eliza the day he'd returned.

When the dinner preparation was finished, Hattie took Eliza and settled her on her lap while Calvin did the same with Little Harriet. They said a prayer over the meal and, one-handed, they began to eat while simultaneously keeping their bowls and plates out of reach of the babies. If they had a girl of all work, she could entertain the babies while Calvin and Hattie enjoyed their evening meal together.

"I'm sorry about the stew," Hattie said after her second bite. It wasn't terrible, but it wasn't very good. Calvin had only taken one bite before moving on to the corn bread.

"It is fine." He didn't look up.

"I overcooked the corn bread."

"The flavor is good."

He was being more patient than kind, and Hattie put down her spoon, overwhelmed by all her failings. She had worked so hard, and yet her husband wasn't returning to a happy wife and loving children as much as he was entering a lion's den. She felt like her whole life was on edge.

"Calvin," she said, waiting for him to look up from his meal. "I think we should hire some help. A girl of all work, perhaps, who can assist with the babies and washing and, especially, the cooking."

He looked at his food and shook his head. "We've spoken of this before. We can't afford the expense."

"Can we afford not to?" she said, keeping her voice level and shifting Eliza so that the baby rested against her shoulder. The baby was sucking her thumb and had closed her eyes, which Hattie should prevent if she hoped to keep the girls to their eight o'clock bedtime. "I work from sunup to sundown and still never finish the work that needs me. What I do accomplish is poor quality and not an adequate reflection of the time I invest. We could build a room off the kitchen she could use, which would reduce the cost and —"

Calvin did not look up as he interrupted. "It reduces the *pay*, Hattie, but not the cost to house a servant. Room and board is not free. We still must provide the meals and the daily incidentals of life."

She did not like that he sounded like a father speaking to his child. "I feel it would be worth the expense to have the house in order and edible meals on the table."

Before lifting his head, Calvin took a breath and then let it out, as though controlling his temper, which only served to tighten Hattie's rising defenses. They had not argued since his return, but the change in the air around them was reminiscent of those early months of marriage when they argued nearly every day. Calvin put down his spoon and straightened. Little Harriet was sucking on the shoulder of his coat.

"As much as I would like to return to an orderly house and have decent meals, there is no money for help, Hattie. My salary has been taken back to its 1835 levels due to this financial crisis, and there is no room for excesses now that prices are on the rise. I am not being cheap, as I know you like to accuse me. We simply cannot afford to hire help."

The financial climate of the country had been a growing concern for some time, and

Lane Seminary had not avoided the difficulties as banks failed and unemployment rose. Despite her awareness of the Panic of 1837, Hattie was too familiar with Calvin's skinflint ways to fully trust this reason. She'd read the papers about how the East and South had been affected, but it seemed to her that Ohio had avoided the worst. Besides, Calvin had drawn a full salary during his absence, and though he'd spent more on his travels than either of them had expected, there must still be some left over.

"It is not an excess, it is a necessity," she said, "and if I were freed up from this drudgery, I could write and bring in some income of my own."

"Not income paid at regular intervals that would assure our ability to pay for ongoing help." He shook his head. "I understand you are used to servants, but although the Beechers may think so, they are truly not necessary to run a household. My mother cared for her own home and children while doing the wash and sewing for half a dozen other families. It is not a matter of needing help, it is a matter of using your time more wisely."

Hattie tried to relax the hand that was suddenly clenching the spoon like an axe. "Using my time more wisely? You say that as though I am primping and lollygagging all day long when I am instead rushing here and there and back again all hours of the day. Then you come home and cast a critical eye about the place. Everything I do is inferior to your standards, and I feel it like a knife in my heart every day."

His expression remained neutral, which only increased her frustration. "When I first began working at Bowdoin Library, I felt much the same way. I could never get through the tasks of the day. But with focus and determination, I learned to perform tasks at greater speed and with better accuracy. It is the same thing here. As you focus on the household tasks and set your mind to become proficient, you will improve."

Hattie spoke through clenched teeth, fiercely hating the analytical workings of her husband's mind. "Which means I am not focused now, in your opinion."

Calvin cut a piece of his corn bread. "That is not what I said. We cannot afford more help, Hattie, however much you wish we could. We are already paying for the wet nurse — twelve dollars a month, which is an astounding cost. Now, if you could take *that* task upon yourself then perhaps we could see about another arrangement, but as long as we are paying that woman, there is not space for this discussion."

Hattie looked at him while repeating the words in her mind. "Do you think I have the wet nurse for convenience, Calvin?"

He looked up and held her eyes. "Don't you?"

"I have the wet nurse because I cannot produce enough milk for both girls on my own. If not for Mina, our girls would be hungry."

The look he gave her was skeptical, but she knew he would not argue on female issues, and she renewed her determination never to admit — *ever* — that she might have more capability.

"I understand," he said, though she did not think he did. "Mina is a *necessity.*"

Hattie narrowed her eyes. A great pounding response was coiling in her chest even though she felt pinpricks of guilt for her own dishonesty. She justified herself with the fact that feeding both girls herself would take, literally, all day. There would be no time for anything else. Never mind that she continued to put off the wash until it absolutely had to be done, or that she spent a great deal of time each day playing with the girls or reading the books Isabella provided her with from the lending library.

Hattie was simply not the domestic sort, and the sooner Calvin understood that and hired a woman who was, the sooner they could get on with their lives together.

Hattie was formulating an additional argument for Mina's services when Little Harriet finally reached the edge of Calvin's bowl, pulling the stew into her and her father's lap. In an instant Calvin was on his feet, Little Harriet was screaming, and stew was everywhere. Hattie startled and began to rise, then thought better of it and settled Eliza, who was falling asleep, back into her lap. She focused on her own bowl of ill-flavored stew, which was not hot enough to have hurt the baby when it spilled.

"Hattie!" he said sharply. "Help me with this — take her."

She raised her eyes to see Calvin holding a screaming Harriet over the kitchen table. Bits of stew dripped from the hem of Little Harriet's dress onto the pan of corn bread. Hattie's heart clenched at the sight of her daughter in distress, but then she met Calvin's eyes. "I'm sorry, *darling,* but I am very *focused,* for the moment, on eating my stew, and I am determined to finish it as *efficiently* as possible. There are rags in the cupboard, however." She turned her eyes back to her bowl and tried to hide her smug smile.

CHAPTER NINETEEN

March 6, 1837

The next day, Hattie turned a blind eye to the housekeeping. Instead, she "focused" on making a delicious chicken and potato pie for dinner and doing the wash, which she put up on lines strung through the living room so the clothes would not freeze outside.

She played with the babies in front of the fire, throwing a bright ball against the wall for almost an hour, and then read to them from her collection of Hans Christian Andersen stories. The girls napped at the same time that afternoon, which allowed Hattie to also catch an hour of sleep she desperately needed. When they woke, she made a maple cake for the night's dessert, ignored cleaning the kitchen afterward, and read *The Journal* edition from three days ago with Little Harriet on her lap and Eliza on the blanket at her feet. Little Harriet

217

kept grabbing for the paper, which meant Hattie had to hold it out of reach, making it difficult to read, but she was determined.

When Calvin came home, she jumped up to kiss him hello, having to duck under the clothesline to reach him. The clothes had been dry for hours, but she'd kept them on the line all the same. She ignored his silent criticism as he surveyed the mess.

"Dinner's ready," Hattie said, leading the way under the crisscrossing lines into the kitchen where she'd kept the pie in the still-warm oven. She was very pleased with both the pie and the cake, which was glazed and waiting beneath a large bowl so that Calvin would be surprised. They settled the girls on a blanket at the head of the table, where the girls kicked and cooed. Little Harriet looked at the brightly painted flowers on the wooden rattle Hattie's brother Edward had sent from Illinois, shook it, then stuck it in her mouth. The side table and stove top were piled with dishes, but the table was set and the house smelled delicious.

Calvin prayed over the meal and cut a bite. His shoulders relaxed as he chewed thoughtfully. "This is very good, Hattie."

"Thank you," she said, cutting a bite for herself and feeling proud of her efforts. "I took your counsel to heart and focused on dinner, wash, and playing with our daughters today."

Calvin complimented the meal again, and the girls' behavior, but said nothing of the wash. They spoke of his work — they'd found the two missing books in another office — and the board had given final approval for his expenses for the European trip. It was a load off his mind to no longer have to defend himself. When he finished eating the cake — two pieces — he thanked Hattie again for preparing dinner, then went into the parlor to sit by the fire and read, as he always did.

Hattie heard his footsteps stop and smiled at the mental picture of him looking at his chair currently covered in little girl dresses and hats she'd set to dry by the fire.

"If the clothing on your chair is dry," she called, "would you be a dear and fold them, please? The gowns go in the second drawer in the girls' room, the caps in the third."

Calvin said nothing.

Hattie smugly served herself another piece of cake and wondered what focus she could choose for tomorrow that would keep her husband from being too comfortable when he returned home.

You're a smart girl, she told herself. *Surely you can think of something.*

■ ■ ■ ■

For the next several days, Hattie continued to focus on specific tasks and ignore other ones. They had bread and butter for dinner on the day she cleaned the kitchen. The next day she spilled some dried onions on the kitchen floor — accidentally, of course. But since Hattie hadn't chosen sweeping to be one of her tasks that day, the vegetables crunched underfoot. The bean soup she'd made had only been passable despite her dedication to it; they both ate extra griddle cakes to compensate. Hattie played with the girls every day, enjoyed tea with Mrs. Allen one day and with Mary Dutton the next. On Monday she ignored nearly everything and took the girls to see Catharine and Granny Beecher. She needed a break.

The first time Hattie had called her new stepmother "Granny Beecher," the woman had made a sour expression, which made it impossible for Harriet not to make sure the name stuck. The woman, to her credit, had grown into it, and while she and Hattie had little love for one another, they both doted on the Beecher granddaughters and could come together on neutral ground.

Lunch had been set out at the Beecher

house — chicken sandwiches and roasted potatoes — when they arrived, and Hattie enjoyed a nice meal before the party moved into the parlor.

"Thank you for watching the girls," Hattie said once the girls were settled in Catharine and Granny Beecher's respective laps. "I do appreciate the chance to prepare for the Semi-Colon Club meeting."

"Certainly," Catharine said, holding a string of wooden beads just out of Eliza's reach.

Hattie made her way into Father's study. Meetings for the Semi-Colon Club had been sparse the last year, due to Calvin's European trip, the riots which divided some of the members, and now the ongoing financial troubles that were affecting several members. Uncle Samuel Foote, who had hosted the club for years, had been forced to sell his mansion, which had so easily accommodated the group. No one had said as much, but tonight might be the last meeting for the literary group.

Hattie settled at the desk, cut a blank piece of paper from her father's stores, and smoothed it across the desktop. She'd had flits of thoughts and ideas the last few weeks as she'd tried to prepare for the meeting, but no time to make notes or explore the thoughts to see if they would support a narrative. Writing required a different focus from reading, which was easier to stop and start. It seemed these days she struggled to maintain her focus for either activity.

She often used humor for her Club writings, but the current tension of her home life made the idea feel out of place. Perhaps, instead, she could write an insightful piece about how living beyond one's means was the culprit of the current financial climate. But it would be rubbing salt on a wound for Uncle Samuel, not to mention the other members who had been affected.

Though Hattie disliked Calvin's constant penny-pinching, she could concede that his thrift had spared them the difficulty of adapting as much as other people who could no longer afford the comfort they'd come to expect as their due. Conceding that, however, did not mean Calvin was right about their not being able to afford help — *that* was being a skinflint and, if she might be so bold in her thoughts, a tyrant. Hattie had not written anything for months, and so despite her willingness to cover the costs of a hired girl, she had no income to pay for employment on an ongoing basis. Calvin had said as much, and she knew he was right.

Perhaps that is what she would write about: the difficulty a woman faced when she needed help but her husband would not agree. But even as her hand hovered over the page, she questioned the wisdom of that. Taking her marital difficulties public was disloyal.

For another fifteen minutes, Hattie paced from the window to the desk and back again, conjuring and rejecting one idea after another and growing increasingly frustrated with her indecision. Finally, she determined to write about the rather mundane topic of modern cookstoves. She'd been researching them since Lane said they would replace the decrepit one in her house.

She had only penned a few lines before there was a knock at the study door. She covered what she'd done, mostly to hide how little there was of it, and looked up when Catharine poked her head in.

"I'm afraid Little Harriet's soiled herself through her clothing, and Eliza will not be settled with either of us. Did you get some writing done?"

Hattie glanced at the clock. She'd been in the study for an entire hour! She forced a smile and casually folded the paper in half while screaming silently in her mind. It wasn't Catharine or Granny Beecher's fault that Hattie had forgotten how to use her brain for anything but babies and housework. Having some time to herself, though unproductive, would have to be good enough for today.

"I did, thank you." How far she had come from writing editorials and inserting herself into public conversations. At least she could look forward to being among adults tonight — Mina was going to watch the girls.

Hattie bundled up two unhappy babies and brought them home. Soon she would not be able to carry both babies at once, even for such a short walk. Then she would be stuck at home on days when she could not take the baby carriage.

By the time she got home, both girls were screaming, her own temper was pitched, and it was nearly an hour before the girls were cleaned and fed and settled on the kitchen floor — which she'd had to sweep. She would have to make hotcakes for dinner, for the third time this week. It was as she was gathering her ingredients that she saw the letter on the table, tucked between dirty dishes from that morning and a basket of thread she'd put up so that Little Harriet would not unwind all the spools.

Hattie knew the letter was from Calvin. He must have come home for lunch. Likely he had been disappointed. Hattie had not made bread since last week and what was left was quite dried out. Perhaps she would focus on making bread tomorrow. Before she opened the letter, she wondered if it might be an apology. The last week, though less demanding on Hattie since she was no longer trying to do everything, had been uncomfortable. The tension was Calvin's fault, of course, but Hattie was still forced to endure it.

Dear Harriet,

There are certain points in which we are so exactly unlike that our peculiarities impinge against each other and sometimes produce painful collisions when neither party is conscious of any intention to disoblige the other.

1) I am naturally anxious, to the extent of needlessly taking much thought beforehand. You are hopeful, to the extent of being heedless of the future and thinking only of the present.

2) I am naturally very methodical as to time and place for everything, and anything out of time or out of place is excessively annoying to me. This is a feeling to which you are a stranger. You have no idea of either time or place. I want

prayers and meals at a particular time, and every piece of furniture in its own place. You can have morning prayer any time between sunrise and noon without the least inconvenience to yourself. And as to place, it seems to be your special delight to keep everything in the house on the move, and your special torment to allow anything to retain the same position a week together. Permanency is my delight — yours, everlasting change.

3) I am naturally particular, you are naturally slack — and you often give me inexpressible torment without knowing it. You have vexed me beyond all endurance often by taking up my newspapers, and instead of folding them properly and putting them in their place, you either drop them all sprawling on the floor or ball them all up into one wobble, squelching them on the table like an old hen with her guts and gizzard squeezed out.

I do not know how to resolve these differences, but I must have order and the ability to predict aspects of our daily life. I fear that we shall never find equal ground if we continue to have contention. With the goal of resolution, I have, this morning, sent a request to my mother for her to join us here in Cincinnati for a time. I feel she can help us with the girls, but also she can show you how a woman can manage her own household. I've asked that she try to arrive by the end of next month if possible. I hope we can manage until then without being childish or unkind in our actions toward one another.

Sincerely,
Calvin

CHAPTER TWENTY

Though Hattie was affronted at first that Calvin had invited his mother to teach Hattie how to run her home, by the time Calvin returned from Lane she had come to terms with his idea. She'd made eggs and griddle cakes for dinner, but Eliza was in a poor mood so Calvin ate while Hattie bounced the baby, and then Calvin took the baby so Hattie could eat. She almost felt guilty for the excellent lunch she'd had at the Beechers' in light of the poor dinner she'd provided. Almost.

"So," Calvin said between Eliza's fits. He sat across from Hattie and bounced the baby on his knee. There was an eagerness in his expression that made Hattie wonder if he were hoping for an argument. She was determined not to let him have his way. "I imagine you read my letter?"

She noted the challenge in his voice, but pretended not to. "I agree that you are anxious, methodical, and particular, but I don't regard those things as superior to my easy nature. If you would care for your own newspapers, that alone might resolve a great deal of the tension — keep the guts and gizzards from being so offensive." She smiled warmly at him. He narrowed his eyes. Hattie continued. "As to having your mother come to stay, I think it an excellent idea."

He tried to hide his surprise but was not altogether successful, and she gave herself a point. "You do?"

"Yes," Hattie said, smiling at him. "I have exchanged several pleasant letters with your mother this last year and find her a good and practical woman. She said that she felt I was a good match for you due to my intellect and accomplishments that ran parallel to your own. It was a kind thing to say, wouldn't you agree?"

Calvin said nothing, but watched her warily. She returned her attention to her plate. Eliza began fussing again, and Calvin stood and began walking back and forth across the kitchen to keep the baby calm. "You think she will side with you," he said after a minute.

"Yes," Hattie said with a crisp nod. "I do. I think she will see the amount of work two babies require, realize that God did not bless me with domestic skills, and recommend that we hire someone who will do a better job at housekeeping than I do in order that I might instead focus on the gifts God *has* given me — gifts that are such a compliment to your own." Though she'd attempted to keep a jesting tone, by the end she no longer felt so light. "I have not picked up a pen in months, Calvin, aside from the family letters, and even then I have to content myself with only a line or two. Since I can't hire help, a family member to assist me in what you have deemed my responsibilities is the next best thing."

"My letter did not upset you, then."

"Only in that you seem to feel your temperament is the one that all things must bow to, but I expect your mother will straighten that out as well."

He tightened his jaw and continued pacing and bouncing the baby.

Hattie finished her eggs and began to clear the table, ready to change the subject and hoping he would follow her lead. She did not want to fill the evening with tired bickering and repeated postulations of duress. "Did you get anything written for the meeting tonight?"

Calvin accepted Hattie's olive branch and shook his head, glancing at her. Eliza had finally stopped fussing but he kept pacing. "I am still trying to catch up with everything neglected in my absence. I had no idea how much work I would have waiting for me when I returned. It's been exhausting."

Hattie noted the fatigue around his eyes. He often helped her with the babies at night, though he could not feed them, and she realized that she hadn't thought much about what his days at Lane were like. The slump of his shoulders and bend in his neck confirmed what she'd never thought to notice — he was worn out, too. Not having time for oneself and one's interests was a challenge they both were facing.

He turned at the far end of the room. "Did you get anything written?"

She looked away from those tired eyes that made her feel self-centered and small in her complaints. "I tried. Catharine and Granny Beecher agreed to watch the girls, but I hadn't time to gather any thoughts so I'll have nothing to read either."

She wrung out a rag from the warm pot of water on the stove so that she might wipe down the girls' hands and then the table, but met Calvin's eyes in the process. He smiled at her, a weary smile that seemed to bind them together in the role of spending a great deal of time *not* doing the things

231

they loved. Hattie returned the smile self-consciously, then applied herself to the task of wiping down Little Harriet, who did not appreciate her mother's desire for tidiness.

Calvin continued his pacing. "I don't think reading will be the focus of tonight's meeting anyway," he said. "It will be a wonder if anyone has had energy for writing this month."

It was, in fact, a solemn evening that bore little resemblance to the high-spirited gatherings the group had experienced in the past. Uncle Samuel was moving to a smaller house and many of his furnishings were gone, either sold on the cheap or packed for the move, and, in the end, there was no reading done at all. Instead the group of friends spoke of all the changes taking place. Salmon P. Chase was increasingly involved in the Anti-Slavery Society and soliciting club members to join. Calvin spent much of the night talking to Hattie's father about his delayed salary and the lack of progress being made toward securing a larger house for his family.

"My mother is coming to stay with us for a spell," Hattie heard him say as she crossed the room to talk with Aunt Elizabeth. "We shall have five people living in a four-room house, President. It is abominable."

Hattie did not listen for her father's answer because she knew what it would be: "Then don't bring your mother out."

But Hattie *was* looking forward to Mother Stowe joining them. Certainly two women could realign Calvin's high expectations, and perhaps both parents would get more rest if there were a third person to help them manage their brood. Perhaps Mother Stowe *could* teach her how to manage her time better so she did not spend every day ticking through the things she was going to put off. Calvin had said on several occasions that his wishes for an organized household were for her benefit as much as anyone's. Maybe — just maybe — he was right.

Hattie settled into a seat within the grouping of mismatched household chairs near the hearth and listened to the conversation between Aunt Elizabeth, Catharine, and Mrs. Beecher. They spoke of Catharine's essay regarding the women's duty to the anti-slavery movement. Hattie hadn't read it yet but wished she had. Did she feel a twinge of jealousy that Catharine could put her voice onto paper so freely?

"I think it a splendid contribution to have so many voices being taken up for the cause," Aunt Elizabeth said. "And proof that the campaign is not only an issue for men. As women and mothers, with nurturing hearts and godly natures, we have a unique ability to feel the horror being done to these poor creatures, and I'm proud as can be that you spoke up."

Mrs. Beecher huffed, drawing the attention of the other women but then acting as though she hadn't done so intentionally. "Well, I don't mean to disagree, of course." Which meant that she *did* mean to disagree. "But I don't see how a woman's voice on this issue makes any difference at all. Men make the laws and therefore enact the changes. For women to waste the breath for such debates is pointless when there is no power. We must trust in our men to set things right and keep our efforts centered on hearth and home."

Hattie felt Catharine bristle.

Catharine sat up in her straight-backed chair. "Women are responsible for raising the next generation. We are the first teachers a child will ever know. If we can open their hearts to the right of a thing, change will come because of it."

Hattie reflected on how the principle of teaching ones' children was a cornerstone of Catharine's school and her view of a woman's role — but one she hadn't wanted for Hattie. Catharine felt any woman capable of what Hattie, as it turned out, was not very capable of after all. What would she think if she knew how poorly Hattie was fulfilling the roles that any other woman could do?

Mrs. Beecher huffed a breath again and shook her head. "Fathers, in their role as patriarch of their families, can open their children's hearts. Writing to women and suggesting that they throw off the natural order of their home is apt to lead to frustrations — both with marriages and the women themselves. It would be better to write of things relevant for women, as Hattie has done."

Hattie hadn't expected to be drawn into the discussion and felt all eyes in the circle come around to her. Mrs. Beecher continued. "Hattie has had the good sense to write of domestic issues that assist women in their own household management. Mr. Beecher showed me her article on Bible reading at home that she wrote last year."

The unique circumstance of hearing even mild praise from her stepmother quite caught Hattie's tongue enough that she could only smile and nod in response.

Catharine's jaw tightened. "A variety of

voices can be heard on a variety of subjects."

"But what is the point of upsetting women with talk of the harsh conditions of slavery? A Southern woman will not change her ways because of it, and a Northern woman will say it has no relevance to her life. As I said, there is no power within women to change public policy, which means that dozens of women simply end up unsettled about something they have no power to combat. I find that a waste of energy and, quite frankly, a threat to the very atmosphere of a loving home, which is where a woman's focus ought to be. I'm not saying you don't have a talent for words, Catharine — of course you do — but I would suggest that you ponder on what God would have you use that talent for. Stirring up contention without opportunity of improving a situation? Or focusing a woman's energy on the aspects of life over which she has command?" She settled back into her chair, a self-satisfied smile on her face. "I, for one, see the merit of only one of those choices, yet that merit is of infinite worth as it takes command of the very feminine virtues God has set upon each of us."

The small group fell silent, only Mrs. Beecher unaware of the offense of her statements. She took a dainty sip of her tea.

Hattie and Aunt Elizabeth shared an impotent look.

Finally, when the tension was thick enough to stir into a cake, Catharine spoke. "My belief in every woman owning her voice is proved herewith. If you'll excuse me." She pushed herself from the chair and quit the group. Hattie watched until Catharine disappeared into the kitchen before she shared another awkward look with Aunt Elizabeth, asking silently with her eyes how they might excuse themselves, too.

"Poor Catharine." Lydia Beecher shook her head. "I pity that woman's lack of vision. She's never been a mother, so she cannot understand where a woman's priority must always lie. After all, an unsettled mother makes for an unsettled home. Surely you agree with me on this, Hattie, do you not?"

An hour later, as Calvin and Hattie made their way from the President's House — they'd refused Father's offer to drop them at their doorstep due to the mild weather — Hattie relayed the women's conversation. "I didn't know what to say," she said, still frustrated by her silence. "I wish I'd read the essay so I better understood Catharine's premise, but I felt badly for her. She's trying so hard to get on with that woman."

"I read Catharine's essay a few weeks back."

Hattie looked up at him, his hat momentarily silhouetted by the light of a window as they walked beside it. "You did? You didn't tell me that."

"Didn't I?" Calvin said, shrugging. "Oh, well, I don't necessarily disagree with her charge that mothers should raise their children with an understanding of the evils of slavery, but I think Mrs. Beecher has a point as well. What good does it to do amplify the feelings of women who have no voice in the debate? I don't know that we should be content to wait generations for such teaching to pay off, and at the same time a Northern Christian woman is teaching her child of the ills of slavery, a Southern mother is teaching her children that it is the proper order of things."

"So a woman has no place in the argument," Hattie said, feeling the same offense she had before.

Calvin patted her hand tucked by his elbow. "That is what a woman has a husband for, Hattie, to argue in her place."

Hattie faced forward, and they walked a few steps in silence. "Catharine has no husband," she said, her voice holding an edge she did not try to hide. "But I believe she has as much right to her opinions as any man."

"Of course she has the right to her opinions. It is the question of whether or not sharing those opinions has value to anyone else. See, here you are getting upset about this, which only goes to prove my point, as well as Mrs. Beecher's."

They turned a corner, and she could see their house squatting in the darkness, waiting for them to arrive. Why did it look like such a shriveled thing this time of night?

He paused for a breath, which in Hattie's mind only amplified the condescending tone. "As a single woman, it is understandable that Catharine fights to be heard — she has no one else to speak for her. And, as I've said before, you Beechers were raised to proselytize. However, you are a married woman and therefore there is no need for you to worry about such things."

"I worried about them plenty in your absence, Calvin. One cannot turn off one's convictions as though it were a damper on a stove."

"I am here to worry for you now, so do not fret about it. We are of one mind on this topic and, I assure you, I am committed to do what I can without putting our family in harm's way. You then, spared of such concern, can focus on those things divinely appointed to your sex."

"And what are those appointments?" Hattie said, unsure if Calvin was ignorant of her rising fury or simply uncaring. Hadn't he once said he admired her opinions on things and her determination to be heard? Had those been the words of a courting man who now wanted his wife under his thumb?

"Hearth and home, just as Mrs. Beecher said. I don't see how any mother and wife has room for additional considerations."

Hattie was tired of fighting with her husband. Mother Stowe would come soon and dispel the growing tension. "Do you have Catharine's article?" Hattie asked as they turned up the short walk to their house.

"I believe so," Calvin said. "In the box of papers, I think." He looked at her as they stopped in front of the recessed door. "Surely you don't want to read it tonight. It is so very late."

She knew what he was really saying: "Surely you will come to bed with me, where we can recover from the tensions of the day in a way pleasing to us both."

"I think I will stay up." Hattie released his arm, keeping to herself how tired she was.

"But do go on to bed without me." She gave him a tight smile and let herself into the house before he could respond.

Her gaze settled on Mina, who was sewing, a sleeping infant wrapped in blankets on either side. Why couldn't Hattie ever get them into such complacence? If one slept, the other fidgeted, when that one was still, the other would take her turn. She forced herself to smile to hide yet another insecurity.

Calvin stepped inside behind her, silent.

"Thank you, Mina, for staying with the girls this evening," Hattie said. "It was a most educational night."

CHAPTER TWENTY-ONE

April 28, 1837

It was nearly two months before Hepzibah Stowe was able to make the arrangements to come to Cincinnati. Calvin and Hattie called a truce during the interim, much as they had a year earlier when Calvin was preparing for his European tour, both of them expecting resolution once his mother joined the household.

Hattie chose a task or two to complete each day but preserved time for visiting, shopping, and reading — never mind that as the girls got older she had less and less time to do anything of her own choosing. She made sure to have *something* for dinner when Calvin came home — sometimes toast and cheese, other times a portion from the Beecher table. She let the housework pile up, then panicked when she couldn't find something amid the family's scattered belongings piled everywhere. When things got to be in such a state as she could not manage them at all, she begged her family to help her, which they did. Calvin took to picking up after himself more than usual, which Hattie thought a fair solution despite the fact that he pouted about it. Silently.

They did not read together in the evenings as they used to, both of them irritated with the other by the time the day came to a close. Hattie sometimes went to an event with a friend, leaving Calvin with the girls. He would agree with a tight look, then sit down with his German books and pretend she'd already left. There were times Hattie felt horrible for disappointing him. When she looked around her house filled with clutter and half-done tasks, she would feel the anxiety created by the disorder rise within her. She never said as much to Calvin, though, and repeated to herself that she was not a cook or a housekeeper and her hands were kept very full and very busy with her daughters. Would Calvin really have her choose a swept floor over the cleanliness and happiness of the girls?

Multiple times a day, she would repeat in her mind, "Just wait until Mother Stowe comes!" Mother Stowe was surely like Aunt Esther: soft, conciliatory, and easy. Hattie could picture Mother Stowe saying, "That's what I'm here for, darling. Now, where shall I start?"

She and Calvin grew more distant, the house grew more disorderly, and Hattie tried with all her might to ignore both crumbling aspects of her life. She managed to write an article for *Gody's Monthly Magazine,* which had recently been taken over by Sarah Josepha Hales. Now there was a married woman with a voice *and* a career. Hattie could be like her, couldn't she? When she told Calvin, he asked if Mrs. Hale had twin daughters or if her already underpaid husband had been slapped with a pay freeze? It was the first time Hattie had sensed shame from Calvin about their situation. She'd been so surprised she hadn't known what to say, and they did not speak of it again.

Everything would be better when Mother Stowe arrived, she told herself.

Today, however, she did not need to repeat the mantra because today was the day Mother Stowe was arriving! Calvin had moved the girls' cradles into their bedroom, leaving what had been the nursery for Mother Stowe. The Beecher household had allowed them to borrow a bed, bureau, and wardrobe to furnish the small room. Hattie purchased a new rug and a side table, which

Calvin complained about.

"Your worry does you no credit," Hattie had told him as she'd removed a pan of overcooked potatoes from the oven after he'd learned of the furnishings she'd purchased. "God will provide."

"For things we don't need?" Calvin had countered with a huff. "So far, it's me who's providing."

Hattie had reprimanded him his lack of faith, and they'd eaten in silence. The burnt potatoes were chewy, but she was careful not to make a face.

Tempers had worn thin, to be sure, but now salvation was at hand. Hattie would have help, Calvin would realize how unfair he was in assuming she didn't need it, and they would come together better than they had before. Already she could imagine his apology, hat in hand: "I didn't realize, Hattie. Can you ever forgive me?"

She would say, "Yes, of course I can." And things would be as they'd been before . . .

But the fantasy got her to thinking: when *was* before? Before his European trip? No, they had argued over the household back then too. Before they were married? That wasn't fair; there had been nothing to argue about. Back then it had seemed obvious that she would assume the role of wife as though it were a new dress — uncomfortable at first but soon feeling like a part of her own person. She hadn't imagined Calvin would be so demanding. She hadn't imagined she would find domestic chores so vexing.

Hattie shook her head, refusing to let her thoughts mire yet again. Calvin was probably already meeting Mother Stowe at the pier by now. Things were about to get better than they had ever been *before*.

Hattie turned her attention to the girls, outfitted in matching dresses she'd spent last week sewing — to the peril of wash day, bread baking, and bed making. They would all have gone with Calvin to the docks except for the spring rainstorm that kept her and the girls at home. Hattie put more effort than usual in arranging the mantel, attempting to tidy the clutter, and sweeping the floor, which she realized had not been swept in well over a week. Eventually her efforts deteriorated, and she lay on a quilt in the middle of the parlor floor while Eliza chewed on her little leather shoe and Little Harriet rolled from her back to her front and bent her knees beneath her.

"You'll be crawling any time," Hattie said, coming to her hands and knees in hopes that would show her daughter the way of it. Little Harriet was already sitting up. They were both growing so fast.

The front door creaked open, and Hattie hurried to stand, only to entangle her feet in her skirts and stumble. She grabbed at the chair to keep from falling. She laughed at the spectacle she surely made and pushed a lock of hair off her face in order to look at the new arrivals.

To Hattie's chagrin, her stumble was not shared in smiles with the newcomers. Calvin looked embarrassed, causing her to straighten even more. Hattie quickly shifted her gaze to his mother, a tiny woman with his same blue eyes and a patient smile on her face.

"Welcome," Hattie said, moving forward with her hands out. Hepzibah Stowe took the proffered hands, but did not initiate an embrace like Hattie thought she might, like Aunt Esther would have. Instead she held Hattie at arm's length and gave Hattie's hands a slight squeeze.

"Mother, this is my Hattie," Calvin said.

My Hattie. Hattie flicked him an approving glance for the endearment before looking back at her mother-in-law. "I am so glad to meet you, Mother Stowe. May I call you Mother Stowe or would you prefer something else?"

"Mother Stowe is fine," she said, then

released Hattie's hands and looked past her toward the babies still on the quilt, reminding Hattie of the other introductions waiting to be made — generational introductions.

Hattie turned toward the girls with pride while Calvin crossed the floor toward the little mischiefs. He picked up Eliza, then turned toward his mother with the infant in his arms. "This is Little Eliza," he said.

Mother Stowe came forward and took the infant with practiced ease. She smiled into the little face. "Oh, what a beautiful tribute to our first Eliza."

Hattie's smile froze, but she did not allow mention of Eliza to unravel her. She had birthed the *beautiful tribute,* after all, no matter who she was named for. Hattie bent down and picked up her other daughter, eager to show off her own namesake. "And this is Little Harriet," she said, walking toward her mother-in-law.

Mother Stowe shifted Eliza so she might reach out and brush Little Harriet's cheek. "Oh, she is a dear."

Harriet blinked and pulled into Hattie's shoulder, her soft brown curls caught up in a fountain on the top of her head, tickling Hattie's chin.

Hattie beamed and shared a triumphant

look with Calvin. She felt a tiny bit sorry for him. He still expected that Mother Stowe would somehow validate his assertions that Hattie could run the household and manage the children on her own. Hattie fully expected a rude awakening on her husband's part but hoped he would not take it too hard. She was ready to forgive him and move forward. Perhaps the intimate portions of their marriage, which had been lacking these last weeks, would also be restored. She could only hope.

"I made the dresses myself," Hattie said, pulling down the round collar on Little Harriet's dress that she'd stuck into her mouth. The collar wasn't quite symmetrical, but then she'd made it first. Eliza's was a better version since she'd had a more practiced hand.

"Oh, did you, now," Mother Stowe said. She pinched the hem between her thumb and forefinger, rubbing the fabric slightly. "Your first attempt at children's clothing?"

Hattie blinked.

Mother Stowe met her eye with a smile. "Oh, don't feel badly, dear, smaller items simply require more attention to detail and narrower seams, that's all. I'll be happy to show you."

"Mother sewed all of our clothing when

we were growing up as well as for several other families. You couldn't want for a better teacher, Hattie." Calvin fairly beamed with pride.

Envy crawled out from a dark corner in Hattie's soul. Did he ever feel proud of *Hattie's* accomplishments? Did he ever brag about *her*?

Just then she caught Mother Stowe looking past the babies into the corner where Hattie had stacked different folds of fabric, her yarns, and a box of shoes a neighbor had brought over for the girls. Hattie didn't want her daughters wearing used shoes but had not yet determined what to do about them. Right then, she wished she'd done something other than store them in the living room. Mother Stowe obviously did not approve.

Hattie thought of the pans currently stacked haphazardly on the kitchen counter and wondered how she might keep her mother-in-law from seeing them. She'd told Calvin that she didn't see the point in putting the pans in cupboards when she was just going to get them out again, but it now felt lazy to have accepted that as a form of organization. At least once a week she knocked over the stack, causing the pans to tumble to the floor in a great cacophony that scared the babies. After the pans fell, Hattie would put them in the cupboards, but when she used them next, they would stack into the same tower all over again.

Hattie forced a smile to cover the wobbling insecurity that was beginning to seep into her joints.

Mother Stowe did not seem much like Aunt Esther after all. Aunt Esther always put people's feelings ahead of work. She would say "I was made for work and have accepted God's role." Hattie took that as validation that some women were *not* made for work. Herself included, of course.

"I'll take your bag to your room, Mother, then fetch your trunk." Calvin reached down for his mother's carpetbag and headed for the stairs.

Hattie watched him go with a kind of panic. The two women looked at one another while shifting their weight back and forth, rocking the babies they each held. Mother Stowe's smile looked genuine, but Hattie was on guard now that her naïve expectations had been proven foolish. She waited a few seconds for Mother Stowe to say something, then realized she was waiting for Hattie.

"I appreciate you coming all this way," Hattie said. "We can use the help."

"Oh, I'm happy to help. Order and efficiency in all things is the key to harmonious living."

"Yes, I'm afraid with the babies I've had so many other demands on my time that —"

"The Good Lord has entrusted you with a great deal, Hattie, and it is your duty to become equal to those blessings." She looked from Hattie to the quilt spread out on the floor and pulled her eyebrows together. "Do you always put such fine quilts on the floor? I would hate to see it spoiled from misuse. Perhaps the first order of business will be determining the proper use and storage of what you already have. Oh, and the sewing, of course." She attempted to flatten Eliza's collar — the better collar of the two — and frowned. "Most certainly the sewing."

Chapter Twenty-Two

May 3, 1837

Within the first week, Hattie realized that Mother Stowe was no ally. The tension between them, however, did not interfere with Mother Stowe giving orders and instructions. "This is the way one folds a dishcloth, Hattie." She would say it as though folding said cloth improperly was something that had never been done before Hattie had managed to find a way.

"Floors are to be swept morning *and* night."

"Rugs *always* go outside during sweeping."

"One plants flowers only after she has maximized her garden space with vegetables and has room to spare."

She actually pulled out the violets Hattie had already planted — her dream had been to see a great purple meadow come summer — and gave them to their neighbor,

Mrs. Allen, who had empty pots beside her front porch. Hattie hadn't delivered the plants and instead sat down to read the paper in her mother-in-law's absence. She hadn't even gotten through the first page before Mother Stowe was back, scowling at Hattie for not having finished polishing door handles throughout the house — that was a job to be done twice a week.

"Set pleats with vinegar, *of course.*"

"Afternoon tea *only* when guests are visiting."

"You need to stop inviting so many guests for tea, Hattie. No wonder you can't keep up with the housework."

Every room of Hattie's house and every process of her organization, such as it was, had been criticized and unraveled. Hattie's protests of liking her dishcloths in this drawer was ignored. Preference had no bearing on what was *right,* and dishcloths should be stored to the right of the stove.

Hattie complained to Calvin, but all he said was that his mother was an expert and one should never refuse education from an expert. His tone was similar to the one Hattie sometimes used when talking to her sister Isabella, who complained that her poor grades were because her teachers did not like her or who simply *had* to have a new pair of shoes to match her dress and would fairly *die* from embarrassment otherwise. Adorable complaints. One-day-you'll-understand facial expressions.

Hattie had woken tired and grumpy from being up three times in the night. Having the girls in their bedroom was proving more difficult than it had been when they were newborns. Every whimper woke her up and then she would lie there, willing herself to go back to sleep while listening for another sound that would confirm the baby was truly rousing. Calvin had gotten used to it after the first few nights, and she hoped to do the same, but so far she remained too alert.

Today, however, despite her fatigue, Hattie was determined to have some power over her household. The question was where. She actually appreciated the breakfast routine that had her and the girls ready for Mina when she came for the breakfast feeding. Usually Hattie was running wildly to open the door while pushing her arms into the sleeves of her dressing gown. The nap schedule Mother Stowe had implemented for the girls was also nice. Hattie knew exactly when they would sleep and for how long instead of waiting for their moods to set the time and then being faced with the inevitable over-tired baby who could not be settled.

By the time Hattie was dressed, she decided she would insist on jotting down ideas for an article on vegetable starts while the girls took their morning nap. That was where she would elbow her way to the front and demand consideration — with writing. Hattie *was* determined, but then Mother Stowe announced they would be oiling the furniture right after breakfast, and when the girls were ready to nap, they were too far into the task to stop.

They spent the morning oiling every piece of wooden furniture in the house with lemon oil, then following up with beeswax. The old blocky furniture revived rather well and smelled divine, but the task took hours.

As soon as they finished, Mother Stowe was on to the next task — teaching Hattie how to make Calvin's favorite dinner: corn chowder. Calvin had never said corn chowder was his favorite, and Hattie ground her teeth as Mother Stowe criticized the way she rehydrated the dried corn. Equal parts water and milk were required to retain the correct flavors. Everyone knew that. Everyone but Hattie.

Calvin came home for lunch, praising the soup frontwards and back, but didn't seem to notice that Hattie said next to nothing during the meal. She attended to the girls as soon as they lost patience with their little blanket nests in the corner — one invention of Hattie's that Mother Stowe agreed with.

After Calvin left, the women cleaned the kitchen according to Mother Stowe's sense of order, all the way down to polishing the bright surfaces of the stove with leather. Mother Stowe insisted it should be done after each meal, even though the stove was so old there was nothing bright left of the handles and knobs. "A little time and attention might bring out the shine," Mother Stowe said when Hattie complained. "One never knows until she tries. In a few more months, it will look good as new." Three months of thrice daily polishing?

Hattie couldn't take it. "I have some writing to work on during the girls' afternoon naps today," she said, hating that she felt like a student at the Litchfield Female Academy again, talking to her instructor.

Mother Stowe pursed her lips. "I was going to show you how to make a rag rug, Hattie."

"We can do it after the girls wake up," Hattie said, but she had actually been looking forward to that task. Mother Stowe had brought the most beautifully braided rug as a housewarming present, and Hattie loved the idea of learning how to make one of her own. Wouldn't her family be impressed? But she'd made her decision to write today in order to show Mother Stowe and Calvin that there must be a place for the pen in her life. She needed to stick with her plan.

"I must get some writing done, Mother," Hattie explained. "I used to write every day, and now —"

"Every day?" Mother Stowe cut in, her eyebrows jumping up her forehead.

"Yes," Hattie said, but she shifted uncomfortably. She hadn't actually written every day since she'd written her geography more than four years ago, and she'd written very little this last year. She didn't have the Semi-Colon Club to write for anymore and no prospects for publication, but that didn't change the fact that she *needed* to write. A letter to Georgiana perhaps. She hadn't responded to the last letter she'd received nearly two weeks ago. "I have several dear friends back in Connecticut whom I wish to correspond with."

"Letter writing is a task to be done at the end of the day," Mother Stowe said as though, once again, such a thing was obvious.

"I am so exhausted by the end of the day

I haven't the energy. But today, while the girls sleep, I can take the time by the window in the parlor." She hated that she felt the need to add, "It is not frivolous to write a letter to a dear friend."

Mother Stowe pursed her lips. "I would think a dear friend would be more impressed with your choosing your household over your own enjoyment, but then perhaps I am simply old-fashioned. I suppose we can work on the rugs another day, and I can tighten the ropes on my bed instead. Of course, we'll need to attend to the ropes on your bed together after the girls wake up."

"The ropes are tight enough," Hattie said. "We only brought your bed from the President's House two weeks ago."

"I think I know when my bed ropes need tightening, Hattie," Mother Stowe said, hands on her hips. "And it should be done once a month, regardless. When did you last tighten the ropes on your bed?"

Hattie was silent. She had actually never tightened bed ropes in her life.

"As I thought." Mother Stowe nodded tightly, turning toward the stairs. "Go on with your letter. I'll be fine."

Hattie watched her go, determined not to give into the guilt she felt leaving an old woman to do a task that did not sound easy to do alone. Tightening the ropes required removing the tick, didn't it? Then using a tool to pull the ropes against the pegs. *Never mind,* Hattie said to herself. Mother Stowe didn't *have* to tighten the ropes today, she was choosing to. And Hattie was choosing to write a letter.

Hattie retrieved her writing supplies, which Mother Stowe had boxed and stored in the hall closet, and laid them out on the kitchen table. She heard a bump from upstairs but ignored it as she dipped her quill in the ink. She wrote *Dear Georgiana,* then let her pen hover over the page. What could she say?

It wasn't appropriate to complain about her mother-in-law — irritation aside, she was a great help. There was nothing to say about Calvin, they were near strangers these days it seemed, and the reality hit inside her stomach like a drumbeat. She wouldn't let the rhythm capture her. She would write this letter!

Dear Georgiana,
   I am sitting at the table in the kitchen, a better version than the last cottage offered, but not much improved. Still no varnish, but a dark stain seals the wood to some degree — there are no splinters.

The twins — my little mischiefs — are blessedly asleep, and Mother Stowe is . . .

Hattie tapped her pen. Would she admit that she was letting Mother Stowe tighten ropes by herself? Would she admit that she hadn't known Calvin's favorite meal was corn chowder? Hattie shook her head, hating the feeling that her writing was indulgent. She'd never felt that way in all her life, and would not give in to it now. She turned back to her paper.

. . . are blessedly asleep, and Mother Stowe is upstairs. The girls are nearly seven months old now. I can hardly believe how much they've grown. With their growing out of dresses and shoes at an alarming rate, I wonder at how my life will be in another seven months. They should be walking by then; Little Harriet will be crawling soon. I confess that I do not know how I shall manage them then.

Would Mother Stowe still be here in seven months? Calvin had said nothing about how long she planned to stay. What if she meant to stay forever? Hattie let out a long breath, infused with fear and prayer.

Hattie finished the letter, which did not say half of what she wanted to say, and sealed it for the post. Perhaps they could take the girls in the baby carriage that afternoon and make a trip to the Walnut Hills post office, which was only a few blocks away. Only when Hattie was finished did she go upstairs where she found Mother Stowe dusting her room. She looked up and gave Hattie a polite smile.

"Dusting is better done in the morning," Mother Stowe said. "The still air keeps the dust from simply churning about and resettling itself. How often do you dust, Hattie?"

"Um, well, weekly, of course." Hattie hated to dust and ignored the task for the most part. Calvin had once drawn a heart in the dust on their dresser. She'd dismissed the sweetness of sentiment because she'd known he'd meant to make a point.

Mother Stowe's eyebrows flew upward. "Weekly?" she said, shaking her head. "That will never do, Hattie, never. You must dust every day. Twice a day in the summer when the roads are more in use. And you must use a cloth, not that feather duster I saw in the cupboard downstairs. Come here, and I'll show you how it's done. There is a very specific motion to dusting correctly."

Hattie nodded and obediently crossed the

floor, fatigue pulling at her arms and legs. Was this truly her destiny? Daily dusting, polishing, cooking, cleaning, organizing. The only saving grace of the day was that they were going to dinner at the President's House tonight. That meant no lesson on the *proper* order to prepare the different dishes of the meal, set the table, arrange the salt shakers, and place the chairs the perfect distance from the table until the family was ready to sit down.

Calvin returned from Lane only a few minutes before they had to leave again, oblivious to the tension in the house. Surely he would notice at some point that Hattie had said barely a word to him all day. Certainly he would look her way, notice the tightness of her expression, and ask, "Whatever is the matter, dearest?" But he didn't. Instead he pushed the baby carriage and listened to his mother's update of yet another person of their acquaintance back in Massachusetts.

Hattie trailed a few steps behind them, glaring at the backs of their heads and wishing she could turn around and go home. An evening by herself at the cottage would be welcome, and maybe then Calvin would realize all was not well. If she had the evening to herself, she could read or perhaps write another letter. To an editor, perhaps. But she'd likely sleep. She was so tired.

The family oohed and aahed over the little darlings before dinner, then Isabella and the boys took the babies upstairs so the adults might eat. The meal was delicious, but Hattie only picked at her food. She wondered how long it had taken Cook to make this meal. Did Cook truly enjoy the process? Did she find satisfaction in the work?

"Not hungry tonight, Hattie?"

She looked up into Catharine's face, which was curious, but also concerned.

Hattie didn't want Catharine's sympathy and forced a smile while cutting a large bite of the roast beef. "It is excellent," she said, directing her gaze and her comment to Mrs. Beecher, even though she'd had nothing to do with preparing the meal. Why did one thank the hostess and not the person who had actually done the cooking? She put the bite in her mouth and chewed thoughtfully.

Mrs. Beecher smiled her tight smile that was as much a part of her as her long fingers and narrow shoulders.

"Mother taught Hattie how to make corn chowder today," Calvin said.

Hattie looked across the table at Calvin, who smiled at her with such pride that the meat stuck in her throat.

"Well, that is something," Father said, a teasing note in his voice. "Hattie cooking." His deep, bellowing laugh normally made Hattie smile. Tonight it was at her expense, however, and the embarrassment was jagged. She kept her eyes on her plate. How did he think she and Calvin had food to eat if she wasn't cooking it? The only thing Calvin knew how to make was eggs and toast, hot cakes, and bacon.

"Anyone can learn to cook," Mother Stowe added. "It simply takes an open mind and willing hand."

"Mother did all our cooking when I was a child," Calvin said. "Hattie could not have a better teacher."

Hattie half expected a button from his waistcoat to shoot from his chest and ping against his water glass he was so proud.

"That is excellent," Father said with an appreciative nod. "And so generous for you to have come all this way to teach her, Mrs. Stowe."

"I'm glad to help," Mother Stowe said. "It is a blessing to bless the lives of people you love. A woman's efforts are never of greater value than in her own home, and it is a privilege to help bring that to pass for my Calvin and his family. I want nothing but their comfort."

Hattie felt ready to burst with irritation at being defamed — never mind subtly — in front of her family and no one, not one person, standing up for her. She looked to Catharine, surely she would side with Hattie, but she instead held her eyes rather pointedly. She lifted one eyebrow as though to say, "Did I not warn you?"

Hattie returned to her plate and forced herself to take three more bites while ignoring the conversation. One. Two. Three. Then she set her fork and knife across her plate. "Might I be excused, Father," she said as though she were still a child in his home. "I would like to check on the girls before we gather in the parlor."

"Certainly," Father said, making a shooing motion with his hand.

Hattie wasn't out of the room before the discussion had turned to the Old School Presbyterians and the New School faction, of which her father was a part. She stood at the base of the stairs with her hand on the rail, intending to see to the children as she said she would, but her eye caught the door of her father's study. Moments later she was closing the door behind her and walking to the shelves that covered three of the four walls. Books. Information. Words. Thoughts other than housekeeping and cooking and washing.

She clasped her hands behind her back and let her eyes drift over the titles on the bindings, pausing on those familiar to her. With each memory of having read a specific volume, a pinprick of light seemed to break through the heavy veil in her mind. She'd first read *Arabian Nights* in secret, knowing her father would disapprove; he'd been against novels at the time. She had read the beloved story over and over and over again, hiding it under her bed, in her workbasket, behind the wardrobe. How old had she been? Seven?

Then Catharine had snuck young Hattie a copy of *Ivanhoe.* How she had adored that story, too. She'd once sat high up in the branches of a cherry tree for hours to finish it before dark, even though she'd read it three times already. She'd heard her family looking for her and not said a word in hopes she might finish one more page. Father had discovered her and was furious that she was reading a novel. She begged him to read it before he forbade her from its pages. To her surprise, he did so. He loved it, too, and hence the ban against novels was lifted. Hattie owned a copy of nearly every book Walter Scott had written, or rather *Sir* Walter Scott — he'd been knighted now.

How long had it been since she had last visited with the dear friends she'd found in the pages of her favorite books? When she did read these days, it was usually a newspaper, or perhaps an article or essay — something small she could finish in a limited time. Though there'd been almost none of that since Mother Stowe had joined the household. When she had been able to write these last months, it had been frantic, like a squirrel gathering nuts for winter. Thoughts and words used to dance through her mind like heathens around a fire. That fire felt as though it had gone out.

Her eyes landed on Father's leather bound copy of Cotton Mather's *Magnalia Christi Americana.* She ran her fingers across the Latin title and repeated the English subtitle: *The Ecclesiastical History of New England America.* Another dear friend, long forgotten, but powerful in the process of her heart's conversion to Christianity when she'd been young. She felt guilty for having abandoned the words she'd once loved, hollow with longing. She pulled the book from the shelf and settled herself in a chair by the window. No candles had been lit in the study, which was often unused at night, but there was some daylight left by which she could see.

I WRITE the Wonders of the CHRISTIAN
RELIGION, flying from the Depravations
of Europe, to the American Strand: And,
assisted by the Holy Author of that Religion, I do, with all Conscience of Truth,
required therein by Him, who is the Truth
itself, Report the Wonderful Displays of
His Infinite Power, Wisdom, Goodness,
and Faithfulness, wherewith His Divine
Providence hath Irradiated an Indian Wil-
derness . . .

"There you are."

Hattie looked up, shattering the world that
was creeping up around her with every page
she'd turned. How long had she been reading — five minutes? An hour? She closed
the book somewhat guilty, somewhat reluctant, and smiled sheepishly at her father
even though, of anyone, he would understand. Even approve.

"We thought you were with the children,
but Isabella brought them to the parlor and
said she hadn't seen you."

"I'm afraid your library seduced me
before I made my way upstairs." Hattie
removed her finger from where she'd kept
her place in the book, realizing she would

not be reading more tonight. She smoothed a hand over the beloved cover and tried to formulate a plan that would allow her to read it another day. But when? When would chores not fill every waking minute? When would Mother Stowe be content to just sit and let Hattie sit? When would the girls not be vying for her waking moments, and stealing too many of the nightly moments too? When would she not be so ragged by the end of a day that she would have enough energy of mind to indulge herself in the words on the page? She stood and made her way to the shelf, feeling petulant.

"Is everything all right, Hattie?"

She replaced the volume and faced her father, who stood near the door, watching her as if trying to read her thoughts. Hattie was tempted to give a flippant answer: "Of course I am all right. Why would I not be all right?" but she felt too tightly wound. She had not been able to speak her mind in her letter to Georgiana, but she could scarcely keep in her words now.

"No, Father, I am not all right. In fact, it seems I am rather all wrong. I do not cook as I should, or clean as any other woman would. I am clumsy and lazy and rather silly in the way I do the things I manage to accomplish. I do not mind my children correctly or care for my husband the way that I should, and everyone who is cursed enough to have to deal with me seems to find me quite aggravating." She lifted her chin, defiance filling her chest as she thought of what he'd said at dinner. "Even you make jokes at my expense. I've not a single soldier in my camp. How is that?"

She had expected Father to be surprised at her candor, perhaps even shocked, but instead he clasped his hands behind his back and took a deep breath. A ponderous breath. A breath meant to precede a sermon. "I have said often enough that you would have made a fine minister, Hattie. How I wish my sons had your gift for words and ability for learning. But God, in His wisdom, which only He can know, made you a woman."

Hattie felt her stomach sink. Her bold words had been wasted.

Father continued. "I have watched you resist your God-given roles from the start of this marriage, Hattie, and while I sympathize with the difficulty of fitting yourself in a role that you find less than stimulating, I also blame myself. I should have insisted you were better trained in the domestic arts so you could better manage your life. If I could go back in time and repair it, I would do so, but I cannot and so there is nothing left for any of us to do but adjust to the present circumstance."

Hattie blinked back the tears that had formed. "I am to ignore every gift God has given me in exchange for clean floors and tight bed ropes?"

"You are to do your duty for your husband and your children," Father clarified. "Clean floors and tight bed ropes are a part of that, yes, and to pretend they are not is beneath your intelligence. Surely you can see that."

She looked toward the window. The setting sun cast a pink and orange glow across the landscape and painted everything in shades that were not their natural colors. "Even if it swallows me?" she asked, then turned back to face her father, the man who had encouraged her, who had sacrificed that she might receive the best education available to daughters. "Even if doing my duty seems to take from me everything that *is* me? I am becoming lost to myself, Father, a stranger in my own skin. Am I to give myself over completely to the work that is required of me? Is that truly what God wants?"

"We are told in the Bible that he who loses his life for Christ's sake will find it."

"And it is for Christ that I scour my

floorboards and pull weeds from my garden?"

"Adam was told to live the days of his life by the sweat of his brow. Does it feel somehow more righteous to live your life frivolously? To spend your time doing nothing of purpose?"

"Learning is 'nothing of purpose'?" Hattie said, grateful to feel anger. Righteous indignation. "Writing is of no value? Using these gifts God gave me is now accounted as sin?"

Father let out a breath. "You are a wife, Hattie, with a husband who needs assurance that his home is cared for as he leaves to support you. You are a mother with children dependent on you for their most basic needs. If you are not to care for your family, who is?"

"Calvin will not let me hire help," Hattie said, pushing away the guilt of talking of their personal disagreements. "He gives me no pocket money to spend as I like. I feel like a child expected to do the work of two women. How is that justified?"

"He is the head of your household, and you vowed your obedience to him."

She closed her eyes, wanting to rage and cry and scream. *Am I so alone?* Catharine's words from her wedding day came back again: *"What woman has a voice left?"* She'd told Catharine she knew she could make her own way but was choosing not to. Was this what she'd chosen? Hattie's mind grew still.

Was this what I chose? Is there any other choice I can make now?

Nothing answered her. Nothing but empty loneliness and regret. She hated herself for feeling this way.

Do I love Calvin? Yes.

Do I love my children? Yes.

Do I have any other choice but to do what must be done? No.

"Hattie."

She opened her eyes. Father had stepped closer to her and put a hand on her shoulder. "I know it is hard to see now, but one day your children will not need your every moment. One day, you will get done in an hour what now takes you half a day. When that time comes, you can return to your study, your reading, your writing. Those gifts will wait for you and bring you joy. But now, at this time in your life, you have a family who needs you and loves you. You have a mother-in-law who has left everything she knows to help you. Don't let pride block your way in this. It will only bring heartache and misery to everyone. Stand up. Invest in a new type of education, and find your purpose and your joy within it."

Hattie sucked all her emotions into a tight ball within her chest, and Father smiled as if he knew exactly what she'd done and approved of it. *"That's a good girl,"* his smile said as if she were a child once again. *"Do what you're told, and we'll all be better for it."*

His real words drowned out the imagined ones: "Lose yourself in the work God has given you, Hattie, and make your family proud. You are a Beecher, and Beechers trust in God and do good. Your good, right now, is caring for your husband and children. Embrace it, and everything else will be all right. You'll see."

Hattie said nothing. She was trapped.

Father steered her toward the door with an arm around her back, seemingly convinced that she saw things his way. "Now, let us go into the parlor and enjoy the evening, shall we."

Hattie didn't nod her agreement, but she didn't need to. No one cared what she thought anyway.

CHAPTER TWENTY-THREE

After Father's lecture, Hattie did what everyone seemed to expect of her — she gave in. She bottled up her frustration, became more attentive to Mother Stowe's teachings, and waited to feel the joy. It did not come. Not after a week. Not after two weeks. Hattie grew quieter every day. And more tired every day. She read her Bible but felt nothing. She cared for her children and felt nothing. She cleaned house and cooked dinner and kissed her husband, all without feeling anything at all. Her house was clean and dinner was hot. Everyone seemed to be happy with the arrangement, so why should she not be?

"We shall try again in the morning," Mother Stowe said at nearly nine o'clock near the end of Hattie's third week of surrender, over a month into her mother-in-law's stay. They were finally working on the rag rugs Hattie had once looked forward to making. Any enthusiasm for the project was lost, however. It was simply one more chore to be completed. The babies had been asleep for an hour already, and Hattie was so tired she could barely focus. Little Harriet had not slept well the last few nights. Hattie would walk her across the floor, nurse as best she could, and finally get her back to sleep only to have her wake again an hour later.

Calvin often took turns with the girls. Hattie didn't know how she would get through the nights without his help, and their shared attention to their daughters was a soft place in their relationship, a reminder that they were partners still. But he could not feed their daughters, and so Hattie found little reprieve no matter how much she appreciated his help. She remembered that at one time she'd believed she could produce more milk if she was of a mind to do so, but now that did not seem to be true. She barely managed two feedings a day and wondered if she had somehow prophesied this turn of things.

"Thank you, Mother Stowe," Hattie said politely as she stood from the table, which was piled with scraps of Hattie's old dresses that would be repurposed into the rugs.

Calvin looked up from his book and

smiled approvingly. Was it her imagination or did she also see concern as well? Probably not — he was more content than he had ever been. She was glad for the encouragement he offered toward her accomplishments, but she herself took little satisfaction in the tasks. She wanted to ask if Calvin would be coming to bed with her, but she wouldn't say as much in front of his mother. Besides, he'd taken to staying up to read while she fell into bed as soon as she could every night. Perhaps it didn't matter if Calvin came to bed or not.

Little Harriet was up three times that night. Hattie nursed until she was completely dry and tried not to cry from the numbing fatigue. Calvin took the baby downstairs in the early morning hours so Hattie could rest, and at some point must have settled the child and come back to bed. When the sound of Mother Stowe bustling around downstairs woke Hattie, Calvin was warm beside her and both girls were silent in their cradles.

Hattie snuggled up to Calvin, heartened by his help the night before and wanting to keep the grateful warmth of that moment between them. Calvin rolled over and wrapped his arms around her. She closed her eyes, savoring the simple closeness, wishing they could remain this way for an hour or more. Something in the half-waking of morning felt nostalgic and sultry, like the early months of their marriage had been when they were so free and easy. Right now it didn't seem so long ago.

The smell of him and the tickle of his breath in her wild morning hair teased her with optimism. Perhaps today she would keep up with her mother-in-law and find the satisfaction Hepzibah Stowe took in an orderly household. One of the girls shifted, causing her cradle to rock in the early morning light, and Hattie let out a breath. The day had begun. She moved toward the side of the bed, but Calvin pulled her tighter against him and kissed her hair, melting her within his embrace. She turned in his arms so they faced one another. "Mmm," she said, leaning in for a kiss.

He smiled with his eyes still closed, kissed her, and then rolled so that he hovered over her and blinked open his blue eyes. He lowered his face to hers and took her breath away with a kiss she felt — *she felt.* It had been so long since she'd felt anything. The household chores and mother-in-law downstairs and babies and tasks of the day were fading from her tired mind when there was a rap on the bedroom door.

As though the knock were a shot, Calvin jumped to his feet and pulled his dressing gown from the chair. Hattie had barely moved before he was halfway across the floor. "Y-yes? Mother?"

"Could you fetch me some water, Calvin? We forgot to bring in a pail last night, and I need to make coffee."

Hattie shared a cringing look with Calvin. It was his job to fetch water, but Hattie's job to remind him; Mother Stowe said so. Could not the woman have waited ten more minutes?

"Certainly." Calvin came back to the side of the bed to kiss Hattie one more time before sliding his feet into his slippers and leaving the room.

Hattie let out a breath, and with it the joy she'd held for a moment or two. She remembered why it was easier to feel nothing and sat up in bed as regret replaced the indulgent feelings she'd dared entertain. She swung her feet over the side only to take hold of the headboard to stop the room from spinning. Her stomach rolled, and she blinked several times to orient herself, then went perfectly still.

"No," she breathed to the morning stillness as a memory of similar sensations

descended upon her, and the room settled
back onto its foundation. *I am still breastfeeding the twins.* She couldn't get pregnant
when she was still nursing. Her courses
hadn't returned since the girls' birth. *Surely
I am not . . .*

She stood up, and the ground shifted
along with her stomach. Seconds passed
before she regained her balance. Those eight
days she'd tried to talk herself out of her
first pregnancy, just over a year ago, were
not far enough away for her to have forgotten. Nor the weeks of dizziness and wobbly
stomach that followed. *I can't be pregnant
again.* But she could. Calvin had been home
four months, and she'd had a wet nurse,
leaving her with only noon and night feedings. Had her determination not to be
tethered to breastfeeding made her susceptible to another pregnancy?

Hattie sat back down on the bed and put
her hands over her middle, which was
unchanged from what it had been a week or
a month ago. Tears threatened, but she
blinked them away. *Perhaps I did not eat
enough last night.* She'd had no appetite for
weeks. *Maybe it is just the incredible fatigue
translating into physical symptoms.* But she
knew. She'd just been too busy to notice

until now.

A mewing sounded from the cradles, and she closed her eyes as reality overwhelmed her. She'd been so tired when she was pregnant with the twins, but she was more worn now than she had ever been in her life. How would Mother Stowe take the news? Just thinking about it made her cheeks flame. She'd already had a honeymoon baby — two! Now she would have a back-from-Europe-baby to prove just how much she and Calvin had missed each other.

And yet . . . the twins had made them a family. Hattie loved being a mother. Father had reminded her that she had a duty, and duty must come first. *This* was reason enough to let go of her last bits of avoidance and disinterest regarding all Mother Stowe was trying to teach her. She was determined to make this work, to have a happy house, happy husband, and happy children.

"It will be fine," Hattie said as she rose to her feet a second time. The room still spun, and the bed called to her. She remembered how she'd been able to lie in bed for hours every morning when she was expecting the twins. Little Harriet's garbled baby singing reminded her that she would get no such rest this time around. "I shall make it work," she told herself as she crossed the cool floorboards towards the cradles and pushed aside the rising emotions she had no time for. "I shall have to."

CHAPTER TWENTY-FOUR

Hattie didn't tell Calvin her news, or rather *their* news. She could be wrong, though after another week of shifting floors and the need to nibble biscuits until noon she had less and less doubt. It seemed that every day brought greater fatigue, and yet her determination to be capable of this grew equally stronger.

Mother Stowe continued to execute her training sessions, Hattie tried harder than ever to learn, and neither noticed the increasing silence between them. *Three babies,* Hattie repeated in her head day in and day out. *Three!* She hadn't mastered managing a household with only her and Calvin. She hadn't done well managing a household with two babies. Now she would have three? Learning what Mother Stowe had to teach her was more important than ever, which meant her own incompetence was more irritating than ever.

On Thursday, once the girls had gone down for their morning nap, Mother Stowe pointed out the need to sand the wooden floor — literally. Scrubbing sand across the floorboards once or twice a year helped to season the wood and, by the looks of things, no one had done the task in years. Unfortunately they had no sand or scouring stones, but Mother Stowe promised she would locate some immediately. "You'll be glad we did it before high summer is upon us," she had said while bustling to their next task. "It's a hot and sweaty job as it is."

Hattie wanted to sleep — she was so tired — but she followed Mother Stowe into the kitchen, then turned sharply when there was a knock at the front door. Salvation! She hurried to the door, pulling it open to reveal Isabella.

"Bella," Hattie said, enfolding her sister in her arms and holding on longer than usual. Fifteen-year-old Bella was already taller than Hattie. The duration of the embrace was on the verge of awkward before Hattie pulled back. "What a pleasant surprise."

Bella's dimples showed in her smile, then she held out two letters. "Catharine said I should bring these to you. She picked them up this morning when she went to the post office." Bella glanced past Hattie into the house. "Mornin', Mrs. Stowe."

Hattie glanced over her shoulder to see her mother-in-law standing in the doorway of the kitchen, polishing a fork with the corner of her apron.

"Good morning, Isabella, dear," Mother Stowe said with the kind of smile older people reserved for children.

Bella turned her attention back to Hattie. "Mrs. Beecher wanted me to invite you all to dinner tonight. Cook's been smoking a brisket since yesterday."

Hattie's mouth watered, which surprised her since nothing had sounded good for weeks. She opened her mouth to answer, but Mother Stowe spoke first.

"Thank Mrs. Beecher for the invitation, but we've already started on our dinner tonight. Maybe another evening."

Hattie almost argued, but Mother Stowe *had* killed a chicken that morning. It was draining in the backyard as they spoke and would need to be plucked, skinned, and deboned for tonight's chicken stew. Hattie knew she wouldn't eat a bite. The cooking smells would leave her ill by the time dinner was served, to say nothing of the revolting awareness that the chicken they would eat today had laid eggs yesterday.

"All right," Bella said, disappointed. "I'll

tell her." She shifted her weight. "Can I see the babies?"

"They're napping, Isabella," Mother Stowe said from closer behind Hattie than she'd been before. "They always sleep from ten until noon. Perhaps another day."

Hattie tried not to clench her jaw and reminded herself that Mother Stowe did not mean to be controlling or even rude, she just prized schedules and efficiency. And Hattie needed to learn that. Fast.

"Sorry, Bella," Hattie said, showing solidarity with her mother-in-law. She looked at the letters from Catharine and thought of all the years she'd been as carefree and easy as Bella was now, though she had already been teaching at Catharine's first school back then. She didn't dare think of the unhampered hours for long. "Tell Catharine thank you for sending the letters, and thank Mrs. Beecher for issuing the invitation."

They said their good-byes, shared another embrace, and then Hattie closed the door. She looked through the letters. The first was for Calvin from a Mr. Reynolds back east, but the second letter was addressed to Hattie from Mr. Leavitt, editor of the *New York Evangelist.* Hattie had published an article in that newspaper almost two years ago. *He wrote me?* The unexpectedness of his correspondence was almost breathtaking.

"I need a moment," Hattie said, hurrying to the chair by the fire as a rush of excitement made her skin nearly sizzle. She put Calvin's letter aside before breaking the seal on the one from Mr. Leavitt. Mother Stowe returned to the kitchen without a word, and Hattie tried to ignore the woman's disapproval. She unfolded the letter, the energy and anticipation nearly overwhelming her as she scanned the contents. The smile on her lips felt unfamiliar as she finished reading, then she went to the top again and read once more.

Mr. Leavitt wanted her to write an article! He was requesting *her*. He said how much his readers enjoyed her domestic style and would she be interested in writing about opportunities for girls' education, and then perhaps something about where Cincinnati was after the race riots of the year before. The deadlines were tight — six weeks for the first and only eight weeks for the other — but he had the space reserved in the September and October editions and hoped she would be interested.

Was she interested? Hattie tried to remember the last time she'd written for anyone but family. Had the Franklin letters from almost a year ago been her last foray? No, that couldn't be right. But as she thought back, she realized that *was* the last time she'd written more than a letter. She'd started a few pieces since then, but jotting down her first ideas wasn't real writing. Real writing was taking that first draft, turning and twisting it on itself until it revealed a new creature, then taking that version and spinning it again. By the end of the process, the final result bore little resemblance to the humbler beginnings, and it was that part — the finished piece — that filled Hattie with enough pride and energy to want to start again on something new. Her collection of New England stories had been all but forgotten, the written pages patiently waiting in her cedar chest.

Hattie's smile grew. *He came to me. He likes my style.* She stood, ready to fetch her writing supplies and respond that very minute until she heard one of the girls fussing upstairs. She looked at the letter in her hand, then up the stairs, then through the kitchen doorway to where Mother Stowe was gathering the ingredients for the ginger cake they were going to make for that night's dinner. The excitement of the moment faded in light of reality, but Hattie reached for the enthusiasm, gripping the slippery tendrils.

Later, she promised herself as she tucked the letter into her apron pocket. *I'll find time to think on this later.*

Little Harriet was getting her first tooth and determined to make sure everyone knew of her discomfort. Eliza was calm in the face of her sister's storm — she was a bit behind her younger sister by way of development — but Hattie hadn't fastened her diaper correctly so all the linens from her cradle had to be removed after her morning nap. They were set soaking outside in the yard. Mother Stowe fastened the next diaper while showing Hattie — again — how to do it securely. Mina came for the two o'clock feeding, and then the girls went down for their afternoon nap, something Mother Stowe expected they'd be giving up soon. Hattie could not bear to think of that loss.

While the twins slept, Mother Stowe demonstrated deboning a chicken wing, thigh, and breast, then told Hattie to do the same with the remaining pieces. Preparing meat was not one of Hattie's favored tasks, and something she'd certainly never done prior to her marriage. That meat in general was not agreeing with her this last week added a level of trepidation, but she was determined to see it through. The dangling carrot of Mr. Leavitt's letter fueled her motivation.

It is not a difficult job, she told herself, pulling the bowl with the offending appendages toward her. *Only a repulsive one.*

With two fingers, Hattie picked up the remaining breast piece, which had seemed to be the easiest one to debone when Mother Stowe had done it. She picked up the knife and made the first incision. Her stomach seized. She exhaled through her nose then took a breath through her mouth and pressed the knife in until it hit the bone. Then she began cutting. Through tendons. Across bone. Her stomach heaved. She breathed deeper. Exhaled longer.

"That's enough cutting. Now use your fingers to separate the meat from the bone — you retain more meat that way."

Hattie's stomach turned over completely, and she dropped the chicken and the knife and ran for the yard. She tripped over her skirts and stumbled against the door when she reached it, which prevented her from pulling it open in time. What little she'd eaten that day came up and out and . . . everywhere.

"Good gracious," Mother Stowe said from behind, pressing the shame.

Throat burning and head spinning, Hattie turned the knob and stepped past her mess before she retched again in the yard, the rough brick of the house holding her up but only just. The warmth of the day did her no favors, and before Mother Stowe could follow her out, she was heaving again, bent in half with a hand to her stomach as though that might help. When Mother Stowe handed her a cold rag, Hattie nearly cried with relief. She wiped her mouth, then folded the cloth, clean side out, and pressed it against her forehead. She concentrated on taking long deep breaths so her stomach would settle like a ship on a calming sea instead of a stormy one.

"I suspected."

The softness of Mother Stowe's voice gave Hattie enough hope to meet the woman's expression, which was compassionate. Hattie could only meet her eye a moment before she looked away, wishing she didn't feel so embarrassed. She shook her head in place of responding. What could she say?

"Does Calvin know?"

Hattie shook her head again.

"Don't you think he should?"

"I wanted to be sure." Hattie wondered if she would ever do anything to anyone's level of approval. She tried to hold back her tears.

Mother Stowe's hand on her shoulder took her by surprise, and she looked up.

"You're doing well, Hattie."

The tears fell freely, and something inside her seemed to shift, releasing a pressure that had been building steadily for weeks. "I am?"

"It's not easy to have another woman in your home, I know that, and you're being very attentive. Not that you don't have a great deal to learn, but every mother has to learn as she goes. You just need to learn faster than most."

Hattie cried harder, but not in self-reproach this time. Fear, certainly, but also relief. Mother Stowe was reaching out to her, and the connection felt like air filling up a barrel that had been closed up tight. "That does not bring me much comfort, Mother Stowe. I am not made to work this way."

"You are learning. Obviously God thinks you capable, and Calvin certainly thinks so, too. Now you have more reason than ever to put your full effort into learning what you must do." Mother Stowe spoke as though it were just a decision Hattie needed to make. Was she right? Hadn't Hattie made that decision already?

Hattie let out a staccato breath. It did

seem as though everything was pointing her to the same direction — cook, clean, care, wash, dust, sweep, serve, sleep, wake up, and do it again. When would her heart reach for it?

Mother Stowe removed her hand. "Now, take a moment while I clean up the mess in the doorway and then come back inside. We need to finish the chicken."

Hattie turned wide eyes to her. Had Mother Stowe not noticed how Hattie had reacted to the chicken?

"Diligence is the first step in conquering any obstacle. I'll wait for you inside. We need to hurry and finish before the girls wake up."

Hattie took three minutes to feel sorry for herself, then she stood up straight despite the dizziness she felt and turned back to the house. She gagged throughout the rest of the deboning process, but there was nothing left for her to retch. Mother Stowe made biscuits to go with the chicken stew. Hattie didn't understand why Mother Stowe couldn't prepare the chicken and let Hattie do the biscuits, but she said nothing.

"We'll set the bones to simmer overnight for stock," Mother Stowe said after Hattie had finished pulling the meat from the bones.

Three children. Two years. She was so tired her hands shook.

The girls woke up, and it was a relief to move on to another task, though if they'd woken up half an hour earlier perhaps Hattie could have used them as a reason not to dry heave through the last of the chicken.

"Dinner will be late," Mother Stowe said as the two women trudged up the stairs to gather the girls. "But at least we have a good reason this time."

This time, Hattie repeated.

Hattie told Calvin as soon as he came home. They sat together in the yard while Mother Stowe put dinner on the table. Sitting beside her husband and feeling the evening breeze slide over her skin should feel rapturous after the toil of the day, but her nerves were taut and everything else felt achy and numb.

"This is excellent news, Hattie," Calvin said, taking her hand and squeezing it. "How the Lord has blessed us."

She faced him, wanting the words to seep into her bones, but she could see the trepidation in his eyes. "Three children in two years," she said.

"Yes, a great blessing."

They sat in silence, and she wished he'd

tell her what he really thought — that it would be expensive, that they both felt stretched so thin, that there was no extra time in the day to fit in the care of another baby. And with the financial turmoil, and the pay freeze, and no help and . . .

Hattie took a breath and pushed a polite smile to her lips. She remembered when Calvin had learned of her last pregnancy on the same day he'd received his travel details. He'd needed her to be strong then, and she felt the same need from him now. Perhaps if she were strong for him, she would feel stronger too.

"I have been trying to think of late just how blessed we are." Saying it made her feel better. "We have your mother here to help, and our home is cozy and well built. Last summer, when all the riots were happening and there was so much fear in the air, I was so glad to be in my father's house. And now I am so glad to be in your house, Calvin. And we will be all right. We will rise to this. We will make it work." *I will make the Beechers — and the Stowes — proud.*

Calvin gave her hand another squeeze and looked up into the branches of the oak tree. "We *will* make it work," he said, then lapsed into silence.

Hattie leaned her head upon his shoulder,

trying not to cry while holding back her fears and exhaustion. She wished they could talk like friends again. Parenthood seemed to have eclipsed so many things.

Hours later, after everyone else was asleep, Hattie sat down at the writing desk her father had given her when the twins were born. The house was still and empty, allowing her concussive thoughts to settle and line themselves up in her mind. There was no point in delaying her response to Mr. Leavitt's letter now that she'd accepted the inevitable, but she did not want Calvin to know. He would agree now wasn't the time and that might raise her defenses. Hopefully Mr. Leavitt would receive her response in time to find another writer for the articles.

She took up her pen, dipped it in the inkwell, and tried not to let her tears drip onto the paper as she explained to Mr. Leavitt that she would not be able to meet the deadline on the article he wanted about girls' education. The topic he'd chosen was ironic; she wondered why her own education had been deemed so important when she was unable to use it. Perhaps her father was right when he said he should have been more attentive to having her learn domestic arts rather than literary ones.

I do hope that when my time allows for me to contribute to your newspaper in the future we might continue the relationship we have had to this point.

Hattie set down the pen and wiped at her eyes with her hand. When would she ever have time to do anything but this day-to-day drudgery? She looked through the quiet house. In another six hours, it would wake and she'd begin again what she'd already done all day today.

I will learn to love it, she told herself. Begged. Pleaded, with a heavy heart, laden with prayer, that she might live up to her responsibilities.

She picked up her pen and finished her letter, thanking him once more. She tried to draw strength from the fact that everyone around her — Mother Stowe, Calvin, even Father — believed she could learn to manage her household and family. Thousands of women lived this same life day after day and, presumably, found joy in it. Her mother had. Her stepmother had. Calvin's mother did. Hattie would put her faith in theirs and do the best she could.

As she finished her letter, she wound up her aspirations like a ball of yarn. Tight. Wadded. And shoved it out of sight. She signed her name to the bottom of the letter, which felt like both a contract and sentence. Her ambition protested a final time as she dusted the ink dry, but she turned her back on it. There was no time for her own pursuits. Perhaps not for years.

But . . .

But nothing, she scolded. *But nothing.*

CHAPTER TWENTY-FIVE

Despite staying up late to write the letter to Mr. Leavitt and being up twice with both babies in the night, Hattie stumbled out of bed at six thirty the next morning. The morning blurred with Mother Stowe's agenda — beating the rugs, sweeping and mopping the floors, baking two loaves of bread, a sewing lesson to make Sunday frocks for the girls, Bible study, and then gardening.

For Hattie's continued nausea, Mother Stowe brewed a kettle of peppermint tea, which Hattie sipped on throughout the day. It did help with her roiling stomach, but she would have given anything to lie on a blanket in the yard with the girls and simply rest her tired bones. Calvin came home for lunch — egg sandwiches — and then Catharine stopped by with the latest Beecher family letter while Mother Stowe and Hattie were alternatingly entertaining the girls and making corn cakes to go with that night's beef stew.

Catharine cooed over the girls for a few minutes, and then Hattie walked her to the door, wiping her hands on her apron. "Thank you for bringing the letter," she said on the threshold, leaning against the door-jamb so it might hold her up for a moment. "I'm sure reading it will be the most invigorating thing I've done all week." Maybe tonight, after the girls had gone to sleep, she could read it by the fire. But then she would miss out on the sleep she dearly needed. Would the lack be worth it? "And thank you for taking my letter to the post office for me." She looked at the letter to Mr. Leavitt in Catharine's hand.

Catharine slipped the letter into her handbag. "Are you all right, Hattie?"

"Of course," Hattie said, but the smile she gave was false, and she felt sure Catharine knew it. She pushed herself up from the doorway. There was nothing Catharine could do to help Hattie measure up to what Calvin and his mother wanted her to be.

Catharine glanced past Hattie. "How are things working with Mrs. Stowe? She's been here several weeks now."

"She is teaching me a great many things. She's a very efficient woman."

"Yes, she does seem to be. Your household has never seemed so . . . efficient."

Hattie nodded, unwilling to say anything that would seem ungrateful.

"And you are all right, Hattie? You are happy?"

Hattie took a deep breath and forced her smile bigger. "Why would I not be happy?"

Catharine held her eyes for a moment, then Mother Stowe called for Hattie. The griddle was nearly ready for the corn cakes. Catharine reached out and put a hand on Hattie's arm. "I shall add you to my prayers — that you might find your place."

My place, Hattie repeated as she watched Catharine move up Gilbert Street. She ached to have her sister come back. *My place. Do I have a place?*

She closed the door. As soon as she returned to the kitchen, Mother Stowe began explaining how to make the corn cake batter. Hattie tried to be attentive, but her mind kept wandering back to the idea of having a place.

"Hattie? Are you listening?"

Hattie looked at her mother-in-law's frustrated expression.

"Yes, Mother Stowe."

They spent an hour making the cakes, then covered them with a cloth and set them aside. Hattie tried to put the babies down for their afternoon nap, but Little Harriet was in a temper, which kept Eliza from falling asleep, and Mother Stowe finally insisted they bring them into the kitchen. "When they are tired, they'll sleep."

Hattie wasn't so sure. Little Harriet had been out of sorts for almost a week. There was the tooth, but Hattie sensed there was something more. She'd suggested trying the baby — now seven months old — on gruel, thinking she was simply not being filled by milk any longer. Mother Stowe had insisted the baby was too young.

"Now we shall start the stew so it will be ready when Calvin comes home. Remember, an early start ensures a punctual meal."

Hattie nodded.

Two hours later, the stew was simmering on the stove, and the kitchen was a disaster. The girls had not gone down for their naps despite three attempts, and Mother Stowe's system of cleaning the dishes as they were finished with them had fallen by the wayside. Nearly every bowl in the house had been used, and the kitchen looked the way Hattie used to keep it before Mother Stowe had come. It was a relief to see Mother Stowe frazzled, a fussy baby on one hip and her gray hair falling out of her bun.

"I have an idea," Hattie said. Mother Stowe pushed a stray lock of hair off her face, but her expression was open. "If you would take the girls out in the baby carriage, I believe they will settle down and perhaps sleep. I shall take responsibility for cleaning the kitchen in your absence."

She expected Mother Stowe to protest, but she was apparently more frustrated than even Hattie had realized.

"I would not mind a bit of air," she said.

Hattie helped ready the girls, who settled down once they seemed to realize what was happening — they loved going outside. Hattie placed the girls so that Eliza's head was at one end of the baby carriage and her sister's was at the other. They were so used to kicking one another that they did not seem to mind the arrangement. Hattie saw the three of them out the door, then closed it behind her and took a deep breath.

Silence. Solitude. Space.

In the kitchen, she began organizing the dishes according to size, just as Mother Stowe had shown her. She went outside to fetch some water for the cleaning and set a few bowls to soak before checking the stew, which was simmering nicely. She adjusted the damper to run the stove a bit hotter to cook the carrots through. She started washing the utensils when the letter Catharine had dropped off earlier caught her eye. It was sitting on the sideboard, out of the way and forgotten. Hattie could take ten minutes to read updates from her family. It would be a reward for having turned down Mr. Leavitt's invitation.

She hurried from the kitchen to her writing desk in the parlor, where the afternoon sun lit up the room. She smoothed out the family letter and savored every report from her siblings, longing for those days when they all lived in one house and crossed one another's paths so easily. Now they were spread all over the country, with William in Putnam, Mary in Connecticut, and everyone else sprinkled in between.

When she finished reading, she fetched her writing supplies and readied her pen while considering each word of her own update. Rather than list her complaints, she bragged about having her household in such fine order thanks to Mother Stowe's help. It did not feel so repressive when she wrote about it, and she reminded herself that she *should* be proud. She might not enjoy that household management had become the focus of her life, but she did appreciate knowing where to find things. Using her pen seemed to connect her thoughts together in a way that helped her to better understand them.

When the front door opened, she expected to see Mother Stowe, but it was Calvin.

"Calvin, dear," she said, smiling up at him and feeling lighter than she had in so very long. She did not even feel as tired. "You're home early."

"It is five thirty," he said, hanging up his hat and coat. Then he sniffed the air. Hattie did too, noting the acrid smell. In a moment she realized that an hour had passed since she'd first unfolded the family letter. *An hour!* She jumped to her feet, dropping the pen, and raced for the kitchen.

"No, no, no," she muttered as she ran for the pot. The stew had boiled over and burned into a crust on the top of the stove. *Perhaps the insides are not destroyed,* she told herself, but when she opened the lid, she saw that a great deal of the soup had boiled out. She tasted what was left — a bit sour. Hattie added some water, stirred, added some onion powder and a pinch of cayenne. When she'd done all she could, she turned to see Calvin standing in the doorway, arms crossed and face drawn into a scowl.

"Where is Mother?"

"She took the girls out in the baby carriage. They have been perfectly terrible all day."

He locked his eyes on Hattie, compelling her to explain.

"I said I would clean the kitchen and finish dinner while she took the girls out, but I took a break to write on the family letter and lost track of the time."

His expression did not soften.

She refused to apologize.

The silence stretched tight.

Calvin took a deep breath, and when he spoke, the calmness was forced. "I have been at my office for ten hours, arguing with the board about our house, fighting for our income not to be reduced any further, encouraging students to do their best work, and yet I come home to a disaster — *again.* How much of this am I supposed to tolerate, Hattie? I've brought my mother to help, I've walked the floor with the babies during the night, and yet I am faced with chaos in place of comfort — *again.* I am not asking for anything more than any other man in my place would request. Why is it so difficult? Why can you not do the work first and then attend your letter? Why is everything so very complicated with you?"

As he spoke, Hattie's feelings became

thicker and heavier in her chest and mixed with her fatigue and determination that did not seem to matter to anyone. She'd worked harder these last weeks than she ever had before, and yet it was not enough. Never enough. There was a time when she would have been angry at what felt like Calvin's determination to ignore her efforts. But she felt too tired to try to make him see. She was too tired for much of anything. "Why did you marry me, Calvin?" she asked without preamble.

He pulled his eyebrows together as though the question made no sense. A twist of anger entered the heavy, sticky place inside her that didn't want to argue and took control. Maybe she *did* want to argue. Maybe they needed to quarrel so she might speak her mind.

She said it again, a level louder. "Why did *you* marry *me*?"

"You are changing the subject."

"No, I am not. It is the same subject we have hashed and thrashed a thousand times since you returned from Europe, and a fair amount before you left. Why did you *marry* me?"

"I am talking about the state of the kitchen," he said, waving his arm around the room, which *was* in shambles. The acrid smell of the burnt stew continued to testify against her.

"I am talking about the state of our union," Hattie said. "And I believe it comes down to a rather simple, if not difficult, truth — I am not Eliza, Calvin. I will never be Eliza."

His neck got darker, and his jaw clenched. "I have never compared you to Eliza, Hattie. She has nothing to do with this."

"She has everything to do with this. She and every other woman who becomes a man's wife and loses her own identity. I am not one of those women. I am not Eliza Tyler, and naming my child for her or wishing I were like her will not change me into a reincarnation of her. I will not be a wife who waits in the parlor for you to come home and light the lamps for me. I will not be the woman who spends my days cooking and cleaning for the sole purpose that your mood will be light when you enter the house. I will not be the woman who will warm your breakfast and heat your bed and bear your children without an opinion or a thought about my part in the equation, yet you seemed determine to believe that I will be — that you can bully and belittle me into becoming a drone."

"I have never reduced you to —"

"Yes, Calvin. You have." She paused for a breath. "And you compare me to Eliza — I see it in your eyes. Would you like to know why *I* married *you*?"

He said nothing.

"I married you because I believed that you *celebrated* the fact that I was not every other woman — that I was not Eliza, even. You praised my intellect, you enjoyed discussing any number of topics with me. I believed that as your wife I would be more than a cook and housekeeper. I believed I would have a voice in our home. I would take up my pen. I could be *me* within *us*.

"I loved the tenderness with which you treated Eliza, and the respect in your voice when you spoke of your mother. I admired the way you learned so quickly, the way you worshiped God, and I knew you would be a good husband and father. I appreciated your steadiness against my eccentricities, your order against my chaos, but I expected that we would find a middle place. I expected that you would tolerate newspapers left on the chair from the night before, that hotcakes for dinner would not be offensive, and that you would help me make room for my writing pursuits and intellectual ability."

She felt tears rising as she put words to ethereal expectations she had never pinned down quite like this. "I never imagined that you would disapprove of me the way you do, that I would become a complication in my own home. I never imagined I would have three children in two years." She put a hand to her stomach, the change noticeable only to herself. "I never imagined that your comfort would mean more to you than my happiness, but I am *drowning.* No matter what I do, it is not enough, and there is no time for me to think or read or write. There is nothing in this home of ours for me — *just me,* just Harriet."

The fire drained from Calvin's face, and his expression was finally concerned if not compassionate. She held his eyes and wiped at her own, praying that the unexpected words had found their way to his heart but also feeling anxious for having said them. Now the words were out there like so many wild pigs to be contained and slaughtered at will.

"I don't know what you want me to say, Hattie." His tone was resigned and careful. "We *will* have three children in two years. I *have* to support us; you *have* to manage this house. I am not asking you to give up your interests, but I *need* you to manage this household so that I can fulfill my role and responsibility. I would like to write, too.

I would like to read at will. I would like a place for just me, just Calvin, but we are parents and partners and are no longer able to pursue a selfish course. I do not understand how you ever thought that marrying me would not change the hours in your day. I cannot simply fix it because you want it fixed. I need you to meet me half way, and I am running out of ideas. I brought my mother from Massachusetts, for heaven's sake, and still you cannot manage your *eccentricities,* as you call them, enough to care for our home and family. You said you wanted help, I found you some, and still I return to chaos."

"One time."

"The *one time* my mother has not held your hand through every minute of the day."

He didn't hear me. He doesn't care. Hattie let out a breath that deflated her like a discarded pillowcase. She had nothing left to say. She turned and made her way from the room, exhausted and spent and used up. She felt Calvin watching her leave; he didn't try to stop her. She went to their bedroom and climbed under the covers. Fully clothed, she pulled the quilts up to her chin and wondered how she had ever managed to speak with so much fire. Mother Stowe would be back with the girls any minute, so there was no time for self-pity, but she buried her face in the bedclothes and cried all the same, sobbing as she mourned the expectations she'd built up for herself and rued the fact that she could not be Eliza or Hepzibah Stowe. If she could be changed into one of *them,* would she be happy?

As the emotion peeled off her like skin, she thought of something she *hadn't* told Calvin in her rant. One of the reasons she married him was because God told her to. Why would He do such a thing when it was so very obvious to everyone that she was unequal to the task? Why had He given her a mind and a passionate heart that beat within her only to have her destiny bend to the man she'd fallen in love with and the children they had made together? Did God know her at all? Did anyone?

CHAPTER TWENTY-SIX

Calvin sat in his favorite chair in front of the cold fireplace, trying to ignore the day's heat that was still trapped in the house. Hattie was in the bedroom, probably crying. Mother wasn't back from her outing with the girls. Calvin was miserable.

He closed his eyes and leaned his head against the back of the chair, picturing Hattie when he'd lost his temper half an hour ago. She'd been defensive at first and then just got sad. She'd seemed to shrink before his eyes, yet he hadn't stopped.

"Why did you marry me?"

He felt hollow with the lack of answer. So much had happened since he'd fallen in love with Hattie. It had seemed so easy, then. She filled the void Eliza had left, she challenged him intellectually, she thought deeper than any woman he'd ever met. He'd wanted to be with her every minute he could. He'd wanted to spend the rest of his life with her because he felt like a better *Calvin* when she was with him. It felt so selfish now. So . . . ignorant.

He hadn't thought about how Hattie would manage a home and her time and support him in his responsibilities. Ugh, that was selfish too. Everything was about him. But it wasn't. It was about them, wasn't it? Wasn't it about how he supported her with a house and security and representation of their rights? Wasn't it about how he helped her fulfill her dreams of children and purpose within a family? He knew she had wanted those things. How could he do everything — manage his career and a home and a family?

Before Mother had come, he'd worked all day, then returned home to what felt like another job. He'd needed help, and Hattie had seemed determined not to give it to him. He'd truly believed that Mother would show Hattie the way to a happier home for both of them. Could she not understand how important that was to their ongoing happiness?

He thought back to what Hattie had said about why she'd married him — because he admired her intellect, because he celebrated her gifts and talents. Because he saw *her* within *them.* She said he didn't see that anymore, that he only wanted her to cook and clean. That he compared her to Eliza. The thought made his stomach burn, and he put a hand to his head, which had begun to ache. He'd said he didn't compare Hattie to Eliza, but he did. And it wasn't right. And he couldn't seem to help it, and —

The front door opened, and he straightened in his chair. When he saw the nose of the baby carriage, he got up and hurried to help his mother inside. It was awkward navigating the bulky piece of equipment in the narrow confines of the parlor but they managed, and then Calvin helped move the girls to the old quilt that Mother approved of putting on the floor. His hands slowed as he remembered the first night she'd come, how she'd said the quilt Hattie had put on the floor was too fine. He remembered the way Hattie's face had fallen. Catching himself and coming back to present, he continued what he was doing, pulling a few of the fabric toys from the basket for the girls to play with.

"I wouldn't have stayed out so long if they hadn't slept so well," Mother said, unpinning her bonnet and sighing with relief. Her cheeks were red and tiny beads of perspiration showed on her forehead. "I swear as soon as we left the house they settled right down. You know, sometimes I wonder if they pick up on Hattie's disorganized nature and can't settle down in her company."

"Don't do that, Mother."

She looked at him, her hands stilling as she fixed her hair. "Don't do what?"

"Criticize Hattie. She's trying." Calvin lowered himself to the blanket. He stacked three blocks, then smiled when Little Harriet managed to kick them over.

Mother pursed her lips and gave a little shrug of her shoulders. She turned to the kitchen, but almost immediately returned, her hands on her hips. "She burned the stew?" She shook her head and took a deep breath. "Where is she, anyway? She promised she'd have the kitchen clean and everything ready. The table isn't even set but I see she found her writing pen, now, didn't she?" She pointed toward the writing desk where the letter Hattie had been working on when Calvin returned lay forlorn and forgotten.

"Hattie's not feeling well, Mother. She's gone to bed."

Mother Stowe pulled her eyebrows together. "It is barely six o'clock." She sighed loudly and came into the room. "Calvin, dear, I know you don't want me to —"

"Mother," he cut her off and looked up

317

from the blanket. He spoke slowly. "Hattie wasn't feeling well. She went to bed. Can we make the best of the evening, please?"

Mother lifted her chin. "Of course," she said. "But you've got your hands full with her, Calvin, and I won't be here forever. Justifying her excuses will not do either of you any good in the long run."

Calvin turned his attention back to the girls and stacked the blocks again without replying. Little Harriet kicked the blocks over again, smiling at her triumphant accomplishment. Calvin looked at the scattered blocks and wished everything were so easy to put back together.

Chapter Twenty-Seven

Hattie fell asleep somewhere amid her tears and woke hours later, confused and disoriented, her eyes scratchy and swollen. She sat up in bed, blinked in the darkness, then heard the cries from the cradle. Sleepy cries that would only get louder. She put a hand to her aching head and remembered the argument with Calvin. Remembrance felt like stones tied to her ankles and wrists. She looked to the side of the bed, just able to make out his form. He might as well still be in Europe for the closeness she felt. It had only been days ago that she'd felt warm and safe in his arms, yet she couldn't bring those feelings back. She couldn't remember what it was like to feel the tingle of anticipation when he came home at the end of the day or the excitement of his touch. Did he miss that? Did he want it back?

The baby cried again, and she got out of bed, realizing she was still in her day dress.

She nursed Little Harriet, wishing she could make more milk. Mother Stowe had said it was only a matter of determination, that nursing more often would refresh her stores faster, but it did not seem to be working, and Hattie worried that her baby was left hungry.

When Little Harriet was asleep in her cradle, Hattie took off her dress and pulled on a nightgown. She'd just slipped back into bed when Eliza began whimpering. Hattie closed her eyes against the tears that instantly filled her eyes. She was so tired. So spent. But she stood and made her way to the second cradle, knowing she had no milk for this child. She picked up Eliza and cooed softly as she sat in the rocking chair, hoping that the little one wasn't hungry and could be settled with some attention.

Hattie began rocking slowly, closing her eyes and letting her head rest against the chair. She woke some time later with a start when the baby in her arms slipped. Frightened, Hattie gathered Eliza to her chest, blinking rapidly in the dark room. She looked at the infant in her arms, blessedly asleep, and tried to settle back against the chair. What if she'd slipped from Hattie's arms entirely? What if she'd fallen to the wooden floor?

Hattie rocked a few more minutes, but was frightened by what could have been. She put Eliza into the cradle before returning to her own bed. When she slid beneath the covers, Calvin rolled over and draped his arm over her waist. She pushed him away. He tried to scoot closer, and she pushed at him again.

"It is too hot," she said, though it wasn't. "Stay to your own side." She turned away from him.

He said nothing, but she felt sure he was awake. The argument from that evening had cut her deeply and left her raw and bleeding.

"Hattie," he whispered in the dark.

She closed her eyes, even though he couldn't see her, and tried to breathe as if she were asleep. She felt his hand brush the sleeve of her nightgown, and she pulled away. She did not want to be touched. She did not want his pity. What she did want was compassion and companionship and to be heard. Her hope of any of those things, though, was dry and brittle. Eventually, Calvin rolled away from her. She tried to make sense of the regret and relief that tangled together at his decision to give her the distance she didn't really want.

■ ■ ■ ■

When she heard Mother Stowe downstairs the next morning, Hattie did not wait to savor the last few minutes of waking and instead got out of bed quickly, before Calvin could speak to her. She did not have the energy to fix all that felt broken between them. Hattie gathered Little Harriet, always the early riser, and took her to the parlor.

Mother Stowe's silent disapproval barely touched Hattie as she methodically went about her morning chores. Hattie wondered if Calvin had told his mother of their argument. If he had, Mother Stowe would surely have sided with him. They likely shook their heads over the stew Hattie had ruined and commented on how impossible she was. Hattie was outnumbered in her own home.

Hattie brought wood in from the shed, fried bacon, saved the fat for when she'd make soap later that week, swept the kitchen, and put the girls' dirty linens in the barrel outside to soak. She was so tired and nauseated that she wanted to put off the washing to the end of the week, but what else was there to do but take care of it today? She served Calvin his breakfast and ignored his concerned gaze that followed her around the kitchen. Hattie poured Mother Stowe's coffee, hushed Little Harriet after Eliza poked her in the eye, and pulled up her hair when a lock of it fell into her eyes. By eight o'clock in the morning, she longed for the end of the day when she could sleep again.

Calvin kissed her on the forehead before leaving for work. She did not meet his eyes. Mother Stowe started the outside fire for the wash. Hattie inspected each room for laundry and thought of the article she'd turned down last week. Would they ever ask her to write another?

One foot before the other. Finish a task. Start on the next. Don't stop. Don't think. Don't you dare feel anything.

Mina came for the girls' feeding and agreed to take the babies home with her so Hattie and Mother Stowe might do the washing without babies to manage. The task was much faster without the little mischiefs underfoot, but the women did not talk as they went about their work. Hattie began thinking of a poem about the colors swirling together in the big washing pot, but stopped herself. She was not a poet. She was not a writer. She was a mother and a laundress and a cook. Her attempt to convince Calvin that she was more than a domestic drudge had fallen on deaf ears. Maybe he was right, and their partnership did not allow for the individual identity she craved.

Her stomach was queasy despite the peppermint tea she'd had, and as the heat of the day increased, she felt dizzy but would not take a break when Mother Stowe was working so hard. Hattie rinsed the clothes and was hanging them on the line when she stumbled to the side, catching herself on the post. A swirl of dizziness made her feel disconnected from herself.

"Are you all right, dear?"

"Yes," Hattie said without hesitation, straightening quickly and determined not to give her mother-in-law any reason for criticism. She continued hanging the clothes but was increasingly alarmed by the way the line moved and weaved before her eyes. More than once she reached for the line and took hold of nothing at all. Blinking quickly to clear her eyes, she squinted at the offending clothesline — a slice through the backdrop of beech trees and the flourishing vegetable garden.

"Are you sure you're all right?" Mother Stowe asked again.

"Yes," Hattie snapped. "I'm fine." But then she stepped to the side, forgetting that was where she'd put the basket of wet clothes. She lost her already precarious balance and reached for something to support herself but found nothing.

Her hip hit first, then her shoulder, before she rolled onto her stomach. She inhaled dirt and grit, then coughed and put her palms against the ground. She tried to push herself up, but her arms would not lift her, and after a few attempts, she let herself drop back onto the dirt, which felt cool against her face. She was so tired. Perhaps she would rest a few moments and let her strength return before she'd get back to her feet. Then she would finish hanging the wash before they baked the bread and swept the floors and made the beds and . . .

Just a few moments.

Just a few more.

Chapter Twenty-Eight

"She is exhausted, Calvin, can you not see that?"

Hattie's eyes fluttered open, but it took her a moment to realize where she was. Last she remembered, she was hanging clothes on the line. Now she was inside. On the sofa? *A taller woman would never have fit,* she thought as she continued to reorient herself to where she was. She stretched her toes and realized someone had taken off her shoes.

"I shall write to William and see if she can visit for a time."

Catharine's voice, Hattie was sure of it. But what was this about their brother William?

"She can rest here," Calvin was saying. "We'll move the cradles from the room and make her comfortable."

"She can't rest in this house," Catharine said sharply. "And she has a responsibility to her health above all. She had two babies not nine months ago, Calvin, and is now growing another. Have you no knowledge of what that takes from a woman's body? She nearly fell into that washing fire — do you not understand that?"

"Of course I do," Calvin defended from wherever ethereal location he stood. Hattie felt lost within a void. Unable to focus. "But — the babies."

"Will go with the wet nurse. Hattie's barely making any milk as it is — don't tell me you haven't noticed. She told me last week she was barely able to feed each of them once a day."

"Surely that's not my affair."

"Is it not, Mr. Stowe? Then you are a pathetic husband."

"Now, now." Mother's Stowe's voice rose in defense of her son.

Were Hattie not still swirling into consciousness she'd have been irritated at her mother-in-law's tone. Instead she was a disconnected eavesdropper on a conversation that must be taking place in the kitchen since she was in the parlor. Pulling apart what she'd heard, she tried to make sense of what had happened. She fell? She was brought inside? Calvin was called home? Catharine had come too?

Mother Stowe continued, "Calvin is doing the best that he can."

"As is Hattie, and look what it's done to her! She is skin and bone and a baby besides, wasting away in front of you and yet you refuse to see it."

There was silence, and then Catharine took up the campaign again, repeating much of what she'd already said but explaining it all in more detail. Calvin and Mother Stowe did not interrupt her, and Hattie's awareness sharpened until she was fully aware of where she was and what had happened. When Catharine finally stopped speaking, a heavy silence hung within the house.

"I am writing to William to ask that he have Hattie for a visit so she might recuperate," Catharine said. "And I am taking Hattie home for now so she might get some *rest*."

Hattie waited for Calvin to argue that this was her home, this was where she belonged, but he didn't.

"I need to clean up the wash," Mother Stowe said. "Calvin, why don't you help me?"

Calvin said nothing, and Hattie heard them leave through the kitchen door. She felt her chin start to quiver that he'd followed his mother's instruction instead of coming to her. She was more of a burden now than ever before.

A moment later, Catharine came into the parlor and though she seemed startled to find Hattie awake, she recovered quickly and knelt beside her. She took Hattie's hand in hers and smiled as a mother might. For a moment, Catharine was sixteen years old again and trying to explain to four-year-old Hattie that their mother had gone to heaven, but everything would be all right.

"How are you feeling, dearest?" Catharine asked, brushing Hattie's hair from her forehead.

Hattie considered this. "Tired, and my head aches."

"You took a nasty fall."

Hattie nodded so Catharine would know she was aware of what had happened.

"Have you had anything to eat today?"

Hattie considered that and then shook her head; she hadn't even thought of eating. There was too much else to do.

"And the baby is making you ill?"

Hattie nodded, touching her stomach, which swelled gently against her hand. "Worse than last time, which seems impossible." She paused, realizing that she hadn't told her family yet that she was pregnant again. Had Calvin told them? "I was going to tell you, I promise."

Catharine shook her head. "Never mind that. It seems perfectly reasonable to me that this time is harder; you had rest and a household of help last time. Not two babies and a husband and a house to manage." She looked as though she might say more but stopped herself, took a breath, and then forced a smile. "I'm going home to get a room ready and will send George and Henry to fetch you."

Hattie shook her head. Though she longed for rescue, she could not leave.

"Don't be stubborn, Hattie."

It was the softness rather than the censure in Catharine's voice that stopped Hattie's growing argument.

When Catharine spoke next, she lowered her voice. "I will not let him run you into the ground, do you understand me? You owe it to yourself, and your children, and even him — the idiot that he is — to preserve your health. Let him miss you. Let yourself recover from all you've been through and better prepare to welcome this new little one. I am not giving this advice lightly, Hattie, but I am *begging* you to take the course I'm prescribing and allow yourself some rest. It may very well save your life."

Hattie was struck by the sincerity and fear in Catharine's voice. Was it as serious as all of that? She didn't trust her own determination, which made it much easier to trust Catharine's. "Calvin has not treated me poorly, Catharine."

Catharine pursed her lips. "He has not treated you well and does not seem to realize the seriousness of this situation. Come home so that he might have the chance. You are both functioning like a spoke in a wheel going around and around so fast neither of you can see clearly. You both need rest."

"But the babies." Hattie tried to rise, but Catharine put a hand on her shoulder. "They went with Mina for the morning."

"I'll send word for Mina to bring them to the President's House later this afternoon. We'll decide a course from there." She squeezed Hattie's shoulder, then leaned in and kissed her forehead. "We will get you well, Hattie. We will."

CHAPTER TWENTY-NINE

Mina kept the girls for three days, and Hattie slept the blissful sleep of the over-worked and undernourished. Dr. Drake came and confirmed that the baby within Hattie was fine. He also confirmed that the baby would get its nourishment at Hattie's expense. To care for the child growing within her, she had to care for herself better than she'd done, which meant she could not continue nursing the twins. What little milk Hattie had left was quickly gone, and Hattie cried.

She would not hold her precious girls to her breast ever again; it felt like yet another failure heaped upon so many others. Though she slept and ate regularly, her thoughts were tired and dark. She missed her little cottage and her own bed. Though she was grateful to have people taking care of her, she also felt foolish for needing that care. She was a mother now and should be acting as such, not playing the role of child again.

Calvin wanted Hattie to come home and promised to care for her there, but Catharine would not allow it and Hattie gave no opinion. More than once he left his visits frustrated — with her, with himself, with Catharine. He hadn't spoken of the pressure he was under at Lane, but Hattie knew that having his household in order allowed him to feel focused and capable at work. She felt guilty for being the reason that had come to an end and the guilt reverberated through Hattie's dried-up chest and made her cry all over again. She had never known such sorrow and seemed to find no relief.

Mother Stowe did not come to visit, and though Hattie wished she did not care, some part of her had hoped that Mother Stowe might fill the missing place of a mother in Hattie's own life. Mourning the loss of that relationship was one more burden heaped upon the moldering pile of regret and unfulfilled expectations.

On the third day, as Hattie was expecting the return of her daughters with both eagerness and trepidation, Father came to Hattie's room. His demeanor was somber as he pulled a chair to her bedside and took her hand.

"I have counseled with Calvin," he said, "and we have agreed that you going to stay with William for a time is the best course."

Tears sprang to her eyes, and Hattie shook her head. She'd known such a plan was being considered, Catharine had suggested it the day of Hattie's fall, but little had been said since then. "I can't leave Harriet and Eliza."

"Mina's child is weaned, and she has plenty of milk for the both of them. I've made arrangements to compensate her — many wet nurses only care for other women's children in their own home."

Hattie's chin trembled and tears rolled down her face. *I failed.*

"Calvin will fetch them for a few hours after work most evenings. Mina says she will introduce them to porridge so they will sleep better at night."

Hattie had wondered if Little Harriet was not getting enough to eat, but hadn't trusted her own judgment. "Mother Stowe said that they were too young."

Father shook his head. "She has agreed to the idea, and Mina assures everyone that both girls are ready for the transition."

"We cannot afford the expense, Papa," Hattie said, grasping another objection. "Calvin is already so worried about —"

"I can," Father said with an authoritative nod. "And it is an investment in your health, Hattie. You must recover your strength or you will lose everything, do you understand?"

Hattie held his eyes. "You told me to rise to my responsibilities," she whispered. "You told me to do my part and make the Beechers proud."

Father looked at the floor and scuffed his shoe against the wood. "It would not be the first time I did not see the forest through the wealth of trees, Hattie." He met her gaze with a repentant look. "I want to defend that I didn't understand the toll it was taking, but in truth I gave you the only advice I know to give — get to work and forget yourself. It is all I have ever done, but I realize now that it might not be the remedy for every situation. I'm sorry I did not try harder to find out if it was fitting for yours."

"Catharine convinced you," Hattie said, knowing he had not changed his opinion on his own.

"I wish she hadn't needed to. Forgive me. Perfectionism is a sin, and I feel that I have told you to seek it out. Your health first, Hattie, then the balance of your home, which only you and Calvin can create together."

She closed her eyes and let the tears fall — tears she could ascribe to more than one cause. Father had released her from the charge that she uphold the family name. But she was being sent away. Some part of her was glad for it, which made her feel worse. "How long must I go?" she whispered.

"A month, maybe more. I've arranged your transportation to begin tomorrow. Henry will escort you. William and Katherine are readying a room."

Hattie nodded, but she felt like a child needing to be coddled and cared for by the adults around her. How had she let this happen? How had everything become so undone? "Is Calvin angry?"

"Calvin is a student in this too, Hattie. He agrees that you need rest and that much has been asked of you."

"I can't go without his approval, Father," she said, opening her eyes. "I am not yours anymore, I am his and he must have a say in my well-being."

"He has agreed to this course, Hattie, and has overcome the majority of his protests but . . . your marriage was very new when he left for Europe, and there was little time for either of you to find your footing once he returned. He must come to terms with his idealistic expectations — supported by his mother, I'm afraid — and you must allow him the chance to do so while also finding balance of your own. Take this time to recover your strength and allow you both to meet the other halfway so that you might bring out the best in one another instead of continuing the discord that seems to have taken root."

"Is common ground possible?" Hattie said, vocalizing the fear that had nagged at her from the start. "We are so different, Father. We value different things and expect the other to support what they cannot understand."

"You made a covenant with God when you married Calvin, Hattie — a *covenant.* More than a promise, a covenant means that He will fulfill his part as you fulfill yours. He can heal the pain between you and preserve your family as you both go to Him with your challenges and hardships and trust in Him to lift you above them."

"Is not leaving my family a breach of that very covenant?"

"You will not be gone for long. Only enough for you and Calvin to both learn to look a mile ahead instead of a single step. Calvin is a good man; I would never have agreed to your marrying him if I did not believe the two of you were well-suited. But as you said, he is overwhelmed. The financial decline has affected all of us, your family being forced to reside in such a small space has caused conflict, and the demands upon him are high both at the seminary and at home. I will look in on Calvin as often as possible and advise him as best I can on his part in this. We will all see that your daughters are well cared for. *You* need to take care of their mother physically and spiritually so that she might return to them whole and happy again. Can you do your part and let the rest of us do ours?"

Hattie hesitated, but after a few moments she nodded — was there any other course? They could not go on as they had been. Her father's faith made up for the faith she lacked.

Father brushed his hand tenderly across her forehead. "You're a fine woman, Hattie, and Calvin is a fine man. Everything will be all right."

CHAPTER THIRTY

June 9, 1837

Hattie made sure to take four bites of everything on the dinner tray Catharine had brought up to her room. She didn't want to eat but understood that she needed to, and so, like a good little soldier, she did. When she finished, she stood up and took the tray to the table beside the door. She was likely well enough to join the family downstairs for meals. It had been three days and she'd done little but sleep and eat. It was the effort of dressing and making conversation and trying to ignore the concerned looks on everyone's faces around the dinner table that kept her to her room. She had just settled back into bed when there was a light knock on the door. She sat up straight and smoothed her hair as the door opened.

Her eyes locked with Calvin's as he came into the room, and she felt a blooming of love in her chest for this man. All the things her father had said came back to her, and she took hold of the faith he had in them to make this work. Surely their love for one another — though not enough on its own — still counted toward their potential success.

Calvin was holding Little Harriet, who trilled and reached out for Hattie as soon as she saw her. Hattie looked at her daughter and felt tears come to her eyes while she put her arms out. Mother Stowe also came in, holding Eliza. Both of the adults had cautious expressions on their faces, like they didn't know what to say. Hattie hated the discomfort, but didn't want it to overshadow the moment. She would leave for Putnam in the morning; tonight she was saying good-bye to her family.

She swallowed the lump in her throat and forced her smile brighter as Calvin reached her and carefully put Little Harriet in her arms. She gathered her baby against her, cooing in her ear and holding her close for as long as Little Harriet would allow it, which wasn't more than a few moments. Soon enough Little Harriet was pushing back. She patted Hattie's cheeks, went in for another quick hug, and then pushed away entirely so she might explore the bed. Calvin sat on the edge of the bed so he might grab the hem of the baby's gown if she explored too close to the edge. When Hattie put out her arms for Eliza, Mother Stowe brought her over.

Always the more still of the girls, Eliza snuggled into Hattie's shoulder, seemingly content to stay there indefinitely. Hattie hugged her close, closing her eyes and inhaling the smell of her. She made eye contact with Calvin. "Thank you for bringing them," she said. "I've missed them so much."

Calvin smiled weakly. He didn't hold her eyes for long.

"Well, then, I'll go on to the parlor," Mother Stowe said, taking a step back. She smiled at Hattie, sincere but careful, and Hattie thanked her for her help. Mother Stowe nodded, then left the room, shutting the door quietly behind her.

For a few minutes, Hattie and Calvin distracted themselves from each other by playing with the girls, keeping them from going over the edge of the bed, and laughing at their energy. Hattie tried to think of something to say to break the fragile tension between them, but couldn't think of anything that sounded both easy and important. She glanced at him a dozen times, but his attention was always centered on one of the girls. When Little Harriet lost interest in the bedclothes and her mother, Calvin put her on the floor. Immediately she began crawling toward the chair on the other side of the room. Calvin stood, shadowing her new explorations. Eliza was content to sit upon the bed and grab fistfuls of the covers.

"I wish I could see you off in the morning," Calvin said, his voice sounding strange in the room and disappointingly formal.

"You have a class at that time," Hattie said as Eliza reached for her.

Calvin nodded, still watching Little Harriet. They fell silent again. They'd never managed small talk well, but she wondered if they were prepared for deeper conversation. Leaving for a month gave her the push she needed. "What will I do without all of you?" Saying it out loud brought tears to her eyes, and she was blinking through them when Calvin sat at the edge of the bed.

"What will all of us do without *you*?" he asked, placing a hand on her knee beneath the quilt.

Hattie shifted Eliza to the side so she could wipe at her eyes. "You'll be fine," she said, trying to laugh through the words. "Mother Stowe will get twice as much done without having me in the way, and Mina will meet every other need."

"Oh, Hattie."

Hattie met his gaze with her blurry eyes and felt the floodgates open all over again. "I'm sorry, Calvin, I'm so sorry. I can't care for our children. I can't care for our house. I can't care for you."

"Shh," Calvin said, scooting closer to her on the bed. Eliza grabbed for him and he pulled the baby onto his lap while putting his arm around Hattie's shoulders.

Hattie felt ridiculous, blubbering through their good-bye, sounding as pathetic as she felt and yet desperate for Calvin to know that she didn't want to go. And yet she did. But she didn't.

A crash from the other side of the room turned both their heads toward Little Harriet, who had managed to pull herself up against the dresser and grab the tatted doily, pulling it, and the book placed upon it, to the floor. She'd fallen hard on her bottom and was stunned for two full seconds before she began to wail. Hattie moved to get out of the bed, but Calvin shook his head, handed Eliza to her, and crossed the room to rescue Little Harriet.

"She's all right," Calvin said after inspecting the child to make sure the book hadn't hit her on its way to the floor. Little Harriet wasn't convinced by her father's assurance and continued to howl, which after a few seconds, led to Eliza whimpering in solidarity.

Hattie tried to comfort Eliza while Calvin crossed back to the bed with Little Harriet in his arms. He shifted the girl to one hip and reached his other arm out for Eliza. Hattie gave him a questioning look — she hadn't been able to hold both babies at once for a while — but he nodded and waved for her to hand Eliza to him. Hattie did so, and soon he was bouncing even more and pacing with both of them. It was such an endearing sight that Hattie put her hand to her mouth to keep from sighing out loud. Oh, that she could see the best of this man all the time and feel the pure admiration and love that she felt right now.

He shushed and cooed and spun around. Hattie laughed, and he looked back at her with his eyebrows up.

"This is entertaining you, my dear?" He was a bit breathless.

Hattie laughed again, the joyful expression on his face lighting the entire room. "Yes, darling, it is." When had she last called him *darling*? When had she felt that was what he was to her?

"Well, then." He added a few steps back and forth, as though he were dancing and began humming a tune.

This is what she would miss. This is what she'd missed all along. Ease. Comfort. Joy. There had been so little of it of late, and the reason she hadn't thought of him as her darling was because he hadn't been that to her. He represented all her weaknesses; he represented difficulty. Her laughter turned to tears — she had no control of her emotions — and when Calvin noticed, he stopped his antics.

"I'll be right back," he said simply and left the room while Hattie tried to get control of herself. She'd done a reasonable job by the time Calvin came back without the babies, a concerned smile on his face as he closed the door behind him.

"I think I better understand why it was so much easier taking care of the girls when you were in this house, Hattie. Many willing hands."

She sniffed and nodded. "But they are *my* children, and it is my —"

"*Our* children."

Calvin came to the bed and urged her to scoot over. For a moment she worried at his intentions, but he sat on top of the covers and pulled her to him. She leaned against his shoulder and closed her eyes, focusing on the feel of his hand on her back, the rise

345

and fall of his chest beneath her cheek. Breathe in. Breathe out. Breathe in.

"Why is life so complicated, Calvin?" she whispered. "How did a simple parlor wedding bring us here?"

He didn't answer right away. Breathe in. Breathe out. "I don't know, Hattie." His voice was just as soft. Just as reverent. With his free hand, he took hold of hers and kissed it before pressing it against his chest. "But there must be a way to make it work. There must be room for Hattie in *us,* and Calvin in *us,* and Eliza and Little Harriet and . . ." His voice trailed off as he paused to take a breath. "I don't know, Hattie." His voice cracked, and he let go of her hand so he could wipe at his eyes. The rise and fall of his chest became staccato, and Hattie cried, too, letting the tears drip onto his shirtfront.

"Let's get you well," he said. "Nothing is more important than that right now."

"Maybe I don't need to leave," Hattie said, feeling more hope than she had in a long time. He'd heard her. It had taken nearly falling into the wash fire, and the Beechers swooping in, but Calvin seemed genuinely aware of her right now in ways he hadn't been. "Maybe I can get well at home, and we can make this work without my go-

346

ing away?"

Calvin was quiet. His hand began rubbing her back again. His breathing evened out. "The arrangements are made," he said, bringing on more tears for Hattie. Did some part of him want her to go just as some part of her wanted to leave? "And . . ." He swallowed. "And as much as I want to say that if you came home we would find our way, it hasn't worked for us yet. Maybe this will."

CHAPTER THIRTY-ONE

June 22, 1837

Hattie sat in the rocking chair on her brother's front porch in Putnam, Ohio, and watched the sun peek over the rolling hills. She'd been waking early all that week — after sleeping in every morning the week prior — and had come to appreciate the unfettered feeling of morning, when the dew was still wet on the grass and the birds were stretching and yawning too. Perhaps that was what Calvin liked about the early morning hours.

Thinking of her husband and the life she'd left him to endure alone brought on the familiar feeling of having failed him, and yet she did feel stronger — just as father had said she would after some rest — and her head was clear. Each day was more hopeful than the last, and she wanted to return to her family in fine form. But when? Two weeks from now? A month? Her heart was pulled between wanting to stay here, where she was rested and cared for, and wanting to go back to those she dearly loved. Could she manage her life in Cincinnati when she returned? Could she be herself *and* Calvin's wife *and* Harriet and Eliza's mother all at the same time?

The evening before she'd left, when Calvin had held her and they had both grasped for hope and tried to believe they'd found it, came back to her, as it often did. She was glad to have a sweet memory to bring with her, instead of the tension and angst of the weeks and months leading up to it. But was it enough? Did he love her *enough*?

She didn't know, and she hated that she didn't know. Love was only one part of this life they shared. There must also be respect and trust and . . . a lot of work.

Hattie wished she had her babies with her so she could sit both of them on her lap and rock back and forth while they all enjoyed the sunrise together. She wished Calvin were in the chair beside her, perhaps with one of the girls on his lap, and they could enjoy just being together in silence and stillness and beauty. Could they ever have that? Little Harriet would want to get down, and she'd go immediately for the steps. Eliza would be content to rock for a while, but she'd eventually wonder what her sister was up to and want to follow. Calvin and Hattie would have to make sure the girls didn't get hurt. It would be easier to go back inside where the walls would contain the little mischiefs. Hattie sighed. What was reality? What was possibility? What was . . . peace?

The screen door creaked on its hinges, and Hattie looked over her shoulder to see her sister-in-law Katherine — spelled with a K to distinguish her from Hattie's sister Catharine with a C. Katherine carried a steaming cup of tea in either hand and handed a cup to Hattie as she sat in the chair next to her. Katherine's hair was still in her sleeping braid and hung down her back, the dark brown and gray winding around one another as though fighting for dominance.

Hattie inhaled the earthy scent of the tea and smiled graciously at her sister-in-law. "Thank you," she said before taking the first sip of the warming goodness. The women had spent surprisingly little time together — Hattie sleeping and keeping to herself a great deal so as not to be more of a burden, and Katherine content to let Hattie keep her own company. That had changed yesterday, however, when Hattie had begun to ask questions about how Katherine managed her home so smoothly. Today was where the answers would begin.

Katherine settled into her seat, and the women watched the expanding sunrise together. When Hattie finished her tea, she set the cup on the small enameled table between their two chairs. She turned toward Katherine. "So we'll start on the kitchen today?"

Katherine nodded, also putting her cup on the table. "And tomorrow, and perhaps Friday, too. There is a great deal to know about managing a kitchen."

Before coming to William's house, Hattie thought she understood what it meant to manage a household. She'd been Mother Stowe's student for weeks, after all, and tried to be attentive for at least *some* of the time. She'd already received more of an education from Katherine than she'd expected. Katherine had a cook, a maid, and a man of all work, leading Hattie to assume that Katherine could spend her time doing as she liked. She belonged to a quilting club, a ladies' auxiliary, and a literary club not much different from the Semi-Colon Club. She and William were also active members of the Anti-Slavery Society in Putnam. Katherine pursued her own interests and hobbies the way Hattie longed to do, but she also spent hours every day managing her help and the aspects of the household not performed by them. Just because one had servants, Katherine had explained, did not mean all the work was done by someone else.

Katherine met with her cook and her maid every morning after breakfast to go over their list of duties. Throughout the day, she checked to make sure their work was done correctly. On Sundays and Thursday afternoons, the help had time off, so Katherine made the meals and the beds and the fires herself. On Wednesdays, she helped the maid with the wash, and on Fridays, she did the household shopping and managed the ledgers. While Katherine did not quilt or indulge in her parlor literature on those days, she could do the work with an air of competence and assurance that eventually she would have time for her own interests. She did not put off household tasks, justify why some chore was not important, or put her own interests first on the days without help. She simply made time for each thing and gave it the proper attention when that time came. She tightened the bed ropes once a year, sanded the floors every three years, and made hotcakes for dinner sometimes. If a chicken needed to be killed, William or one of her sons took responsibility for that task; they had their own work to do around the house.

Hattie wanted that same gracefulness with her time rather than feeling rushed and anxious about what she needed to do. She wanted the awareness of knowing what was going on in her home and with her family, without becoming so focused on some other aspect that meals burned and children went hungry. She wanted the sense of peace that came from things being in their proper place. None of that would happen without her efforts, and she felt humbled enough by circumstance to feel fresh determination toward a solution — a solution she could live with day to day.

She'd once told Mary Dutton that she simply was not skilled in household management, as though that meant she should not have to do it. Such a thought felt ridiculously juvenile to her now, and yet she was learning that she did not have to do it Mother Stowe's way either, with ferocious attention to detail and perfection that left room for nothing but maintaining order.

"I gave Giana the day off, so we'll have the kitchen to ourselves," Katherine said, drawing Hattie's attention back to her. "She has implemented a fantastic order and keeps everything located according to how often it is used. Not every pan is in the same cupboard, you see, because a roasting pan might be used once a week but the frying pan is used for eggs each and every morning, which is why it hangs next to the stove. I'd never had such an organized kitchen before she came to work for us, and I praise every day that we have her."

"And you don't mind cooking when she's not here?"

Katherine shrugged. "I don't cook as she does, that's for certain, but I can make passable meals." She paused, cast a quick look at Hattie, and then faced forward again. "I prefer to leave the preaching to William and your father, but . . ."

Hattie kept her expression open so that her sister-in-law would continue. She sensed some preaching, even if Katherine was attempting to categorize it as something else.

"When my children were small, things were not like they are now, Hattie. I had so much to learn, and so much of my time could not be my own because my children needed me. We couldn't afford the help we have now, and William was busy . . . so busy." She paused, and Hattie sensed she was journeying back in time within her own

354

mind. "I look back now and wonder how I managed it, but I did. I learned what I needed to learn, and you know, I look back now and miss those days." She leaned her head against the back of the rocking chair and looked at Hattie. She let out a long, deep breath.

"I can't imagine twins — or a husband gone to Europe for almost a year — so I don't mean to say that my experience was yours, Hattie, but I do believe that the sacrifices we make as mothers are worthwhile. I have learned so much about myself and the world and God, and while I'm sure I could have learned those things another way if that were my path, I didn't. God blessed me with *this* path, and once I gave myself over to that journey and was willing to learn as I went, I found myself within that journey." She smiled self-consciously. "Have I offended you?"

Hattie shook her head, but she also sighed. "There is just so much and I feel so lost."

Katherine reached out her hand and Hattie took it. "I understand, but you are never truly lost when you are doing good. The Bible tells us to serve and give to the poor and be charitable, but too often we think those admonishments are for those outside our family. I think they count twice as much to those we have covenanted with and brought into that union. Meals and wash and sweeping is God's work as sure as ministering and paying tithes. Your children will grow up, your ability to manage them will grow too, and one day you'll look back and marvel at how much they taught you."

"And my gifts and passions just stay on a shelf and keep until I have time of my own again?" Ten years? Twenty?

Katharine shook her head. "You find a way to use them, Hattie, absolutely you do. But you don't give them so much focus that your family comes second. Perhaps you bargain with Calvin to have a day a month to spend in your father's office, or perhaps Calvin makes dinner twice a week so you can find time to pursue those things that matter to you on those evenings. You look for an hour here and an hour there and you'll learn to make better use of your time than you did when you had days and days at your disposal." She squeezed Hattie's hand. "That is what God does, Hattie. Beauty for ashes. A change of heart instead of a change of circumstance."

Katherine's words did not appease Hattie entirely, but they did add to her hope. A little hope here and a little hope there in time became bigger and stronger and easier to see. "I want to do well," Hattie said. "I want everything you've said to be true."

Katherine smiled and looked back at the peach-colored sky.

They rocked silently for a few more minutes, until Hattie broke the quiet. "Do you know how to make corn chowder, Katherine?"

"It can't be very different from potato chowder, I don't think. It's a particular favorite of yours?"

"Of Calvin's," Hattie clarified. "I'm afraid I was too bitter to listen to his mother's instruction when she tried to teach me."

"Then we shall adventure it together, and when you return home, you can teach Calvin how to make it." She winked before pushing up from her chair. "Give me an hour to get myself ready for the day and feed the children, then we shall set to work."

Hattie pushed herself up as well. "I can make hotcakes reasonably well, and eggs are easy enough so long as I don't let myself become distracted. I'll manage breakfast; you manage yourself."

Katherine paused in surprise, which made Hattie realize how little she'd done to help since she'd come here. Before she could apologize, Katherine smiled. "That would be wonderful, Hattie, thank you."

Hattie followed her into the house and let Katherine point out the basics of the kitchen before she was left alone with the stove and pans and spoons. So many times before, such a scene had sparked resentment and irritation in her, but if Katherine could work without complaint and find joy, then Hattie could as well. She was here to get her feet underneath her once again and rediscover her faith. It was time she got to work.

CHAPTER THIRTY-TWO

July 1, 1837

Dear Calvin,

Forgive me for not writing sooner. The obvious excuse is that I have been convalescing, which I have been, but I have also sat down a dozen times to write and found no words to fill my pen. How do I write the feelings of my heart and do them justice? In this my pen has failed me, and so I shall not speak of them at all. Instead, I shall tell you how fine the weather is here in Putnam; a hundred and fifty miles makes a surprising difference in the discomfort of these summer months. Katherine is an exceptional host; how blessed I am by the many substitute mothers I have had in my life. Especially at times like this when I am reduced to an infantile state once more.

I am gathering my strength to return

to you and our daughters. I miss you all very much. My thoughts are also heavy with Eliza, it now being three years since her passing. I wonder what she thinks of us when she looks down from heaven. I feel a great deal of shame for my part in the troubles we face. I have had time to think of my situation and what I want from this life we share. I choose us, my darling, and the happiness I believe still exists for us. I hope you can believe me and that we can find accord when I return. Katherine is giving me lessons, and her way of management appeals to me. I think I can do better than I've done, and I pray it will be enough.

There I go, attempting to say when I cannot say correctly. I will write no more on that until I can do my feelings justice. Kiss our precious girls for us, thank your mother for caring for you in my place, and be in good health yourself.

Love and affection,
Hattie

Calvin turned up the path, the drooping flowers limp at his side. He watched his feet instead of the headstones lined to the left and right. He knew precisely where to stop and only then did he look upon the stone that served as Eliza's earthly marker.

ELIZA TYLER STOWE
1809–1834

He stared at the stone a long time, then stepped forward and laid the flowers along the front. "Forgive me for staying away," he said and scrubbed a hand over his face. "There are many difficulties for me right now, difficulties I never imagined would besiege me." He paused and let out a heavy breath. "Oh, Eliza, sometimes I envy you."

The words struck him hard, but sometimes the peace of the grave did beckon him when the demons of his present circumstance took hold with their claws. "Hattie is gone to Putnam, and my children are farmed out to a woman who can feed them. I am a man of thirty-five years living with my mother, who coddles and cares for me as she did when I was young. It is a comfort, I admit, but a thin one. I miss you."

The words struck him with guilt and deep shame as he thought of how Hattie had accused him of comparing her to Eliza. Tears rose in his eyes. "I should not miss you, the wife of my youth, but . . ." Unexpected emotion choked him, and he bent his head forward and began to cry. Soon he was kneeling before Eliza's headstone with his head in his hands and his heart spilled out on the ground between them. He missed the ease of their marriage, the way Eliza cared for him much as his mother did.

He sobbed, moving from guilt to grief to longing until he felt expended and empty. He remained on his aching knees and wiped at his eyes with the lapels of his coat. Mother would be displeased when she saw what he'd done to his suit. He focused on the stone again, on Eliza's name.

"Did I silence you, Eliza?" he whispered. "Was I overbearing and selfish and cruel to you without realizing it?" It was a thought he had entertained before. Surely Eliza would have told him if he were unreasonable, wouldn't she? And he only asked of a wife what a thousand other husbands asked of their wives, didn't he?

He thought back to the days of his courtship with Hattie, the way she would debate and discuss her views on a topic. He'd found it astounding to have a woman be so intellectual and confident; Eliza had never engaged in such discourses. She agreed with his thoughts, and there were times, he could admit now, when her acquiescence had aggravated him. He had fallen in love with *Hattie,* not a replacement for Eliza. He'd felt secure in that once, but now he was not so sure that he hadn't been trying to change her into the wife Eliza had been.

"I very much want to do right with what I have, Eliza. My daughters . . . oh, how you would love them. And Hattie — I know you loved her as a bosom friend." He paused, remembering how Eliza and Hattie would visit and laugh in the parlor while Calvin worked on his lessons in the other room. So long ago. So much had changed. "I love her, Eliza, I can't imagine my life without her. But what am I to do with her?"

His mind focused on the preposition: *with.* As though she were a pet or an investment. He shook his head, ashamed of himself. She was *Hattie* before she was his wife. Why was he so determined to change her? A different sentence came to mind: What are you to do *for* her?

He paused in his thoughts and in his breathing. *For* was a very different word than *with.* The words of their marriage ceremony came to his mind: *Have you cleaved unto your wife and no other?*

He thought of Eliza and the times he allowed himself to miss her, the times he thought "Eliza would never . . ." Then he thought of his mother, the way she doted on him, the way he let her. She did not approve of Hattie's efforts, and he had taken advantage of that to fuel his own disapproval. Hattie had said in the horrible argument they'd had the night before she fainted that she needed space for herself within their marriage, parenting, and home. Why did that threaten him? But then they had had those moments in her room at the President's House before she'd left when all was tender and beautiful and his heart was full of love and humility.

. . . love her as Christ loved the church . . .

He stared at the ground and remembered Mother summoning him home because Hattie had fainted while doing the wash. Her skin had been pale as a sheet, her hair wild around her face. She'd looked like a child, and he'd felt . . . angry. As he remembered his reaction, shame fell over him like a drape. He'd been *angry* that he'd had to leave his class. He'd been disappointed in her for causing him distress. He had been put out and inconvenienced yet again by Hattie's inability to fulfill her role. Was he such a cold man that he had no space for compassion?

Catharine had berated him and reminded him that Hattie had birthed twins nine months earlier and was growing another. The doctor had said that Hattie's milk was nearly dry because she was not nourished enough herself to feed three babies. Lyman had come, hat in hand, and spoken of his dead wives and how they haunted him. And Hattie. Hattie had had to travel a hundred and fifty miles to get well. A hundred and fifty miles from him, her husband, who was supposed to love her, care for her, and protect her.

Calvin looked at Eliza's stone again; that was all it was — a stone. A symbol of a life once lived. A life that ended. He thought of when they were first married and how they had learned to find their way together. She had known how to cook three dishes, and he'd never cleaned out a stove before. He'd learned so much in those early years. Had he been judging Hattie for not knowing what Eliza had already learned? Had he expected Hattie to be Eliza instead of a woman to herself?

Calvin had made new covenants when he married Hattie, and he felt keenly that he had failed them. Hattie had not shared the thoughts of her heart in her last letter because he had not proved himself a fitting caretaker. He thought back to what she'd said about drowning, and how offended he'd been. He had seen the confession as her excusing her incompetence. Again. Her contributions were weak. Not enough. Unacceptable.

Already on his knees, Calvin brought his hands to prayer and bowed his head before his Maker. "Dear God in heaven, forgive me my selfishness, my lack of compassion, my cruelty and my unbending nature. Fill me with hope, help me to make amends for the wrong I have done and fix what is broken between Hattie and me. I love her, Lord." He said it and he felt it. Though his eyes were closed, he was aware of Eliza's headstone before him, her body buried beneath it. She *was* gone. Calvin was here, and his family needed him. Hattie needed him. And he needed her, too.

"Forgive me," he prayed again, his voice shaky. "And soften my heart. Help me know what I can do and then give me the strength and patience to do it."

When Calvin walked into the cottage some time later, his mother looked up from her knitting and smiled adoringly at her son. "I wondered if you had lost your way home," she said, patting the space beside her on the sofa. "Come sit a spell; you look wrung out."

She returned to her knitting, but Calvin did not cross the room as she'd instructed and after a few more stitches she looked up again. "Calvin?"

Calvin removed his hat and held it in front of him with both hands. "Mother, we need to talk."

CHAPTER THIRTY-THREE

July 21, 1837

Hattie read over Calvin's last letter as the carriage made its final turn toward the posting station in Cincinnati where Calvin said he would be waiting. He'd said all the right things in the letter — that he was sorry for being so severe, that he loved her for her, that he wanted her to be happy and for them to find a middle ground where they were both content within the promises they had made to one another. She felt guilty for doubting his sincerity — he could not change his nature any easier than she could change hers — but she was rested now.

She'd been physically and spiritually fed at William's. She'd read whole books again, penned an essay about New England for her forgotten collection, and learned some things from Katherine that made her hopeful of finding her way within her own household. She'd desperately missed her children. And a few times a day she would think, "I can't wait to tell Calvin . . ." only to realize that she would not tell Calvin. He'd been a hundred and fifty miles away living their life without her. She missed him but treasured the longing as a sign of hope for them yet.

The worst of the sickness brought on with her pregnancy had passed, and with the chance to sleep full nights, her thinking was clearer than she'd been able to manage for a very long time. She was ready to return home, but she was scared too. Calvin said in his letter that he was devoted to her happiness and had made changes while she was gone. But was he really? Could any one person be devoted to the happiness of someone else? She did not expect him to give up his own needs and desires, but could both of them get what they wanted and needed?

Hattie was a mother, and it had forever changed her. She could not go back to the woman she'd been before Eliza and Harriet. She was also a wife, and even with their differences, she could not imagine a future without Calvin in it. There must be a way to find joy in all her responsibilities and still feel like herself besides. Katherine had nurtured that hope, and now that Hattie was returning to her home and family, she would have the chance to prove it true. Or impossible.

The carriage stopped, and a coachman helped Hattie step down. She adjusted the strings of her reticule while perusing the crowd until her gaze landed upon Calvin. She smiled and felt warm confirmation that she belonged here. He'd said that he'd asked the Beechers not to come, and she was glad for the chance to have a more private welcome. He smiled too, soft and sweet, before he stepped forward from the crowd.

"You look very well, Hattie," he said once they were facing one another.

"I feel well," she said, wishing they were alone so she could put her hand on his cheek. "And I am glad to be home."

He smiled wider, and Hattie took his arm when he offered it. They made small talk as best they could as they traveled back to Walnut Hills in her father's carriage Calvin had borrowed. The girls, Calvin said, were at the Beechers so Hattie might have a chance to get settled. It was a thoughtful gesture on his part, and Hattie thanked him for the consideration even though she was brimming with eagerness to see them.

She did not ask after his mother because

she did not want to fray the accord between them, but she noticed the porch was freshly swept when they arrived at the front door. And one of Mrs. Allen's pots, filled with the violets Mother Stowe had given away, had been put on the Stowes' walk. Hattie smiled at the flowers, then wondered how her vegetables were doing in the back. They should be producing soon.

I am glad Mother Stowe was here when I was not, Hattie told herself, determined to make her relationship with her mother-in-law work.

"I spoke with the board about our house last week," Calvin said. "They assure me it will be ready by the end of the summer."

Hattie met his eye and raised her eyebrows. "Of course that's what they said. And what do you believe?"

"I believe that perhaps they meant the end of *next* summer. I shan't be holding my breath and am determined, instead, to enjoy our cozy lair." Calvin opened the door for her before standing to the side.

"As will I." Hattie stepped past him into the house. She was surprised to see the girls' blanket on the floor with their toys scattered about. There was a stack of books beside Calvin's chair. Hattie took in the state of the parlor with a glance, then turned to look at her husband. "Is Mother Stowe ill?"

He smiled sheepishly but didn't answer as he closed the door on well-oiled hinges.

Hattie walked further into the room, expecting her mother-in-law to come around the corner. After a few moments, however, she realized the house was empty but for Calvin and herself. She turned to face him while undoing the ties of her bonnet. "Is Mother Stowe at the Beechers with the girls?"

Calvin shook his head. "I believe Mother is nearly through Pennsylvania by now. She left two days ago, and I'm afraid I didn't get around to picking up after the girls came home last night."

Hattie's hands stilled in undoing the knotted ribbons. "Left?"

He took a step closer and reached out to help her with the ties. She let her hands fall to her sides and watched his eyes. "I meant what I said when I told you I had made some changes, Hattie." His strong fingers sorted out the knot easily enough, and he gently removed the bonnet from her hair, then removed first one hairpin and then another. He dropped each pin — slovenly, really — to the floor at their feet, and Hattie did not stop him. When the pins were removed and her hair hung down her back, he put his hands into her unruly curls and smiled. "I've missed this." Her entire head tingled with sensation.

He kissed her lightly and lovingly on the lips. "I've missed kissing your fine lips and gazing into your lovely eyes."

Hattie did not know what to say, but anticipation shivered through her chest, and she swallowed.

He smiled. "I've missed *you,* Hattie, and I'm so glad you've returned to us. I can't live without you, you know, and every day of your absence pressed that truth upon me with greater fervency."

"Oh, Calvin." She put a hand against his cheek. "I could not have stayed away much longer, even without your letter asking me back."

"Can you forgive me for running you from your own home?"

She shook her head. "You didn't run me away, Calvin, it's just . . . ." Just what? She still didn't know how to find the words, and yet she was unwilling to keep her thoughts to herself. She must speak up so he could hear her. As lovely as this seduction was, she could not allow it to blind them.

"We will make this work, Hattie. We will."

Pretty words and wished-for endearments,

but . . . "How?" she asked pointedly. "It is the one part that has haunted me. I fear that one of us will have to give up himself or herself to please the other, and that idea is repugnant. I don't want to change you, Calvin, to browbeat and break you to do my will any more than I want to be the one beneath the rod."

Rather than darkening his mood, Calvin seemed to brighten at her words. "Would you like to see the rest of the changes I have made?"

Hattie was surprised at the turn of subject, but followed his lead. "More than your mother's leaving?" It was a relief to know she would not feel Mother Stowe's judgment.

"Oh, yes," Calvin said, his eyes sparkling like a little boy. He took her hand and led her to the kitchen where the pots and pans were orderly and stacked just as Mother Stowe liked them. "I've hired a girl of all work — Anna Smith — to help with the house and the babies. She's been staying with Catharine this week and getting instruction from the cook at the President's House while we waited for you to come home." He gestured to the side of the kitchen where there was a doorway that had not been there before. "Henry and George helped me build a room for her. We might need to add a stove come winter. We left a corner free, just in case, but Lane will cover the cost of necessary improvements in exchange for my no longer beating them over the head with demands for a bigger house."

He began leading Hattie to the stairs, but she pulled back on his hand. "You hired help?"

Calvin turned to face her. "Mother helped me with the vetting process, and Catharine gave her own opinions. Anna is English, young, mild-mannered, and eager to learn. She adores the girls already, but will need some training since she is only eighteen. It was more expensive to hire someone with experience. Anna agreed for a dollar and twenty-five cents a week."

Hattie could not move through her shock fast enough. "But you have been so set against household help. You said it wasn't only because of the expense but because I needed to learn to manage myself."

"Maybe there is not always just one right way to do things. You have been asking for help from the very start, and I have been determined against it. In your absence, I came to realize that I did not have a clear view of what it took to run a household or manage our little mischiefs." He pulled her toward the staircase again. "There is another change I want to show you."

He had to drop her hand for them to navigate the narrow stairwell, but took it again when they arrived at the top. There were two doorways — the one to the left led to the bedroom they shared with the girls and the one to the right had been Mother Stowe's room. Calvin led her to their bedroom door and opened it.

The room was very much as it had been the last time Hattie saw it — the bed, chest, washstand, and bureau — but beneath the window was her writing desk. Calvin had moved it from the parlor downstairs. She walked to it as though drawn by a cord and ran her hand over the smooth surface. It had felt so good to write again when she was in Putnam, but she didn't know how she would fit it into their lives here. She faced Calvin, emotion rising in her chest. "You've made me a space to write."

"The bed is yours too."

Hattie looked at it a moment before turning her confused eyes back to her husband.

"After this baby comes, I will take the bed in the other room — your father agreed to our keeping it — and I will leave our . . . relations to your discretion." He waved his hand toward her growing middle. "I think we have proved that we are very compatible in that area and, therefore, may need to set some boundaries. You can control our future intimacy and, therefore, the timing of our children. We can share the children between both rooms at night until we have a house that fits our family better than this one."

Hattie did not know what to say. Part of her felt rejected, and yet there was no denying the relief that he had — literally — made a place in their home and in their marriage for her. He was giving her the space she needed to find herself within them and the family they were building.

Calvin met her eyes with his deep blue ones, and her heart melted. When he spoke, his voice was soft and sincere. "I don't want to use you up, Hattie, in any way I may have already done." He looked at the floor, and Hattie felt her eyes fill with tears. He nodded toward the desk and spoke before she'd thought of a response.

"I cannot afford Anna's pay with my salary for long, so I took you at your word that you would rather pay for help yourself than be without it. Henry has sent notice to some of his connections, soliciting articles for you to write. Between his connections and your own, you should be able to supplement the household income enough to cover Anna's wages." He looked up again. "She cannot run the household herself, of course, but I hope she will provide you a few hours a day to devote to your pen."

"Oh, Calvin," Hattie said, the words choking her as she crossed the room and threw her arms around his neck. He returned the embrace, holding her close and burying his face in her hair. They stood that way for nearly a minute before she pulled back, her hands on his shoulders. "Thank you," she whispered, feeling seen and understood. Beauty for ashes. Faith and works.

He tucked a lock of her unpinned hair behind her ear. "You asked me why I married you, Hattie, and I gave a poor answer."

Hattie shook her head, not wanting to relive the emotions of that horrible night.

"I married you because I admired your mind, your strength, your determination, and your commitment to family. I married you because you made me feel stronger and smarter and more capable than any other person ever had in my life. I married you because I wanted my journey to be connected to yours." He used his thumb to wipe away the tears she hadn't noticed sliding down her cheeks. "I believed when I married you that I loved you and could not live without you. I *believed* it, but I didn't know. I have come to know it. I love you, Harriet Beecher Stowe, not only because of what you do for me or for our children, but because you are remarkable and you challenge me to be a better man — I need that challenge to improve.

"I do not pretend that we will not cross swords a thousand times more in the future, I do not pretend that my nature is so changed that those aspects of your nature that make me crazy will never again bother me, or that my nature will not vex you greatly too, but I will do better than I have done. I will not forget that you being a woman unto yourself is every bit as important as your being a wife to me and a mother to our children. You *must* be a literary woman, Hattie, it is one of the things you were foreordained to do. I will do everything in my power to support you and hope you will forgive me for having forgotten."

Hattie couldn't speak and instead wrapped her arms around him, tighter than before, holding him as she'd longed to on so many nights when they were apart. She owed him an apology, too, for being so stubborn, for the times she vexed him on purpose or showed such little consideration for how hard he worked to provide for them. She was ashamed of the way she'd behaved, but then she felt his lips on her neck and lost her words for the moment. She promised she would find the words later as she welcomed his affection. He trailed kisses to her ear and then met his lips to hers. The excitement and relief of her homecoming mixed and stirred between them until she was sliding the coat from his arms. Seeing as how she was already expecting, there was little need for a second bedroom just yet.

Though they were alone in the house, Calvin shut the bedroom door and undid his necktie as he crossed the day-lit room. As he joined her beneath their wedding quilt, she felt this would not be the only aspect of their marriage in which they were evenly matched anymore. Her misgivings calmed, her fears receded, and, finally, there was calm and peace and hope between them.

That evening, with their girls returned and Hattie's hair attentively repinned, Calvin sat in his favorite chair by the cold fireplace, the books still stacked beside his chair. He put on his spectacles and looked over the rim at the three women who made up his audience. Hattie sat in the center of a blanket spread on the floor, Eliza in her lap. Little Harriet was crawling and would not be content with the fabric toys she was playing with for long.

Hattie couldn't believe how much the girls had grown in her absence, but she would never forget the way their faces lit up to see her, and the feel of their little arms around her neck. Mina would continue nursing them for as long as necessary, at least until the next Stowe child needed her, but the girls were healthy and happy and growing as they should. They both had porridge each night before bed, allowing them to sleep in a six-hour stretch. Six hours felt like manna from heaven for Hattie. Little Harriet could also tolerate mashed squash and carrots for supper, but Eliza would get an upset stomach.

"Now girls," Calvin said in his schoolmaster tone, drawing all three faces toward him. "This is a very special book, you know. In its original German it is as lyrical as a song."

The girls blinked at him. Eliza shifted more comfortably in Hattie's lap, already having to share it with her little brother or sister. Little Harriet pushed herself to a sitting position and watched her father a moment before putting her plush duck into her mouth. Hattie laughed and answered for the three of them. "We are listening, Papa."

"Very good." Calvin pushed the spectacles up his nose and opened the book — one of the treasures he'd brought home from his European travels. He'd said many times how he would like the family to read it of an evening, but such an evening had never come; they'd been too frantic and filled with other things. Now, with Anna straightening the kitchen after a simple dinner that Hattie was proud to make and Calvin was gracious to receive, Calvin's goal could be realized.

As Calvin began to read the German fairy tale of *Tom Thumb,* Hattie recommitted herself to her goal of melding together her responsibilities to her husband, her children, and herself so that she might keep the comfort she felt right now with her, always.

Epilogue

March 1851

"Freddie, no," Hattie whispered while leaning across three other children in pew twenty-three to lightly slap her son's arm. Her ten-year-old was tearing a paper into bits and watching the pieces flutter to the floor. Upon his mother's reprimand, he huffed and leaned back against the pew with folded arms and a scowl. Hattie sat back, too, but had no sooner caught up with the minister's sermon than seven-year-old Georgiana — Georgie — began whining that Henry was sitting too close.

"Settle down, dear," Hattie said.

"He smells like ham," Georgie said.

"Calvin," Hattie hissed toward her gray-haired husband of some fifteen years, sitting as the other bookend on the pew; he was closer to Georgie than she was. Over the years, he'd become rather expert at blocking out the fidgeting of their children, a trait she found both admirable and irritating. Hattie said his name again, loud enough for some of the parishioners near them to turn their heads. She smiled an apology but kept her focus on her husband and raised her whisper a degree more. "Calvin!"

Calvin blinked, then settled his gaze on her and lifted his eyebrows in a question. She gestured toward Georgie, who was wiping her eyes from the tears caused by her brother's proximity and porcine aroma. Understanding dawned, and Calvin reached across the other children and lifted their youngest daughter onto his lap before he looked intently back at the minister. He bounced the child — though she was getting too big for such things — on his knee with practiced ease.

The baby in Hattie's arms, Charles Edward, named after the baby Samuel Charles whom she'd lost to cholera two years before in Cincinnati, shifted in his sleep. She tucked the blanket around his chin, wondering if she would ever look into his sweet face without mourning the child she'd lost. Six healthy children, a patient and attentive husband, and a writing career never seemed to ease the ache of that loss, which had settled into her bones and thrummed within her heart. But she would not be any less grateful for what she *did* have, which was much. She kissed Charley's downy head and then looked forward again, determined to get some good from the Sunday sermon.

The family had been in Brunswick, Maine, nearly a year now — finally free of Cincinnati, which held dark memories of First Charlie's death. Some of her happiest days had been spent in Ohio, when her children were young and the days ran together. Her sister-in-law Katherine had prophesied that one day Hattie would miss those early years of motherhood; she had been right. Hattie's very heaviest days nearly strangled out those good memories sometimes, but she was getting better at pointing her heart to joy and following that direction.

"We must not be blind to the evil around us, even if we feel our voices are small and indistinct," the minister said, his voice booming within the small church. "We must not shrug our shoulders and look the other way when evil flourishes among the lowly."

His words turned her thoughts from her family — always the first thing on her mind — to the next topic that seemed to be overwhelming her of late — slavery. He might not be talking specifically about slavery, but these days everything Hattie heard seemed to be directed to that most evil and inhumane institution.

Lowly, Hattie thought. *Poor, small, without privilege.*

"We must not say that because our bellies are filled and our eyes are clear that no one else is hungered and burdened."

Hattie nodded, as did several other heads in the congregation of the First Parish Church. It was good to be back in New England among educated and progressive minds. Not that Ohio did not have a representation of that class, but passions ran high, and the divisiveness created more tension than Hattie could stomach. Now firmly in the North again, Hattie felt better understood and yet surprised at how many Northerners still saw slavery as a Southern problem. Many of them were disconnected enough from the institution to feel as though it had no bearing on their own consciences.

The idea that there was something she could do to challenge the ignorance had been niggling and squirming in her chest for weeks, but she could not yet make out what she was meant to do. Certainly the prompting was to write something on this topic, something that people would hear. But what? She wrote articles for magazines. Most of her content was focused around the domestic arts she had learned against her own nature, which ironically made her a good teacher of such things.

Talk to the mothers.

She straightened in her chair. *The mothers?* The Grimke sisters, pioneers in both women's rights and abolitionism, had once said their strength had come in talking to the mothers. Hattie, herself, talked to mothers in everything she wrote.

The minister continued to expound his topic of charity. "As Christians, we are to lift the hands that hang down."

She felt her throat thicken, and her heart began to pound.

"Mourn with those that mourn."

Hattie held Charley closer. She knew the mourning of putting a child in the grave. How much more bitter would it feel to have that child taken from her and sold as so many slave children were? Sold as an animal. As a thing.

Could there be a more excruciating wound?

Talk to the mothers, the fathers, the Christian hearts.

A scene suddenly opened up in Hattie's mind, and the voice of the minister, though it had been rising in passionate volume, began to fade in her ears. The children shifting beside her, even the ache of her own arm beneath Charley's head, became muted, and the air around her seemed to grow still as a terrifying vision caught every bit of her attention.

She saw a large, powerful black man. She felt the goodness of his Christian spirit and the size of his heart — *the slave.* He was bent over a post, his hands clasped in prayer as another black man struck him again and again with a whip. A white man, small and wiry, stood by, watching, reveling — *the master.* Each lash cut through flesh and bone and spirit, shattering and slicing the slave. The master drew power from each blow, his smile growing, his bloodlust surging as though it were as tangible as his long, dirty fingernails.

The slave would not cry out from the pain but continued to pray; his was a heart truly converted. He prayed for deliverance, for forgiveness of his oppressors, and for eternal peace away from the miserable conditions of his mortal life. He had a family, Hattie knew, one he loved as deeply and surely as Hattie loved her own, but they'd been lost to him, and he had not seen them for a very long time. With each lashing, the slave — *Uncle Tom* — became smaller, while the master fed upon the evil action and became bigger. Then the slave crumbled, not even his hands in prayer could hold him up. He withered to the ground and lay still, nearly dead and yet at peace.

The master breathed heavily, steeped in excitement and power — a big man in his own mind. But he was evil. He symbolized the institution itself.

Her mind's eye looked again upon the black man whose body was growing smaller and thinner until he was no more than a baby, the same size as her Charlie had been the day she laid him in an impossibly small casket and watched him be lowered into the ground. The powerful slave man had been some woman's child once. Had his mother known him? Had he been sold from her? What lengths would his poor dear mother have gone to in order to save him from such a fate, if she could?

A jostle brought Hattie back to an awareness of where she was — the church in Brunswick, surrounded by her children who were standing, ready to leave. Calvin stood from his place at the opposite end of the pew. The sermon had ended, yet her thoughts had not caught up with what had unfolded in her mind. Hattie stood out of habit, gathered the children's shoes and books scattered about their pew, and put the family back in order enough to make the walk home to the rented house on Federal Street.

Once outside the walls of the church, the younger Stowe children scampered and ran, free at last, free at last, while Eliza and Harriet, now fourteen years old, rolled their eyes at their siblings and conducted themselves like the young ladies they were.

Calvin fell in step beside Hattie, peering at her with concern. "Are you well, Hattie?"

Hattie nodded. She still felt half here and half in her vision.

"You look as though you have seen a ghost," Calvin continued. "Are you sure you're all right?"

Hattie stopped walking while the children hurried ahead. Harriet and Eliza were capable of supervising the family the rest of the way home. Anna, who had stayed on all these years, had Sunday off, and the girls were used to helping with meals in her absence. "I've seen something, Calvin."

"Seen something?" Calvin repeated. He hitched Georgie higher on his hip and lifted his gray-and-white speckled eyebrows expectantly. He gazed at her with those lovely blue eyes that had mourned with her, celebrated with her, and kept her firmly planted when her flighty spirit became untethered. "What do you mean?"

Hattie looked back at the church, then focused on her husband again. "In church, during the sermon, a . . . a vision opened before me. A slave was . . . beaten to death . . . and . . ." She struggled to find the words she needed to paint this picture. *Pictures.* Yes, that's how she had to tell Uncle Tom's story, through conversation and instruction with a domestic voice and ordinary style that would feel familiar and real. *Talk to the mothers.* She opened her mouth and the words tumbled out, describing what she'd seen and how it made her feel.

"I have to write it, Calvin. I don't know what it will be — the end of a short story, perhaps? Fiction that shows truth in a way people can understand it. But I must write it before it fades. It is . . . important." It was also the Sabbath, and Hattie never wrote on the Sabbath, yet . . .

"Then you must write it down," Calvin said, his expression reverent. He set Georgie down amid the child's protests and reached for the baby in Hattie's arms. Once Charley was settled, Calvin took Georgie's hand and nodded in the direction of their house. "I'll gather the children and see to their luncheon. If it's truly a vision you've received, you cannot wait another moment."

Hattie leaned forward and kissed him soundly, right there on the street. Who would she be without Calvin? She pulled back, shared a smile with her husband, and took quick strides to the house, afraid that at any moment the images would leak from her mind like tea from a cracked kettle and she would lose them forever.

The children had beat her home, but she slipped upstairs before they bombarded her with all their needs and wants. She turned the lock on her bedroom door. Her writing desk was set by the window where she still managed a few hours every day to write. Keeping to a writing schedule allowed her to be free of its gripping passion for the other hours of the day so that she might attend to her other priorities.

For the next two hours, she wrote as furiously as she ever had in her life, capturing the scene that had opened before her, though she wrote it out differently, then immediately going over the recollection and inserting a better word here and reordering a sentence there. When she'd gone over it a third time, she finally felt as though she could breathe normally — that she had captured everything. Inspiration in regards to her writing was not new for Hattie, but she had never experienced something like this, something that felt . . . Godly.

"Of small and simple things are great things brought to pass," Hattie whispered to the air, which fairly shivered around her. She was small and felt very simple living a domestic, middle-class life, but God had called her to this place and she would hold her ground with Him. She would use her words. She would speak her piece and add her voice to those of the protesters crying for vengeance against evil and praying for salvation for the lowly. With her pen still in hand, Hattie positioned it at the top of the paper and wrote the title for the picture God had given her to write.

Uncle Tom's Cabin: Life Among the Lowly.

CONCLUSION

In 1853, amid backlash and criticism that she had exaggerated the cruelty of slavery, Harriet published the book *Key to Uncle Tom's Cabin,* in which she explained the sources and inspiration she used. Critics would continue to claim she exaggerated the circumstances, but over the course of decades, time and first-person accounts would prove that she had no need to embellish the ugly truth of slavery.

A story is often told of her first meeting with President Abraham Lincoln where he said, "So you're the little woman who wrote the book that started this great war." Researchers do not believe this happened, since there are no firsthand accounts, but the quote does sum up the influence many people attributed to her for the Civil War, which would follow a decade after the release of *Uncle Tom's Cabin.*

Calvin and Hattie moved with their family

from Brunswick, Maine, to Hartford, Connecticut, in 1852, where they lived for the rest of their lives. Calvin acted as Hattie's manager after the success of *Uncle Tom's Cabin* and traveled with her across the United States and Europe on a number of speaking tours. His own literary aspirations were either redirected or unrealized as he put his efforts into supporting her career in every way he could, making good on his pronouncement from years earlier that she "must be a literary woman."

Calvin passed away on August 6, 1886, at the age of eighty-four in their house in Hartford. Ten years later, on July 1, 1896, Hattie passed away at age eighty-five, surrounded by her three surviving children, Harriet, Eliza, and Charley, as well as her sister Isabella, who had become a champion for women's suffrage. Her other four children, First Charlie, Henry, Fredrick, and Georgiana, preceded her in death. The twins, Harriet and Eliza, never married.

CHAPTER NOTES

Chapter One

Due to there being several "Harriets" in this story, I chose to call our Harriet by her family nickname: Hattie.

On January 6, 1836, Harriet Elisabeth Beecher became Harriet Beecher Stowe. She and Calvin were married by her father at his Walnut Hills home without much fanfare. On her wedding day, Harriet wrote a letter to her friend Georgiana May, saying that she had been anxious and doubtful until that day and now felt calm and ready for the changes ahead. Harriet was already a teacher and a published author (*Primary Geography for Children,* 1833) with plans for future publications. Because of her abilities and success, her financial security did not depend on marriage as it did for most women of this age. She stood about five feet tall and looked as described here, plain, and somewhat masculine in her features with a prominent cleft in her chin.

Catharine was likely not there for the wedding, and her opinions regarding Harriet's marriage are fictional but reflect a growing belief among early feminists (though they would not use that term for several years) regarding a woman's identity being swallowed up in family responsibility. Many women of this time were "worn out" by the amount of work put upon them, which was a growing reason for women to fear marriage and the inevitability of children. Women had very few rights as individuals, but once they married, what rights they had were represented by their husbands in the public sphere.

Catharine would become a compelling voice in the view that women and mothers had the most influence on the values of children due to their nurturing roles. She would go on to train teachers, advocate for women's rights and public education, and establish kindergarten in the United States. She had been engaged as a young woman, but her fiancé died in a shipwreck near Ireland. She never married.

The only attendees at the wedding were Harriet's family and her friend Mary Dutton. Some of Harriet's siblings did not even know of the wedding until after the fact and originally thought that Calvin had married Catharine, not Harriet.

I made up the part about a borrowed wedding dress and do not know if Aunt Harriet was at the wedding. Aunt Esther was managing Lyman Beecher's household at the time of Hattie's marriage, as she often did when there was not a Mrs. Beecher to do so. Hattie did have a bouquet of orange blossoms.

Chapter Two

A few weeks into her marriage, Harriet told a friend that she and Calvin would sit around the fire and read in the evenings. Calvin loved German biblical literature — though he had to hide it from his theological peers due to its progressive ideas — and they both loved discussion and debate.

One difference in their temperaments that showed up again and again in the resources I studied was Harriet's love of "projects" and amusing herself. Harriet was disorganized, absentminded, and had a high tolerance for clutter. She was raised with hired help who took charge of the tedious aspects of life, allowing her to utilize her time at her own discretion.

Calvin, on the other hand, was extremely frugal and orderly and raised to do for himself. His mother had managed her own home, and he struggled to understand why Harriet could not do the same. Some accounts presented Calvin as lazy and critical, but I tried to reflect his analytical approach no worse than Harriet's sometimes flighty behavior. Her lack of interest in order and systems would be a bone of contention for them for decades. In a letter she wrote to Calvin years later, she said, "I am working hard (for me)."

In addition to writing, Harriet loved to draw and paint, especially during her school years. Roxanne Foote Beecher, Harriet's mother, who died when Harriet was only four years old, was known as a painter in her younger years but set down her brushes when family demands required her full attention. She gave birth to nine children in fifteen years and died after a short battle with consumption. The next Mrs. Beecher bore four children, moved west with Lyman Beecher, and also died of consumption just six months before Calvin and Harriet married.

I am guessing that Lane Seminary had a cafeteria and that Calvin availed himself of it after Eliza's death. Gilly's Pub is of my own creation.

Harriet used the phrase "cultivating indigo" to explain the heavy moods Calvin sometimes experienced. He was particularly susceptible to periods of depression, when his energy lagged and he struggled to think optimistically. Lane Seminary was responsible for a large part of his frustration; he had left a solid position at Dartmouth to come to Cincinnati, buried his first wife, Eliza, in Ohio, and yet the Seminary struggled to keep their promises regarding housing and salary.

The line quoted in this chapter in regard to a companionate marriage is taken from Susan Lebsock's book, *The Free Women of Petersburg: Status and Culture in a Southern Town, 1784–1860,* as referenced in one of my sources. The book was not published until 1984, so it is fiction that Calvin would have encountered the quote used here. Companionate marriages were on the rise in the 1830s as women pursued education, and both men and women looked for intellectual equals as partners in marriage. Since many women were unable to pursue higher education on their own, marrying an intellectual man gave them a chance at an education they could not receive otherwise.

Though they had domestic squabbles, Calvin and Harriet seemed to have had a very satisfying intimate life, as communicated in letters they wrote to one another when they were apart.

Chapter Three

This scene is fictional, but the details regarding the Semi-Colon Club are accurate other than the fact that the pieces were usually read by a male member of the group and rarely by the author. Harriet and Calvin continued to attend meetings together until the club dissolved in 1837.

Calvin struggled with headaches from time to time, but whether they were of the magnitude I show here, I do not know. I used this scene to reflect his struggles, but also Harriet's tendency to put her own needs and desires ahead of other people's.

Harriet's first prose had been published after having been read at a Club meeting in 1834. Club member Judge James Hall encouraged Harriet to enter a contest sponsored by his magazine, *Western Monthly Magazine*. Harriet entered and won fifty dollars. Her piece, "A New England Sketch," was published in April 1834.

The people mentioned by name in this scene — Uncle Samuel Foote, Elizabeth Foote, Mrs. Greene, Mr. Allen, and Mrs. Bingham — were all members of the Semi-Colon Club. Other members of the group went on to achieve remarkable things in their lives: Salmon P. Chase would become secretary of the treasury under President Abraham Lincoln and then a chief justice of the Supreme Court. Elizabeth Blackwell would become the first woman physician in the United States.

Incidentally, the Semi-Colon Club was not named after the punctuation mark. It was based on the fact that Christopher Columbus's Spanish name was Cristóbal Colón. *Colón* discovered new lands, and the members of the club were discovering new things through one another's writings, which had to be "semi" important too.

Chapter Four

In the fall of 1834, Harriet, Calvin, and her father met Reverend John Rankin while traveling to Ripley, Ohio, on Lane business. Whether there or at a later date, Rankin told the story of a slave woman who crossed the breaking ice of the Ohio River with her baby clasped to her chest. Rankin's story would become the template for Eliza Harris in *Uncle Tom's Cabin*.

That Harriet would have written the story at this point in her life and presented it to the meeting or discussed it with Calvin is of my own imagination. In 1836, Harriet was opposed to slavery — all the Beechers were — but she was not yet an avowed abolitionist. From the different accounts of this time in her life, it seemed as though she was soaking up information and experiences about slavery, many of which would be reflected in the book she would write in 1851. Edward relating the experience of a mother drowning herself and her child rather than be put to work "down river" did not happen; I took the story from *Uncle Tom's Cabin,* assuming Hattie may have heard a story like it at some point.

Chapter Five

I did not find any specific thoughts as to how Harriet felt about being pregnant so soon after her wedding, but she said later in life that she often felt overwhelmed and lost in motherhood and wished she and Calvin had had more time together before they started having children. She struggled with her health most of her life, sometimes expressing that she wished she could die to be free of the struggles. She believed she would die young.

Calvin's trip to Europe came about as related here, though this particular scene is fictional. The couple likely knew the specifics soon after their marriage since Harriet had planned to accompany him to New York until realizing she was pregnant. Calvin originally planned to sail from New York the first of May but did not end up leaving until June 8, 1836. That the expenses were split as presented here is of my supposition. Calvin was very thrifty.

In a letter Calvin sent Harriet after leaving Ohio, he insisted they name the child after Eliza Tyler if it were a girl. Naming the first child after a late spouse was common in their day, and I found no indication that Harriet took offense to the suggestion, but she did feel some insecurity regarding Eliza from time to time and so I chose to show it in this scene in a few different ways.

Findley's Furniture Store is of my own creation, but Findley's Market, named for an early settler of the Cincinnati area, James Findley, remains in Cincinnati to this day.

Chapter Six

Cincinnati in 1836 was filled with riots where racial contention led to physical violence. Though a free state, Ohio was just across the Ohio River from Kentucky, a slave-holding state, and was dependent on Southern goods for their economy. Ohio was also located between the South and Canada, where escaped slaves could live free of their masters since Great Britain and all her colonies had abolished slavery. A great many free blacks resided in Ohio, but that led to concerns that they would take jobs away from the whites and that their lack of education and presumed lack of morality would pull down Ohio's ability to progress.

Though slaves could be freed, they were not given the rights of white citizens. Ohio operated under the "Black Code," which required blacks to have sponsorships and pay taxes (though their children could not go to the public schools these taxes served). Limitations were placed on the freed slaves' ability to live and work independently. The blacks who banded together in communities seemed threatening to white citizens, though whites did not want the blacks to live among them either.

For those with anti-slavery sentiments, there was an entire spectrum of feelings about the institution, from simply not participating in slavery themselves to believing it was inherently evil and a crime against humanity and God. A great deal of the tension was between people against slavery, but at varying degrees or with differing opinions on how to fix the problem. And, of course, every person believed they had it right.

George formally joined the Anti-Slavery

Society in 1836 and professed himself an abolitionist. He was the first of the Beecher family to say outright that he believed slavery should end and that blacks should have rights equal to whites within the United States. Henry and Hattie eventually shared George's convictions toward abolition, but they did not officially join the movement for some time.

That Lyman Beecher would be against George's conversion was not directly stated, but at the time he was a vocal proponent of colonization, or deportation, which was contrary to the abolition stance of giving citizenship to the blacks. Instead, the idea advocated that all bonded blacks should be freed but sent somewhere else and assisted in creating their own society.

George was known for his quiet disposition and had come to Ohio after graduating from Yale in order to become a minister, the career Lyman Beecher wanted for all his sons. Less than a decade later, George would be found dead by a self-inflicted gunshot wound in an orchard behind his house. Hattie never accepted that he killed himself, but he struggled with depression through much of his life and felt things very deeply.

Henry, after graduating from Amherst

College, returned to Cincinnati to attend Lane and assumed editorial responsibilities of *The Cincinnati Journal and Luminaries,* which Lyman Beecher took advantage of for his own public posturing.

Chapter Seven

Calvin left Ohio in May and sailed from New York on June 8, 1836. I do not know if he visited his mother on the way or if Harriet slipped him some peppermints to ease the expected seasickness. Harriet did give Calvin a letter to open once he had set sail. One account said she'd sent him a letter for every Sunday he'd be gone in addition to the packets of letters and journal pages she sent throughout his trip. A few of the lines of my version of this letter — regarding his "cultivating indigo" and that she would love to go in his place — are from that very letter she sent; the other lines I filled in to make a full correspondence.

While on the ship, Calvin expressed in letters that he missed both Harriet and Eliza and feared that something might happen to Harriet during childbirth. Whether due to his own ability to rise above his fears or with the help of Harriet's encouragement, he did not allow his fears to interfere with his trip. He took his work seriously and made good use of his time abroad. This trip would be the pinnacle of his career. Upon his return to Ohio, financial difficulty at Lane Seminary led to continued frustrations while a steadily growing family prevented him from moving forward career-wise. Though Calvin had expected to be a literary man in his own right, he would never achieve that goal.

Chapter Eight
The riot on July 5 is documented, but the details — including the parade route and Lincoln Park being in downtown Cincinnati — are my own. Harriet was not present for the parade, but the thoughts expressed in this scene are in keeping with her opinions of the matter as recorded in her letters to Calvin, her editorials, and her journal entries. The riots of 1836 would be referred to on several occasions when Hattie spoke of the injustice toward blacks that she witnessed firsthand.

Chapter Nine
The tract replicated here was distributed on July 17, following the July 12 ransacking of Birney's office, but before the July 31 attack, which ended with the press at the bottom of the Ohio River — forever silenced, though Birney was not. The reference of

Salmon P. Chase blocking entry into the boardinghouse where Birney was living at the time took place on July 31. The mayor's lack of action stretched over a few weeks' time and infuriated Hattie.

There is no specific reference that Hattie was in town to receive the tract, but she did have strong feelings about what was happening in Cincinnati — many of her exact thoughts are included in this letter to Calvin — and it was around this time she began writing as "Franklin" in *The Cincinnati Journal.*

The original Shillito's Dry Goods store opened in 1830. Larger buildings were built over the course of the next two decades until the final seven-story department store became the largest department store west of the Appalachia Mountains. At the time of this story, the store was located on Main Street between Fourth and Fifth Street.

Cincinnati had several nicknames: *Porkopolis* because it was the country's leading hog packing center; *Queen of the West* and *London of the West* because of its marketplace, which was the largest in the west at the time; and *City of Seven Hills* because of the seven hills surrounding Cincinnati, one of which was Walnut Hills, where the Beechers lived and where Lane Seminary was located.

At the time the Beechers moved to Cincinnati, pigs were allowed to run the streets, eating garbage thrown out by the citizens and causing a great deal of havoc. For the New England–bred Beechers it seemed very primitive, though they tried hard to accept the frontier aspects of their new home.

Chapter Ten

The first editorial from Franklin was published in the July 21 edition of *The Cincinnati Journal* and the excerpt printed here is from that original piece. It was Hattie's first foray into public politics, but the response shown here, as well as Mr. Peterson inviting her to a citizen's meeting that was held that night, is of my own creation. I imagine the editorial was well received due to the fact that Hattie went on to write other pieces and later spoke of this as an accomplishment that helped her understand the power of words in the public sphere.

There is no account of Calvin's reaction to her editorials other than her telling him in a letter that it was a "light sketch written in an easy style." Though the tone was light, the content was not.

By this time, Hattie was six months pregnant and unaware she was having twins.

Chapter Eleven

Calvin's letter censuring Hattie is of my own imagination, as is the discussion between her and Catharine upon her return and the terms of her investment in the school. The justifications shown here from Catharine's point of view are in keeping with her feelings regarding Hattie's fault in the failure of the school, which officially closed in 1837. Hattie never received a return of her investment due to some rather creative justifications on Catharine's part that left her with profit and both of her partners with nothing.

Catharine did return to Walnut Hills sometime in 1836 after summering with their sister Mary in Connecticut. Like Aunt Esther, Catharine spent many years of her life traveling between her siblings' families and helping where she could. Unlike Aunt Esther, she was not always as welcome due to her bossy and rigid nature.

Just over a year after Harriet Porter died, Lyman Beecher went back to Connecticut and married for a third time to Mrs. Lydia Beals Jackson, a widow of about fifty years of age, and a decade or so his junior. That Hattie learned about the marriage like this or felt this way about it is fictional.

Chapter Twelve

The newest Mrs. Beecher came to Cincinnati in August or September of 1836. I found no accounts of Hattie's relationship with Lydia Jackson, which says to me that it was likely not an important one in Hattie's life. I portrayed it as conflicted for my own purposes of the story. Catharine and Mrs. Beecher would have conflicts throughout the years as Catharine, unmarried and without a home of her own, felt that her new stepmother made her feel unwelcome in her father's home.

Chapters Thirteen and Fourteen

Hattie didn't discover she was pregnant with twins until after the birth of the first baby on September 29, 1836 — the same day Aunt Esther struggled with cholera. That the babies did not contract the highly contagious disease seems miraculous to me as Dr. Drake attended to both patients throughout the day. Hattie named the first baby Eliza Tyler per Calvin's wishes and then named the second daughter after her sister Isabella, though her name would be changed to Harriet at Calvin's request when he returned to America following his European tour.

The twins likely experienced what is now

called "twin to twin transfusion" as Eliza, born first, was very small while Harriet was robust and healthy. In twin to twin transfusion, the placenta gives more blood (nutrients) to one twin at the expense of the other. It is often a very serious condition that can lead to the death of the malnourished twin. Eliza was small and frail with a tendency toward illness for a good portion of her life. In recounting the events of Hattie's delivery, her sister-in-law Katherine wrote the following: "You are a genius, and therefore cannot be expected to walk in a beaten track."

Chapter Fifteen

This scene is fictional but incorporates many facts. Calvin's journey back from Europe was tedious, and he encountered rough weather due to the season. Calvin was a good sailor and not too affected other than his arrival was delayed a few weeks. He learned of the birth of the twins upon his arrival in New York and immediately sent a letter to Hattie asking that they change Isabella's name to Harriet as a tribute to her. He was thrilled to be a father and eager to return to his family, but he had business that required his attention first. Upon his arrival in New York, he had been away for eight months.

Chapter Sixteen
Calvin did send the letter pronouncing that the second twin be named Harriet, and Harriet told others how tired she was looking after the babies. Everything else in this scene is fictionalized.

Chapter Seventeen
Calvin returned to Cincinnati on February 6, 1837, a year and a month after he and Hattie had married. They had been apart for nearly nine months. The details of their reunion are fictional other than the date and the fact that it would likely have taken place at the President's House.

Chapter Eighteen
The name of the twins' wet nurse was not mentioned in my resources. Whether Hattie was unable to breastfeed her daughters due to lack of milk production or simply used the wet nurse as an excuse to get some help is a matter of debate within her biographies, but she did employ a wet nurse with all of her children, as was common for a woman of her class. Mina was the wet nurse who helped with Hattie and Calvin's third child,

Henry, and she was paid three dollars a week.

"Hold your hosses" was a slang version of "hold your horses," which originated in Homer's *Odyssey*. "Hold your hosses" did not appear in print until 1843.

The details of this house are of my own creation. At this time, the Stowes lived in a brick cottage on Gilbert Street owned by Lane Seminary. They would not receive their promised house — with four bedrooms and an adequate kitchen — until 1839.

Chapter Nineteen

The majority of this letter is taken from one Calvin sent to Hattie sometime during the first two years of their marriage. It was likely later than recorded here, since the original includes a reference to their servant "Anna" in his complaint about the "wobbling newspapers," but it outlines the differences in their temperament and was a basis for much of the story I have written.

The other details of this chapter, and the concluding paragraph of the letter, are of my own creation. Calvin's mother did come to Cincinnati in the spring of 1837, but the invitation was not included in the letter, and it's unclear whether Calvin's intent in his mother's visit was to help teach Hattie how to run a household or simply to get her some help without having to pay for it.

Chapter Twenty

Catharine's article *An Essay on Slavery and Abolitionism with Reference to the Duty of American Females* was published by Henry Perkins in 1837. The idea that Mrs. Beecher would be against it, or Calvin would agree, is of my own creation.

There was a growing movement at this time of women having public voices. Some women — like the Beechers — tended to side with the idea of mothers influencing rising generations through their feminine roles as defined within the bounds of Christianity. Others, such as Angelina and Sarah Grimke, were encouraging women to move beyond their own homes and match the voices of men in a public setting. I used these scenes to show the differing opinions and how I imagine Hattie fit within them. She was devoted to the traditional roles of women and felt women could be powerful within their own homes, but in time she would take her views far beyond her own parlor.

March 6, 1837, would be the last official meeting of the Semi-Colon Club.

Chapter Twenty-One

Hepzibah Stowe quickly sided with Calvin in the arguments regarding household management, and Mother Stowe was indeed diligent in her own housekeeping and did not employ servants of her own. At one point, Harriet wrote a letter to Calvin, accusing him of colluding with his mother against her. The details of this scene are of my imagination.

According to one account, Hepzibah Stowe had nine children, but only two of them lived past infancy. Calvin's father, Samuel Stowe, died when Calvin was six years old, leaving Hepzibah a widow with little choice but self-sufficiency.

Chapter Twenty-Two

Harriet's experiences with *The Arabian Nights* and *Ivanhoe* are from her personal history, except for the detail that she was found reading in a tree. Lyman Beecher was against novels for many years, but changed his mind after reading *Ivanhoe*. Harriet had a "Sir Walter Scott" shelf in her home and adored his novels. She also read Mather's *Magnalia* when she was young, and loved his work.

That Harriet's days with Mother Stowe unfolded as presented here or that Lyman would have put her in her place is a matter of my imagination. He said on more than one occasion that if Harriet had been a son, she'd have made the best preacher of all his children.

Chapter Twenty-Three

Harriet would have discovered her pregnancy with Henry, who would be born the following January, about this time. That these would be her feelings is of my own creation, but I can only imagine how overwhelming it must have been. Even today, a prevailing belief is that women cannot conceive again until their menstrual cycle returns after childbirth, which is often held off while a woman is breastfeeding. Many women have learned this is an unreliable method of birth control. That Harriet would know of this old wives' tale or would be managing any of the nursing for the twins at this point is my own conjecture.

Chapter Twenty-Four

Harriet did write for the *New York Evangelist* at different points in her life, and Mr. James Leavitt was the editor from 1830 to 1837, but the details of this correspondence are fictional as is her decision to put her writing on hold.

Chapters Twenty-Five through Thirty

The reasons for Hattie's trip to Putnam are vague, but she did travel to stay with William and Katherine in June of 1837, a month or so after Calvin's mother had joined them in Cincinnati. She would have been three months pregnant with Henry. The details of her still nursing the twins and having failing health are of my own creation but are based upon struggles she experienced with later pregnancies. There was no fall near the wash fire or accounting of specific arguments between her and Calvin at this time.

Chapter Thirty-One

William and Katherine were actively involved in the Anti-Slavery Society of Putnam, Ohio, a city growing in its abolitionism and position amid the Underground Railroad in 1837. That Katherine managed her household as portrayed here or that Harriet was there for training is of my own imagination. William was nearly a decade older than Harriet and his household would have been much more established than her own.

Chapter Thirty-Two

Harriet and Calvin exchanged letters while she was in Putnam, though this one is of my own creation. Harriet returned from Putnam in July 1837 to find that Mother Stowe had returned to Massachusetts during her absence.

That Calvin made peace with his continued longing for Eliza is also of my own imagination, but it did seem to be after this phase of their marriage that he was able to separate the two women. He was a devoted husband to Harriet, but, I imagine, it was not an easy transition for him to make from having loved Eliza to loving Harriet.

Chapter Thirty-Three

Anna Smith began working for the Stowe family in either 1836 or 1837; that she joined under these circumstances is of my own imagination. She worked for the Stowes for eighteen years and become like a sister to Harriet.

In her autobiography, Harriet talked of Calvin reading the German fairy tales he loved to his family in the evenings. He would translate as he read.

One of my resources mentioned Calvin offering separate bedrooms for the sake of Harriet's health, but I was unable to confirm it. Harriet once told her sister that abstinence was the only method they used to limit their family, but seeing as how they had seven children in fifteen years, and spent a great deal of that time apart as they both took health treatments for months at a time, seems to suggest they were not particularly diligent in the long-term.

At some point in the early years of their marriage, Harriet began to write a few hours a day, but she was very clear to her friends that she did it for the pay. She would rather write and pay someone to do the menial household work than manage the household on her own.

In a letter Calvin once sent to Hattie, he said, "You must be a literary woman!" Over the course of their fifty years of marriage, he would continue to make room for her career within their family and their relationship.

Epilogue

Following the vision in church one Sunday of Uncle Tom's death, Harriet wrote down everything she could remember, believing at the time that she would write some "pictures" to help Northern citizens understand what slavery truly was. In the years that followed, Harriet gave varied accounts of the experience, including exactly what she "saw" and which year the vision took place. I took some of the details Harriet shared and added a few more to create a fully fleshed-out scene.

Not only did Harriet draw upon the story told to her by Mr. Rankin for Eliza's character, but she also used her own experiences employing a former slave woman, Juliette, in Cincinnati. Juliette had confided to Hattie that she'd borne her master's children against her will, then had to leave them behind when he turned her out. After hearing her tale, Calvin and Henry helped Juliette start her journey to Canada, where she would have a better chance of a new life. She would never be reunited with her children, however, who remained slaves to their own father.

The first installment of *Uncle Tom's Cabin* was published in the *National Era* in June 1851 — Hattie had just turned forty years old — and another chapter was presented each week for the next ten months. The serialization drew a large following, and though there was criticism for Hattie's domestic voice and her portrayal of slaves, which many people felt was exaggerated, she ignited people's hearts in a way no other anti-slavery narrative had. She spoke to the mothers, the fathers, and the Christians, often breaking into her own voice to deliver a sermon on Christian duty and appeal to human sympathy.

After the serialization concluded, Harriet met with publishers about turning the serialized chapters into a book. The result was *Uncle Tom's Cabin: Life Among the Lowly*, her first novel, and the beginning of a new life for her and her family as she was thrust into the public eye and literary success.

The novel version of *Uncle Tom's Cabin* sold 300,000 copies in America in the first three months, and 1.5 million copies in England the first year it was available there. Harriet would go on to write nearly thirty additional books and short stories, but *Uncle Tom's Cabin* would forever be known as her greatest work.

TIMELINE

June 14, 1811 Harriet Elisabeth Beecher is born in Litchfield, Connecticut, the seventh child of Reverend Lyman Beecher and his wife, Roxana Foote Beecher.

1816 Roxana Beecher dies of tuberculosis. Harriet is sent to live with Grandmother Foote and Aunt Harriet Foote.

October 30, 1817 Lyman Beecher marries Harriet Porter. He would go on to father four more Beecher children with his new wife.

1819 Harriet begins her formal education at Miss Sarah Pierce's Litchfield's Female Academy at eight years old.

1824 Harriet, age thirteen, moves to Connecticut and attends her sister Catharine's school, the Hartford Female Seminary.

1826 Fifteen-year-old Harriet becomes a teacher at the Hartford Female Seminary.

1832 Harriet moves to Cincinnati, Ohio. She joins a literary group known as the Semi-

Colon Club and meets Calvin and Eliza Stowe.

1833 Harriet's first book, *Primary Geography for Children,* is published.

April 1834 Harriet's short story, "Uncle Lot," wins *Western Literary Magazine's* writing contest and is published as "A Sketch of New England."

August 6, 1834 Eliza Tyler Stowe dies of cholera while Harriet is visiting family in Connecticut.

July 7, 1835 Harriet Porter Beecher, Lyman Beecher's second wife, dies of consumption.

Fall 1835 Calvin and Harriet are engaged.

January 6, 1836 Harriet marries Calvin Stowe.

June 1836 Calvin sails for Europe.

July 1836 Cincinnati riots inspire Hattie to write under the pseudonym "Franklin" for *The Cincinnati Journal.*

September 29, 1836 Harriet gives birth to twin girls named Eliza Tyler and Harriet.

January 14, 1838 Henry Ellis Stowe is born.

May 6, 1840 Frederick William is born.

May 25, 1843 Georgiana May is born.

1843 *The Mayflower,* a collection of short stories, is published.

January 1848 Samuel Charles ("Charlie") is born.

July 26, 1849 Charlie dies.

April 1850 The family moves to Brunswick, Maine.

July 8, 1850 Charles Edward ("Charley") is born.

September 1850 The Fugitive Slave Act is passed, making it a crime to assist anyone escaping slavery.

March 2, 1851 Harriet begins writing *Uncle Tom's Cabin*.

June 5, 1851 First portion of the serialized version of *Uncle Tom's Cabin* is published in *National Era*. Episodes would continue through April 1852.

1852 The family moves to Andover, Massachusetts.

March 20, 1852 The novel version of *Uncle Tom's Cabin* is published. It sells 10,000 copies the first week, and 300,000 by the end of the year.

April 1853 Harriet begins her first European tour with Calvin and her brother, Charles Beecher.

1853 *A Key to Uncle Tom's Cabin* is published.

December 15, 1855 Aunt Esther dies.

1856 *Dred, A Tale of the Great Dismal Swamp* is published.

1856 Harriet takes a second tour of Europe to talk about slavery and explore international copyright for *Uncle Tom's Cabin.*

July 9, 1857 Nineteen-year-old Henry Ellis Stowe drowns while swimming in the Connecticut River.

1859 Harriet takes her third trip to Europe.

1859 *The Minister's Wooing* is published.

December 20, 1860 South Carolina is the first state to secede from the United States.

April 12, 1861 The Civil War begins when Confederate troops attack Union troops at Fort Sumter.

1862 *Agnes of Sorrento* is published.

January 1, 1863 Abraham Lincoln issues the Emancipation Proclamation, freeing slaves.

1864 The Stowes move from Andover to Hartford, Connecticut, and build their home, Oakholm.

January 31, 1865 Congress passes the Thirteenth Amendment to the Constitution, prohibiting slavery.

April 9, 1865 The Confederate army surrenders.

April 14, 1865 President Lincoln is assassinated.

April 15, 1865 Vice President Andrew Johnson is sworn in.

December 6, 1865 Congress ratifies the Thirteenth Amendment to the Constitution, prohibiting slavery.

1866 Chapters of *The Chimney Corner* are published in *Atlantic Monthly,* volume 18.

1869 Harriet and her sister Catharine publish *The American Woman's Home.*

1869 *Old Town Folks* is published.

1870 *Little Pussy Willow, Lady Byron Vindicated,* and *My Wife and I* are published.

1871 *Pink and White Tyranny* is published.

1871 Fredrick William Stowe, a veteran of the Civil War, moves to California. The family never hears from him again.

1872 Harriet contributes to *Six of One by Half a Dozen of the Other.*

1873 The Stowes move to their final home on Forest Street in Hartford.

1873 *Woman in Sacred History* and *Palmetto Leaves* are published.

1875 *Betty's Bright Idea, Deacon Pitkin's Farm, The First Christmas of New England,* and *We and Our Neighbors* are published.

May 12, 1878 Catharine Beecher dies.

1878 *Poganuc People* is published.

August 6, 1886 Calvin Stowe dies in the Stowes' summer home in Florida.

January 13, 1890 Georgiana May dies after a long-term illness and morphine addiction.

1890 *The Poor Life* and *Life of Harriet Beecher Stowe* are published.

429

July 1, 1896 Harriet Beecher Stowe dies in her sleep surrounded by her three living children — Harriet, Eliza, and Charley — her sister Isabella, and her nephew Edward.

1897 *Queer Little Folks* is published.

BIBLIOGRAPHY

Fritz, Jean. *Harriet Beecher Stowe and the Beecher Preachers.* New York: Penguin Putnam Books for Young Readers, 1994.

Hedrick, Joan. *Harriet Beecher Stowe: A Life.* New York: Oxford University Press, Inc., 1994.

Koester, Nancy. *Harriet Beecher Stowe: A Spiritual Life.* Grand Rapids: Wm. B. Eerdmans Publishing Co., 2014.

Rau, Dana Meachen. *Who Was Harriet Beecher Stowe?* New York: Penguin Group, 2015.

Stowe, Harriet Beecher. *Uncle Tom's Cabin; or, Life Among the Lowly.* Cleveland: John P. Jewett & Company, and Jewett, Proctor & Worthington, 1852.

Weld, Theodore Dwight. *American Slavery As It Is.* 1839. Retrieved July 6, 2016, from http://docsouth.unc.edu/neh/weld/weld.html.

ACKNOWLEDGMENTS

For whatever reason, this book came in fits and starts over a nine-month period of time — longer than my other historical romance novels have taken. I struggled to find the story I wanted to tell and then struggled to focus when I found the time. Big thanks to my writing group for reading the early versions, and to Jennifer Moore and Nancy Campbell Allen for reading the full manuscript once I finished. I owe a big thank you to all the writers who have organized the information about Harriet and her family; there was a wealth of information for me to choose from, and I recognize the years of diligence other people put in to this creation.

Big thank you to the Shadow Mountain team who first gave me the idea of stories focused on true events and especially to Lisa Mangum, my editor, and Heidi Taylor, Product Manager, who continue to encourage me — and then make me sound better than I ever could on my own. Thank you to Rachael Ward for the typesetting and Richard Erickson and Heather Ward for the cover. The "look" of any story is an important detail, and I appreciate their time and talents very much.

Thank you to the marketing team and to my agent, Lane Heymont, for championing me on many fronts and helping smooth the sometimes rocky road of publication. I am surrounded by talented and invested team members and so grateful for their help.

Thank you to my Father in Heaven, who has given me so much and helped me grow in so many ways, to my husband, Lee, for his unfailing love and support, and to my kids for giving me a "full" life. I was very impressed by Harriet's determination to "have it all" and I can relate to the richness of both family and publishing success — both are better because of the other. I wouldn't change a thing.

ABOUT THE AUTHOR

Josi S. Kilpack is the author of twenty-five novels and one cookbook and a participant in several co-authored projects and anthologies. She is a four-time Whitney award winner — *Sheep's Clothing* (2007), *Wedding Cake* (2014), and *Lord Fenton's Folly* (2015) for Best Romance and Best Novel of the Year — and the Utah Best in State winner for fiction in 2012. She and her husband, Lee, are the parents of four children.

You can find more information about Josi and her writing at josiskilpack.com.

The employees of Thorndike Press hope you have enjoyed this Large Print book. All our Thorndike, Wheeler, and Kennebec Large Print titles are designed for easy reading, and all our books are made to last. Other Thorndike Press Large Print books are available at your library, through selected bookstores, or directly from us.

For information about titles, please call:
(800) 223-1244

or visit our website at:
gale.com/thorndike

To share your comments, please write:
Publisher
Thorndike Press
10 Water St., Suite 310
Waterville, ME 04901